A BAPTISM OF FIRE

JULIE EVANS

Copyright © Julie Evans 2023
All rights reserved.

All characters and events in this publication are fictitious and any resemblance to real persons, living or dead, is purely coincidental.

This book is sold subject to the condition that it shall not, by way of trade or otherwise, be hired out, lent or resold, or otherwise circulated without the author's/publisher's prior consent in any form of binding or cover other than that in which it is published and without a similar condition including this condition being imposed on the subsequent publisher.

The moral rights of the author have been asserted.

To my children in the sincere hope Philip Larkin wasn't always right!

PROLOGUE

He'd always been trouble. Classic delinquent material. Absent father, mother so needy she was willing to sacrifice her kids for the love of a man. The sort of love that had her working all the hours God sent and dealt her a slap when she answered back. It was no surprise he went off the rails, but what to do about it? How to stop the rot?

All the airy-fairy psychology in the world wouldn't put his sort right. A short, sharp shock was what he'd needed.

No one objected, not really. The boy was a loner with no friends to speak of. Then again, kids, like pups in a litter, always sniff out the runt, don't they? Luckily, a few of us retain those natural born instincts. I can spot a wrong-un at fifty paces, and trust me, the boy was a wrong-un. People try and tell you it's all about nurture or the lack of it in this case, but that's bullshit.

Look at his sister, she had the same stepfather, the same useless mother, but she didn't have that glitch in her makeup. She worked hard at school, held down a part-time job and got herself a place at university. She used her head and stayed on the straight and narrow with the sole aim of getting away from her car crash of a family. Strong, determined and beautiful... oh, so very beautiful. Her only fault, no not fault... weakness, was loving the boy. She would do anything for him. She talked about how she'd get him out of there. She even planned to take him to university with her. Imagine it, a bright young woman with her whole future ahead of her, meant to be having the time of her life, saddled with her worthless kid brother, but she wouldn't see sense... wouldn't hear a word against him. I could see it, though. It was crystal clear to me the day he lit that first fire, the one at the school. He said he didn't do it, said the other lads set him up, but he would, wouldn't he? She believed him. Despite all the evidence pointing in his direction, she was adamant that if he said he didn't do it then he didn't. I knew there and then as I looked into her teary eyes, she wouldn't go to uni, not without him. I knew that waste of space would ruin her whole bloody life and it was down to me to save them both, and that's just what I did, and now, I'm going to have to do it all over again.

ONE

There is a reason why, before mobile phones and the cloud, when asked which one precious item they would save from a burning house, people invariably opted for their photographs. It's the same reason they take the photos in the first place because the past is irreplaceable, it defines us from our first steps to our last breaths. The things we remember and the things we'd rather forget. We can try to hold back the years and lose sleep over our bad choices, but we can never rewind time. It is done and dusted. Nevertheless, there are moments when rewriting our past could transform our future.

The young man sitting on the train that November evening was searching for transformation. He had no need for photographs. His past had survived the furnace. All he had to do to remember was look in the mirror. His history was branded upon his skin.

The tannoy crackled to life, and the nasal recording announced, 'Next station, Truro. Change for connections to Penryn and Falmouth.'

The passengers shuffled in their seats, gathering themselves and their belongings. The student slouched next to him who had missed all the scenery, glued to Instagram on her phone, looked up and stood to heave a rucksack, almost as big as her, from the luggage rack behind.

The movement nudged a heavy-set woman across the aisle who had got on at Bodmin and gossiped incessantly ever since, to finally pause for breath.

'Home for Christmas, love?'

The girl shot her a baffled look as if mystified why anyone

over thirty thought they had the right to engage her in conversation. 'Yeah?' she replied in a tone that sounded more like *what's it to you?*

The woman, impervious to the insult, smiled before turning to pick up where she'd left off. 'They turn the Christmas tree lights on at five thirty and the parade starts at six. We can get a bit of shopping done first, then treat ourselves to a glass of Prosecco at The William before it begins.'

'Make that a pizza and two glasses. I'm not shopping this evening. I've been caught out before,' replied her friend. 'They reduce everything nearer Christmas,' she added in a whisper as if imparting a close-guarded retail secret.

He'd forgotten about the lantern parade. He should have realised when he'd struggled to book the Airbnb, there was something going on. He remembered taking part when he was a kid, how they'd spent weeks crafting the giant lanterns out of waxed paper stretched over willow and wire frames for the procession. The theme that year had been the world's oceans and he'd been one of four picked from his class to carry the lantern in the shape of a Great White Shark.

They were crossing the viaduct now, its solid arms wrapped around the little city like a proud mother. He peered through the train window down at the floodlit cathedral, the fairy-lit terraces cowering in its pious shadow. The place had probably altered; it would be strange if it hadn't after all this time, but he'd put money on the people being the same. The past settled close to the surface in communities like this. If you kicked at the dirt, the dust rose, stifling the appetite for change and settling in the lungs of those who stayed.

They'd be drawing into the station soon. Fifteen years was a long time in anyone's book. He'd left a frightened kid with no idea if he'd ever come back or what he'd face if he did. Now, all grown-up, he was prepared for the worst they could throw at him, but he had no illusions, this was no homecoming. The mayor wouldn't be waiting with a brass band.

He heard the sharp intake of breath from the woman across the aisle as he rose to put on his coat. He turned, clocking her embarrassment as he met her eye. He was used to the reaction. The uncomfortable marriage of disgust and pity.

'Don't worry, missus, it's not catching,' he grinned.

The woman's lips puckered in her struggle to find something to throw back at him. He didn't wait. He moved to the front of the carriage, feeling her eyes pinned to his back like a donkey's tail in a children's party game, as the train wheezed to a halt.

It had started to rain. Not enough to soak you, but enough to frizz hair; the fine drizzle caught in the beam of the platform lights turning the world monochrome. He breathed in deeply with the romantic notion it might conjure an olfactory memory or two. It didn't.

Air is air, you bloody idiot, he thought.

Pulling up his collar, he headed for the exit.

Station Hill was steep, and the granite pavers slippery, but at least his bag had wheels, and the pub where he'd booked a room was at the bottom. A quick change after he'd checked in, then something to eat and an early night. He had an appointment the next morning with Eden Gray, the solicitor he hoped would take on his case, and he needed to be fresh for it.

He spotted the pub as he rounded the corner. Decked in Christmas lights, music blaring, it seemed welcoming enough.

The sweaty heat hit him the minute he opened the door.

The place was buzzing, people wrapped up for the weather, vying for seats near the window to avoid going out in the rain to watch the parade. Families out for the evening relegating the regular boozers to the far corners of the room.

Shaking the rain from his collar, he pushed his way to the bar.

A young woman with crimson braids and a silver ring through her septum hollered above the heads of a couple arguing over the menu.

'What can I get you, love?'

'I'll have a pint of Betty Stogs, thanks. I've booked a room,' he shouted back.

'Right you are,' she said, grabbing a glass, 'I'll get the booking up on the screen in a second.'

She delivered his pint and headed for her laptop.

He took a sip, turning to sneak a peek above the rim of the glass at the packed room, checking for faces he might recognise.

'What's the name?' the girl asked.

He turned back to face her. 'Retallick... Kit Retallick.'

'Well, there's a thing you don't see every day,' a voice boomed from behind. 'The return of the prodigal fucking son.'

The shock of being recognised so soon after arriving hit him like a shot between the eyes. That the individual was someone he had been to school with made it all the more disconcerting. He'd always got on well enough with Rob Davey. He wasn't the sharpest tool in the box or a close friend. He'd played football with him, that was about it. What floored him was that Rob's words sounded like a greeting and not a rebuke.

He was no prodigal son. He was at best the proverbial bad penny and, to many, something far worse, but Rob looked genuinely pleased to see him. It could be the drink talking. From his flushed cheeks and rolling gait, he looked as if he might have been there all afternoon.

'We're over there in the corner by the window,' he gestured, 'me, the missus and a couple of boys you don't know. Why don't you bring your pint and come and join us?'

'Mr Retallick, here's your key. Breakfast is in the bar from seven o'clock until ten thirty.'

The temptation to grab the key from the girl and bolt to his room was overwhelming, but if he allowed himself to be knocked back so easily, let the old insecurities and fears take hold again, he might as well pack his bags and leave right now. His probation officer had said not to expect an easy ride, that in all likelihood there would be a backlash from the local community. She'd even suggested he might consider moving elsewhere. He'd told the woman he'd think about it but knew in his heart he wouldn't.

Rob's friends were waving at him from the corner of the room and he thought there was a likelihood that not following might cause more of a hoo-ha than if he went over, said hello, made his excuses and left. He thrust the key into his pocket.

'Look who we got here, boys. This here's Kit. We were at school together back in the day.'

'What day was that then, Rob, the one day a week you bothered to turn up?' teased the man wearing a Nirvana t-shirt to Kit's left.

'Yeah, yeah, very funny,' said Rob, taking his seat. 'I was just telling this bunch of comedians about the parade when we were kids. How it took us months to make them lanterns and how most of us never got picked to carry the damn things. Did you ever get to carry one, Kit? I know I bloody didn't.'

'Nor me,' Kit lied, taking a nervous sip of his beer.

He noticed the fourth wheel, a pockmarked bloke with a snake tattoo on his forearm, staring.

'Do them scars on your face hurt?' he asked.

Kit resisted the urge to lift his hand and touch them the way he had done when the scars were new and they burned like hot knives all the time. 'Not anymore,' he said.

The redhead Rob had called his missus bucked up, her thickly mascaraed lashes quivering like trapped spiders.

'I think they're sexy,' she grinned, looking Kit up and down as if he were a bus timetable.

Rob shuffled in his seat.

'Go on, ask him how he got 'em.'

Kit took another sip of his beer.

'No, I'm not asking, it's personal, something like that. I don't go round asking you how you got that beer gut, do I?' she said, parting her jelly-red lips into a smile for Kit's benefit.

'Well, we all know how he got that. All bought and paid for,' chipped in the Cobain fan.

'I'll give you a clue, I'm a fire starter, I'm a fire starter,' Rob sang, lolling out his tongue, aping the lead singer of The Prodigy.

'Never heard that one before,' said Kit, trying to make light of it, his stomach clenching. 'Then again,' he continued, hoping to lighten the moment, 'originality was never your strong point, was it, Rob?'

Two young kids on the next table were staring, their mother weighing up whether the tension building next to them warranted a move.

Rob's face turned beetroot as his friends began to laugh and Kit realised he had played this completely wrong and should have kept his mouth shut, let Rob have his cheap shot.

'What's it feel like to be back with the family, eh? Oh no, I forgot, you haven't got a family, they're all fucking dead. Is that original enough for you, weirdo?' Rob snarled.

The woman at the next table shot them a disapproving glare.

'That's enough, keep your voice down,' hissed Rob's girlfriend. 'We don't want to get thrown out. Everywhere else will be packed and we've got a good seat here by the window.'

The table fell silent as Rob took an angry gulp of his beer.

Kit finished his in one and stood to leave.

'Well, nice to see you again, Rob,' he said, hands shaking as he picked up his bag and made his way through the crowds to the stairs at the back of the bar leading to his room.

He was glad to be at the rear of the building, away from the hullabaloo of the parade. He sat on the bed. He could feel the tension building. He needed to calm down.

He inhaled deeply through his nose, then slowly let the air escape through his mouth, in… out, in… out, the way he had been taught by his therapist until he felt that magical click in his head.

TWO

Eden watched spellbound as a schooner in full sail, so tall she could practically reach out and touch it, passed her first-floor office window. There was something magical about the annual candle-lit march to the beat of drums. The way the soft glimmer from the lanterns warmed the darkened streets, licking upturned faces with the velvety candlelight usually reserved for paintings by long-dead Dutch masters.

The city's Festival of Lights took place every November during the run-up to Christmas. It never failed to draw a crowd, and this evening was no exception. It was always fun, but amid the music and revelry, there were often moments of near silence punctuated only by gasps of awe and wonder from those watching, reverent in the knowledge the fantastical effigies would later burn to nothing. Dust to dust, ashes to ashes, a *memento mori* to all.

'Will Daddy be here soon?' quizzed Flora, Eden's seven-year-old niece, face flushed with nervous delight, as she spotted a giant bug with articulated legs spidering through the crowd.

'Of course, he wouldn't want to miss this.'

Flora's dad, Luke Parish, was supposed to be joining them, but it was anyone's guess when he'd turn up. Working as a DCI in the Devon and Cornwall Police had proved incompatible with his increased parental responsibilities. The promotion from DI had supposedly meant more regular hours, but increasingly, Eden found herself on childminding duty. They had drifted into a cosy routine with more than a whiff of domesticity about it. Every now and again, she worried she was too invested in her niece and her father. Luke could, and probably would, soon find someone special to replace her sister, and he'd want his new partner to play a major role in his daughter's life. Where would that leave her?

Most of her friends already had kids. She was lagging on the maternity front. Her mother had convinced her that women had to give up their independence and ambitions when motherhood knocked on the door, but from where Eden stood, her contemporaries were doing a pretty good job of having it all. With flexible hours and homeworking, they effortlessly juggled Zoom meetings and the school run in a way her mother could never have imagined possible.

She, on the other hand, had her work and precious little else but was scared of the alternative. She'd been on a couple of disastrous dates in the last six months, set up by well-meaning friends who she suspected were increasingly uncomfortable with her singleton status. The problem was she'd been where they were now and no longer trusted the concept. She'd thought she and Andrew were a couple until she'd become the other woman because, despite popular belief, the wife was always the afterthought in a three-way relationship. These days amongst couples, she found herself looking for chinks in their relationships almost to reassure herself she wasn't the only one this could happen to. She'd spot the frosty silences in some, the raised eyebrows and involuntary sneers, or watch with interest the elaborate dance of others whose long-practised rhythms were designed to re-enforce their connections, like mating albatrosses. In her experience, these rituals were practised by only two types of couples: those young and in love and those middle-aged and petrified they weren't.

Her divorce had set her back years, financially and emotionally. There was no getting away from it. Andrew's affair had rewound her biological clock, stopping it dead the day he told her he wanted a divorce. Three years on, she had managed to rebuild a life for herself, but as for relationships, that wasn't so easy. Luke and Flora had filled the gap. She had lavished her pent-up maternal feelings on her niece, and Luke was someone she could trust. There were invisible boundaries he would not cross. If all this were to end, she had nothing lined up to replace it.

She could have a baby outside a relationship. Anything was possible these days. But her own past wouldn't allow it. She knew one good parent was better than two mediocre ones and would defend single parenthood to the hilt, but it was not for her.

Her parents' revelation a couple of years before that they had taken her in and made her their own after she had been abandoned by a sixteen-year-old runaway had instilled a need for family. Eccentric and infuriating as they were, her parents had always been there for her. She wanted that for her child.

Despite her nagging concerns, it felt good to be enjoying the night's spectacle with Flora.

She'd finished work early, picked her up from school and headed for the Christmas market. Flora had been thrilled to be out in the dark, milling with the throng amid the sound of brass bands and carol singers, her face rosy with excitement.

The roads had been closed to house the paper chain of stalls lining the cobbled thoroughfare selling everything from hand-crafted jewellery to homemade Christmas chutney. Beneath the cobweb of Christmas lights, they'd scoured each stall looking for a present for her mother, Thea. Eden had subbed her niece, knowing her sister wasn't one of those who subscribed to the thought counting. In the end, they'd settled on a hand-printed silk scarf, which Flora thought cost a tenner but which actually cost thirty quid. She'd blown what was left of her pocket money on a disgusting plastic cone of brightly coloured marshmallows.

Following their noses, they'd found the young farmers' hog

roast turning above a tray of glowing coals. They'd bought brioche buns filled with smoky meat, crackling and apple sauce, which they ate as they snaked their way towards the cathedral and the tree lighting ceremony.

'Dad says apple sauce counts as one of your five-a-day,' said Flora as they waited for the mayor to flick the switch.

Using the same logic, on the walk back, Eden had treated herself to a twist of paper filled with warm caramel toasted nuts, now filling the office with the sweet scent of cinnamon.

'There's Daddy,' Flora squealed, spotting Luke in the street below, picking his way through the spectators, head down, eyes scanning his phone screen.

'Daddy, we're up here,' Flora shouted.

There was no chance Luke could hear her through the thumping percussion.

'Don't worry, he knows we're here. I'll go down and let him in. Don't lean out of the window while I'm gone.'

She knew she could trust her niece to be sensible. The first few years of her life with Thea, before Luke won custody, had been chaotic. The regular bouts of depression and mania Flora had witnessed before Eden's sister saw sense and began to take the medication prescribed for her schizophrenia had left the child craving order and routine the way other kids craved a trip to Disney.

Eden made her way down the stairs, past the walls lined with ancient copies of *Halsbury's Laws* and *All England Reports*. She felt for the light switch in the darkness at the bottom. The electrics in the old building made no sense, the product of countless re-wiring jobs over the decades. Fuses blew regularly. She was always relieved when the place lit up to order.

The thrum of the crowd had evolved to whoops and cheers, raucous laughter and the shouting out of names as people recognised old friends. Eden opened the door gingerly, worried the pavement was so crowded someone might tumble in if she pulled it back too quickly. As she'd thought, she was faced with a wall of backs.

She pushed through, leaving the door ajar, emerging to see Luke circumventing two women who looked like bookends in identical canary-yellow plastic Macs. One winked at the other as he edged past and was forced to press himself a little too close.

'Sorry,' Eden heard him say.

'Don't you worry about it, my 'andsome,' teased the nearer of the two. 'Most fun I've 'ad in ages.'

Both women dissolved into laughter, followed by a fit of synchronised coughing.

'You had a lucky escape there,' Eden smiled as Luke reached her.

'You're telling me.'

They shuffled past the knot of squatters on the threshold, edging the door shut behind them.

'She's upstairs, and before you say anything, she spent her own money on the stuff she bought.'

Flora was as Eden had left her, sitting on the window seat, nose pressed to the glass, watching the cavalcade below. Her face lit up as she ran to her father, wrapping her arms around him.

'I hear you've been shopping,' he said, tipping her chin upward.

'Yes, I bought lots, especially for Mummy.' She ran from him to the seat, pulling the silk scarf from the pink paper bag she'd clutched on the walk back. Luke gave Eden a sideways glance as if to say, *yeah, her own money, right?*

'That's beautiful. Mum will love it.'

Flora beamed.

'I'll go get us a coffee. Do you want juice, Flora?' Eden asked, keen to let the two of them have their moment. Her niece was too engrossed in conversation with her father to answer.

Eden took her time in the tiny kitchenette before balancing the tray and climbing the staircase back to them.

Flora had a mouthful of marshmallows.

'I told her she could have a few then ditch them,' said Luke. 'She's at your mother's tomorrow night, and you know what she's like about sugar.'

Sugar was right up there with nuclear waste as far as Eden's mother was concerned. "The biggest public health scandal of this generation, darling."

Eden had been known to feign agreement whilst surreptitiously sucking a Werther's Original, but even she drew the line at the multicoloured bag of confectioner's tooth-rot Flora was tucking into.

The chatter below seemed to notch up a decibel as the pulsing music faded into the distance and the last of the elaborate lanterns passed through the street.

The crowd, buoyed up by the sense of celebration and more than a few mulled ciders, sounded good-humoured and ebullient as they looped behind the procession, crawling towards the giant pyre waiting at the park. Those outside the pub across the street were getting rowdier too, occasionally bursting into a hesitant rendition of 'Last Christmas'.

'Gonna be a long night for some,' said Luke.

'What do you care? You're off-duty. Not your problem,' said Eden.

Luke smiled. 'You're right. Not my problem.'

'What's happening now, Daddy?' asked Flora, still staring out the window.

'Auntie Eden and I will finish our coffees, then take you up to see the bonfire,' answered Luke, grabbing a couple of digestives from the biscuit barrel.

'No, not that, Daddy. I mean why's that man going the

wrong way? The parade is going towards the park, but he's running this way?'

'Maybe he's looking for someone. You can easily get lost in a big crowd,' said Eden. 'That's why I made sure you held my hand when we walked around the market, remember?'

'But he's running with his lantern and... and... it's on fire, and now everyone is running back this way.'

Luke ditched his coffee and ran towards the window, craning his neck to get a better view down the street. Eden followed.

The crowd seemed to be surging, moving back the way they'd come like a tide on the turn. Willow poles were swaying. A giant grandfather clock tilting like the Tower of Pisa looked ready to topple as the music thumped in the distance. The ruckus seemed to be happening in the middle of the procession. Neither Luke nor Eden could see the man.

'Where was the man, Flora?' asked Luke.

'I don't know. He was there, then he wasn't. I think he must have fallen over.'

Then they spotted him. A man, a huge lantern, rammed down onto his shoulders, staggering blindly through the centre of the crowd, reaching out for help as onlookers clambered over one another to get out of his way. They could hear his high-pitched screams as pain and terror sent him zigzagging from one side of the street to the other, the massive false head alight, flames licking his back.

There were shrieks and cries of panic as the herd stampeded, shrinking to the edges of the pavement banging on doors to be let in.

'What's happening, Daddy?'

Luke grabbed Flora from the window seat, threw her into Eden's arms and stumbled down the stairs.

'Why don't you go sit over there at the desk, Flora? There's nothing to worry about, just someone being silly. There's paper and pens in the drawer,' said Eden, trying to conceal the panic in her voice.

'But aren't we going to see the bonfire?'

'I'm not sure it's going ahead, sweetheart. I think they've called it off because of the rain,' she lied. 'Why don't you make a card for Mummy to go with her present, perhaps a drawing of her wearing her lovely scarf?'

'Okay,' said Flora, buying into the distraction in the way only a small child would.

Eden ran back to the window.

The music had finally halted, replaced by the sound of sirens as an ambulance and three police cars sped down the narrow road. Within minutes, police officers had cleared the crowd from the vicinity.

Luke was some way down the street kneeling beside the man who lay, clothes smouldering, on the ground. Eden recognised the curtains from the downstairs office draped across him. Luke must have had the presence of mind to grab them on his way out. Only the top half of the man's body was visible, his head blackened and charred, engorged with what remained of a smoking wire lantern frame. It was like a scene from a horror movie.

THREE

By the time Luke returned, Flora was curled up asleep in the chair. He looked ashen-faced and exhausted.

'Come on,' he said, lifting Flora, 'The roads are chock-a-block. I'll give you a lift home.'

'You don't have to. I can always sleep here.'

'Don't be daft. I'll turn the siren on, and I've got an ulterior motive. Could you keep Flora overnight? As you might have guessed, I'm back on duty.'

'That poor man. What a thing to happen. I suppose there's bound to be a health and safety inquiry. It could be the last parade we'll see in the city.'

'We've got more to worry about than health and safety. If he dies, this is a murder inquiry.'

'Murder?'

'There's no way this was an accident. Some evil bastard wedged that thing down on his head, doused him with lighter fuel and set him on fire. The question is why?'

A shiver licked the back of Eden's neck. 'Do you know who he is?'

'His wallet was in his trouser pocket along with his lanyard. He works for a charity. We've contacted his wife. I'm meeting her at the hospital after I've dropped you and Flora off.'

Eden imagined the wife getting the phone call, the flash of realisation life would never be the same again.

'I'll drop Flora at school tomorrow if you like. We can get the bus in. I've got her uniform in my bag,' Eden said, remembering Flora had changed in her office after school.

'If you're sure?'

'Positive.'

Wrapped in the muffled horror at what they'd witnessed, neither spoke again until they reached the car.

Luke was right; the temporary road closures had meant people were delayed in exiting the car parks, and long queues had formed. Luke drove with the siren on, past the lines of stationary cars towards the coast and Eden's cliffside home.

'What kind of monster would do such a thing?' Eden said eventually.

'I've no bloody idea or whether it was one person or several.'

'Is there any chance he'll be able to tell you who did it?'

'If there was, I wouldn't be here now, I'd be by his bedside. The burns are only part of the story. The paramedics said his whole body was in shock. They sedated him. I've seen some things on this job, road traffic accidents, knifings, a couple of bad shotgun injuries, but I've never seen anything as horrific. His face had literally melted. It was barely a face at all.'

It was an image, once imagined, was hard to forget. Eden was relieved when they pulled up outside the beach house and glad she'd taken Luke up on the offer of a lift home. She wouldn't have been able to get much sleep in the office with everything that was going on in the street below.

She went on ahead. It was a miserable night shrouded in thick sea mist. Once inside, she flicked on the outside light so Luke, Flora in his arms, could easily negotiate the sandy path up to the door, avoiding the worst of the needling rain.

She kept meaning to get a timer on the light. It was dark by four thirty this time of the year, and while she could walk the path blindfolded, she was aware not everyone, including the Sainsbury's delivery driver, relished the idea of walking the cliff path in the dark.

The old hewer's lookout she'd painstakingly renovated was not to everyone's taste. It was exposed to the elements and isolated, especially in the winter, but Eden loved it. She woke up every day thankful she'd taken the plunge and bought the derelict building when no one else had the stomach for the challenge.

She lifted Flora from Luke's arms and laid her on the sofa.

'I'll carry her up to bed; you go on.'

'Okay, and thanks. I owe you one.'

'Nothing new there then,' she smiled.

Once he'd driven off, she stacked the wood burner and poured herself a large glass of Primitivo.

The stove had been something she'd decided on early on in the renovations and it hadn't disappointed. The fire provided company as well as warmth. Comfort on cold winter nights when the wind howled around the house. But tonight, watching the logs crackle and spit, all she could think of was burning flesh. She shuddered. Knocking back the wine in one, her hand shaking, she wedged the glass into the dishwasher. She still felt queasy, the alcohol tacky on her tongue, and she steadied herself against the kitchen counter before walking back to the lounge to collect Flora.

Eden could smell her niece's sugary marshmallow breath on her neck as she bent to lift her from the sofa. She should make her clean her teeth, but Flora was dead to the world, and it was late. There was no guarantee she'd go back to sleep if she woke her, and they had to be up early for the school bus. She'd have to make sure she made a special effort the next morning.

She contemplated going back downstairs to get a cup of tea and catch the late-night regional news to check if any new information had emerged about the night's events. But after she'd showered and changed into her pyjamas, she couldn't muster the energy, so decided to have an early night herself.

She had a day free of court hearings tomorrow, which generally meant a diary stacked with appointments with clients, new and old. On top of that, there was a mountain of paperwork to get through, so an early night was best all round.

Lying awake in the darkness, she was pretty sure she was one of only a handful of people who knew what happened tonight was an attack and not an accident. She needed to keep shtum about it for now. She half wished Luke hadn't told her. The knowledge was an itch hard not to scratch. She hoped Luke was mistaken. If not, it would be all anyone talked about for months, perhaps even years, once the news got out. They suffered little violent crime in general and virtually no knife or gun crime. When it did happen, the impact was shattering and the effect unsettling. The community would be up in arms, and the fallout would impact her other cases. The local magistrates would feel pressured into dishing out heavier sentences, and the police would be looking for the culprit. Some of her clients were bound to find themselves in the mix, although she couldn't believe anyone she'd represented was capable of this. Nevertheless, if the police were planning on knocking on doors, it stood to reason her life was about to get even busier.

FOUR

DS Denise Charlton was pacing the hospital foyer when Luke arrived. She looked relieved to see him.

'It doesn't look good. He's on the second floor, critical care. If he makes it through the night, he'll be transferred by helicopter to the burn's unit at the Southmead in Bristol, but the doctors don't hold out much hope.'

They walked slowly to the lift. Luke wanted to be fully briefed before he met the wife.

'The victim is a fifty-nine-year-old male, Paul Vincent.'

Luke knew as much from the driving licence he'd taken from the man's wallet at the scene but didn't want to interrupt.

'His wife Amanda is upstairs. They won't let her see him, but she's determined to stay.'

'Has she been given the details?'

'Some but not all. You'll see why when you meet her. She was diagnosed with MS a year ago, and stress makes the symptoms worse. I didn't see the point in adding to her worries, but she knows it was an assault and the prognosis isn't good.'

In the close confines of the lift, Luke could smell the smoke on his coat. He shrugged it off, turned it inside out and folded it under his arm.

Amanda Vincent sat in the corridor outside the doors to intensive care. She was small, frail-looking, her expression that of someone whose life was unravelling and who hadn't a clue why or how to stop it. Nurses ran in and out of the ward. Every time a new one emerged, she looked up, eyes pleading for good news, something to lift the blanket of hopelessness.

Luke set his coat down on the seat opposite.

'Mrs Vincent, I'm Luke Parish, the officer in charge of the investigation into the attack upon your husband. I wonder if we might have a quick chat?'

The woman's face, already leached of colour, paled further as Luke sat next to her. Denise sat on the other side.

'As DS Charlton has explained, we think this was a planned assault. What we don't know is whether your husband was the intended victim or happened to be in the wrong place at the wrong time. I know all this is a terrible shock, but the sooner we begin our investigation, the better chance we have of catching whoever did this.'

The woman twisted a crumpled tissue between her fingers. She didn't look up.

'Is there anyone you can think of who holds a grudge against Paul, someone he has had an argument with, say a colleague from work or a neighbour, somebody he doesn't get on with?'

'No, no one. Paul gets on with everyone. He's a gentle, kind man.' Her voice was soft, fractured with pain and disbelief as she gulped back her tears. 'We have wonderful neighbours, the same ones since we moved into the cul-de-sac ten years ago. Most of them and all his colleagues came to our twentieth wedding anniversary last year. I can't think of anyone who would want to hurt Paul.'

Luke had to keep going. These first few hours were crucial.

'He works for the Samaritans?'

'Yes, he's the regional manager,' sniffed the woman.

'Has he mentioned any threatening or aggressive calls? Anything strange or unusual?'

'He doesn't take many calls himself anymore. That's mostly the job of the volunteers. In any case, he never talks about any of the calls with me or anyone else. He's not allowed to. They're confidential.'

Luke knew the Samaritans' commitment well enough. He

had tried unsuccessfully to get a witness testimony on another case following a domestic assault and had drawn a blank.

He didn't want to press her. The woman seemed to be drifting further away with every question.

'I'm going to grab a coffee from the machine,' he said. 'Denise will sit with you. Would you like me to get you something, a drink or a bar of chocolate to keep you going?'

The woman shook her head.

Luke caught Denise's eye, prompting her to take the baton in his absence.

He headed back down to the ground floor. He hated hospitals at the best of times and even more at night. The constant beep of machinery from the darkened wards, the eye-reddening fluorescent lights bleaching out the colour. For all the effort to portray them as safe harbours, they felt alien and dangerous to him. Where else were you required to sleep in a bedroom full of strangers or keep the doors unlocked at night? CCTV was all well and good, great for nailing someone after the event, but not so great at stopping some bloke off his meds on the rampage. On top of it all, hospitals, by their very nature, welcomed with open arms the worst society could throw up. You only had to poke your head around the door of A&E on a Saturday night at the height of the tourist season to see overwhelmed nurses trying to remain polite in the face of people they would give a wide berth to out of uniform. Abusive piss-soaked drunks and junkies from god knows where demanding attention, not in a fit state to remember their names let alone who their GP was to check their records. Vulnerable and unable to fight back, the sick people on the wards were sitting ducks. Policing their safety, if there was someone out to get them, was a logistics nightmare.

He knew well enough where his fear of hospitals stemmed from. When he was a child, there had been an incident. He was six at the time, recovering from a tonsillectomy on a ward with four or five other children at the old City Hospital in town, long since knocked down and redeveloped. Back then, it had been in transition, a rambling eighteenth-century infirmary, no longer fit for purpose, in the throes of closing. Only minor ops like his were carried out there, and even then, with severe shortages of nursing staff, mothers were encouraged to stay overnight with their kids as unpaid labour. His mum, like all the others, slept on a zed bed in a separate room nearby.

His had been the last op of the day. His mum had been there when he woke to give him a drink through a straw, help him to the loo and put him back to bed. Still groggy, he had drifted quickly back to sleep but had woken abruptly in the middle of the night, disorientated, to find a man walking through the ward. He had looked to the chair by the side of his bed for his mum and, when she wasn't there, had tried to call out for her, but his throat was sore and dry, and he couldn't make a sound. The other children were asleep, unaware of the man walking from bed to bed.

He'd instinctively known it was best if he looked that way too and squinted up his eyes to feign sleep, closing them properly when the man approached. He had kept completely still as he felt him touch his hair, only daring to open his eyes and move when he could no longer hear his breath.

He had said nothing until he was safely in the car with his mum following his discharge later that morning. She had said it was probably a dream brought on by the anaesthetic. He had wanted to believe her but had known it was real. He had never forgotten it and had hated hospitals ever since.

He shuddered.

Feeling safe as a child was all that mattered. He thought of Flora and the years when Thea had custody of her. Thea was never violent or wantonly neglectful, quite the opposite. She was over-emotional, often suffocatingly affectionate, but she was never really there for Flora. She was too selfish and narcissistic to put her daughter first. On good days when she was taking her meds, she'd take pleasure in motherhood, seeing their child as a reflection of herself, an appendage to be paraded before her sycophantic arty friends. Other times, if it suited her, she'd palm Flora off on near strangers to indulge her own need for constant attention.

He was determined to make it up to his daughter. He thanked God he had time. She was young. A few years later and their relationship might have been irretrievable. He would have been one of the thousands of absent fathers struggling without success to build a relationship with a teenage child who didn't want to know.

Eden had helped so much since he'd brought Flora back to Cornwall. She'd encouraged her out of her shell, showing her the kind of unselfish, undemanding love Thea had never been capable of.

He remembered the two of them earlier that evening, excited about the parade, Flora telling him about their shopping spree. Anyone who didn't know their history would have thought they were mother and daughter. When later he had laid his sleeping child in Eden's arms, he'd known she'd be safe.

He'd be lying to himself if he didn't admit he had wondered what it might be like to come home to Eden and Flora after a shift at the station and when his little girl had gone to bed, to settle on the sofa by the fire with a glass of wine picking holes in some cheesy crime drama on the telly.

It would be so easy to reach across to Eden and take her in his arms. He couldn't ignore her beauty, even if she seemed oblivious to it. So unlike Thea, who had always revelled in how pretty she was. There had been times recently when the tension he felt as his hand brushed against hers or he kissed her cheek was almost unbearable.

He'd had to drag himself away in order to avoid making a huge mistake. If she rejected him, something precious could be ruined forever, and Flora would suffer. He couldn't risk that. She was his priority now. She needed to feel safe and loved.

He gulped down the last of his coffee and headed back to the ward, where he and Denise sat with the woman who seemed to grow smaller with each passing hour. By the time her husband was pronounced dead at four in the morning, she was barely there at all. Denise offered to drive her home, but she declined, saying her brother-in-law would pick her up. She would be staying at her sister's. Luke couldn't blame her for not wanting to go home to an empty house. He knew well enough what that was like. A family liaison officer would contact her the next day. For now, he would leave her to deal with her grief as best she could.

The mood was sombre when he and Denise touched base in the car park before going their separate ways.

'Did you manage to get anything more when I was downstairs?'

'Only about his work, nothing relevant to the case. All ancient history. She felt easier talking about the past than what's just happened.'

'Not surprising,' said Luke, taking his car keys from his pocket.

Denise flipped open her notebook.

'Prior to taking early retirement, Paul was a social worker for years. She said he became disillusioned with the heavy caseloads and the constant scapegoating instead of tackling the lack of funding head-on. He'd suffered with depression for a long time before he left, feeling guilty there had been nowhere to put children he suspected were abused or had mental health issues. The fact kids were left in barely functioning families.'

'Same old shit then,' said Luke.

'Afraid so,' echoed Denise. 'I'll have another go tomorrow if you like, once all this has had time to sink in.'

'Check with her sister first. We don't want to push her, not with her condition. In the meantime, let's see if we can get hold of his work records, the cases he covered, to check if any names crop up on our database.'

Luke sidled into the car, wondering if Vincent's past had something to do with this. A disgruntled parent who had lost their kid because of him, or a child ripped from their family who had bided their time to make the man pay for a decision taken years before. At this stage, the motive was anyone's guess. He would have to wait for the toxicology report from the pathologist to see whether Paul Vincent had been drugged. Whether he was or not made little difference. They were dealing with a perpetrator with the confidence and audacity to set a man ablaze in the middle of a crowded street. This was not simply murder. This was a public execution.

FIVE

Agnes Chenoweth parked her car on Hendra Hill by the children's playground. She wouldn't pay the ridiculous daily parking fees the tourists lashed out willy-nilly. She forked out enough in council tax already. If it meant moving the car mid-morning, so be it.

She'd popped into the garage on her way to work to buy a packet of ginger nuts for the office. She'd remember to reimburse herself from petty cash when she got in.

She was always the first to arrive, had been when she worked for Douglas Bassett, and now Eden Gray was the boss, she saw no reason to change the habit of a lifetime. She relished the peace and quiet, the smell of polish when the cleaners had been in the night before, and the chance to get things ready for the day without distractions. She liked to busy herself retrieving files from the cabinets for Eden's appointments and court cases, and when that was done, to make a cup of tea and flick through the paper before the others arrived.

Molly usually turned up at eight-thirty, just before Eden. Keen as mustard that one. Then again, as the new trainee, she was anxious to make a good impression. It could mean the difference between being kept on as a qualified solicitor after her training or not.

Agnes took her usual route along St. George's Road past the old church, recently converted to swanky flats for singletons and young couples. At least it was being used. Like many of the churches in the city, it had been boarded up for years before someone managed to get planning permission to convert it. Looking ahead, she could see the road was closed. Police tape stretched from one pavement to the other, a young officer walking the line.

She'd heard on last night's local radio that a terrible accident had occurred during the lantern parade. A man had suffered fourth-degree burns after his clothes caught fire. According to the morning bulletin, the poor devil had died later in hospital, leaving a wife and two adult children. A terrible tragedy, but hadn't she been saying for years the parade was an accident waiting to happen?

Agnes never attended the festivities herself. It hadn't been a thing when she was growing up. It wasn't one of those old Cornish festivals like Flora Day or the May Day celebrations in Padstow with the Obby Oss. They were proper traditions she always tried to get to. This was a made-up thing designed to get the crowds in for a pre-Christmas shop, and it had a whiff of new-age hippy ritual she could do without. It was always a nuisance getting home from work when the place was heaving with late-night shoppers. Now, because of the police tape, she could not get there in the first place and was gasping for that tea.

She decided to try the gentle art of persuasion. 'Good morning, officer. I need to get to my workplace just down there on the left, the building with the brass plaque,' she said, pointing towards the office only yards away. 'My boss is Eden Gray, the solicitor. You've probably heard of her. She spends a lot of time with you lot down at the station. If I could just nip under your tape, I promise to stick to the pavement. You won't even know I've been there.'

'I'm sorry, madam, but like the tape says, this is a crime scene and no one, not even people working for solicitors, gets past it.'

She didn't like his tone or the way his mouth turned down at the edges when he said the word *solicitor*. 'Crime scene, what do you mean crime scene? The radio said…'

The officer ignored her and began to pace again.

'You're telling me I've got to go all the way around?' she shouted after him.

He didn't bother to turn to face her to answer. 'It's not far,' he shouted over his shoulder. 'You can nip through Victoria Gardens. The path exits at the top of Edward Street by the court, although I suppose working for a *solicitor,* you already know that.'

Cheeky beggar. Give some people a uniform, Agnes thought, but it was clear there was no point arguing with the likes of him. She was already late and he'd said 'crime scene'. Her spirits lifted. At least when she finally got to the office, she'd have a front-seat view of the investigation. Like watching an episode of 'Vera'.

She turned and retraced her steps towards the viaduct before hanging right through the wrought iron gate into Victoria Gardens.

She hadn't visited this place since she was a child. It had been a bit rundown then, although Mother always said it had been a wonderful place when she was growing up. She'd said it had been the venue for concerts and Sunday school tea treats, and there had been a jamboree there to commemorate the end of the war. Agnes remembered kneeling by the fish pond with a stick in her hand, looking for newts while her mother gossiped with her friends in the wooden shelter, drinking from a flask of tea and knitting. Agnes pondered how mothers were always knitting in those days. Whenever they sat longer than five minutes, out came the knitting needles. It was as if that generation felt guilty doing nothing. All those ill-fitting sweaters and itchy scarves. Nowadays they were scrolling on their phones, and what did they have to show for that other than a catalogue of lost time?

This place brought back memories of overwhelming loneliness. Being a 'late surprise', she had always been the only child around. Her own siblings, like her mother's friends' offspring, were all grown up, and Mother always used the excuse she was too old to play with her whenever she took a ball or a skipping rope from the toy box. Looking back, her mother would have only been about forty-five, but forty seemed old then, and her mother was always being mistaken for her gran.

She'd be left to make her own entertainment for what seemed like hours on end and remembered that particular day, the one with the stick, when she'd toppled in the pond. It wasn't deep, but it had been a good ten minutes before anyone noticed, and instead of comfort, she'd received a slap to the back of her legs for ruining her red T-bars. She'd had nightmares about gasping goldfish after that, and from then on, she had never bothered to try and win one at the fair like the other kids.

Shaking away her memories, she tightened her grip on the handbag slung over her shoulder. This place was a no-go zone at night, probably during the daytime too. She'd heard junkies hung out there to score or whatever they called it. No one did much about it. The police certainly didn't seem to be bothered. That young PC who'd sent her off with a flea in her ear would be better occupied sorting that rabble out rather than making law-abiding citizens like her late for work.

The path took a slight incline up towards the pagoda-roofed Victorian bandstand. She had to admit it looked wonderful. The wrought iron railings had been given a fresh coat of paint, their flowers picked out in gold. To be fair, the whole place looked a picture. She wondered if some European money had been chucked at it before Brexit. The beds were all planted up, even though winter was well and truly here. She relaxed a little and thought she might even be tempted to come up here with her sandwiches on fine days. Even the fish pond looked smarter than she remembered.

As she rounded the side of the bandstand where the steps

were, she noticed someone sitting inside slumped against the railings. He looked scruffy, and she wondered if her initial misgivings had been well-founded after all.

She wouldn't look at him. It didn't do to make eye contact with down-and-outs. They took it as their cue to ask for money. She quickened her pace, watching out of the corner of her eye for movement, ready to run if the bundle of rags got up and shuffled towards her. He didn't. He remained seated and oddly still. Despite herself, her eyes were drawn to him as she passed.

Was he asleep? She'd expect his head to be either thrown back or slumped forward if he was, but he sat bolt upright, hands on knees, legs straight, staring ahead, and his eyes... yes, she could see now, his eyes were wide open.

She began to panic. Should she ask if he was alright? He certainly didn't look alright. He was white as a sheet.

Convincing herself it was none of her business, she was about to carry on walking when she noticed his ankles. They were shackled together.

She moved closer, pausing at the bottom of the steps before gripping the handrail to steady herself, feeling the bite of the cold metal as she saw his hands were chained too. She could also see from there that the face was not a face at all but a mask. One of those grinning Guy Fawkes masks popular with protesters and students with a gripe.

She felt a wave of relief. It was a Guy, left there by kids the evening before for a joke. She could smell it now, the smoke on the filthy clothes. She had better report it nonetheless, horrible thing. It could scare some elderly dog-walker half to death.

She wondered whether she should walk back down the path and fetch the young policeman. He probably wouldn't come. No, she'd leave the monkey to his tricks and call the organ grinder, Sergeant Fairchild, at the station. She reached into her bag for her phone. *Now where was it?*

Then it spoke. The voice guttural, little more than a whisper. 'Help me… please someone, help me.'

SIX

Luke had finally crawled into bed at five am, only to be woken with a jolt by a call from Denise just before nine.

'Sorry to wake you, but there's been another assault.'

'Can't someone else deal with it?'

He was having difficulty hiding his annoyance. Ever since his DI, Ross Trenear, had been given the old heave-ho, he'd found himself pulled every which way. He had a mountain of admin on his desk he'd barely looked at in two weeks and was short of detectives on the ground. Not that he minded that part of the job. It was the paperwork he hated. In fact, he was beginning to wish he'd never taken the promotion in the first place.

'If you like, sir, but there are similarities between this and the attack on Paul Vincent. The victim's in hospital, in a pretty bad state. His feet and hands are badly burnt.'

Luke felt a surge of panic as he put Denise on loudspeaker and pulled his trousers from the back of the bedside chair. 'When did this happen?'

'He was found semi-conscious in the bandstand at the top of Victoria Gardens this morning around seven forty-five by Eden Gray's secretary Agnes Chenoweth. It seems she had to cut through there because St. George's Road was sealed off after last night.'

'Have they secured the gardens?'

'Yeah, and forensics are already there. They were around the corner setting up to examine last night's scene when we got the call. They've diverted a couple of their team to examine the bandstand.'

'And the victim, is he conscious now? Does he know who

did this to him?'

'He's been taken to A&E. No one had the chance to talk to him. I thought you'd want to do it yourself.'

'You thought right. Meet me at the hospital in twenty minutes, and good job, Denise, you must be even more knackered than I am.'

'Yeah, but I've got youth on my side, sir. I'm used to all-nighters.'

Luke felt the good-humoured jibe as he put down the phone. He and Denise had skirted around each other when she first joined the team. They'd even met up for the odd drink, although it had never been public knowledge for obvious reasons. They had hit it off, but any romantic notions either may have harboured had come to nothing. There had been one of those defining moments that could have proved tricky to get past if they weren't such pragmatic people. A late night, a couple of bottles of wine and more than enough mutual attraction for them to have hopped into bed only to regret it the next day. But they had wavered, and it had passed, and on reflection, he was relieved. He was sure she felt the same way. He might have missed out on a lover, but he'd gained a good friend, not to mention an excellent detective sergeant.

***

Denise was waiting for him when Luke arrived at the hospital. She squeezed past a trolley in the corridor to join him by the swing doors, notepad in hand.

'The victim is a local man. Graham White, a sixty-six-year-old retired headmaster. He's a widower. I haven't been able to get access, but his daughter has been in there with him. I grabbed her when she came out for the loo. She confirmed he's sedated and said the doctors have told her they think they have managed to save his hands, but they'll need to amputate his feet. Can you imagine?' Denise shuddered. 'She had no idea why anyone would want to do this to her father or why he was at the festival. She said it's not his thing. He'd attended before but only under sufferance as a teacher in one of the participating schools years ago. She called at his flat in Truro yesterday evening to drop off a pasty for him. Apparently, she makes them every Wednesday and takes him one. She has a key and always lets herself in, but he wasn't there. She called his mobile and it went to answerphone so she left a message saying she'd called. She put the pasty on a plate in the kitchen and left. She thought it was unusual for him not to be there but wasn't unduly worried. He's active and has lots of friends. She only lives down the road, so it's not like he was desperate for the visit or anything.'

'What time was this?'

'She checked her phone while I was with her. She left the message at six thirty.'

'Any sign of a struggle? Anything not where it should be?'

'I asked her and she said no. She said he's not the tidiest, but as far as she could tell, there was nothing unusual.'

'Right.'

'Do you think it's something to do with the festival?' asked Denise.

'What do you mean?'

'I suppose what I mean is, do you think it's over?'

'We can't be certain of anything. The parade may have been nothing more than a useful distraction. The crowds, the music, people milling about in fancy dress without suspicion. Unless White knows who did this or we find witnesses, we might never be able to trace his attackers, especially if they wore costumes. We'll be stuck with questioning the usual suspects. Sad bastards who we know like setting fires, vandals and junkies who hang around the park.'

'But surely the two attacks must be related?'

'I think so, and so do you, obviously, but we'll keep that under our hats until we find a connection between the victims or turn up some evidence.'

Denise nodded.

'If these are random victims with no connection, we've got big problems. The less we reveal, the better at present until we know what the hell we're dealing with. The last thing we need is panic, not to mention an influx of wannabe confessions and media madness.'

'I get it.'

'I assume someone is taking a statement from Agnes Chenoweth? That woman doesn't miss much. She'll have come away with more than most witnesses, although she might not remember everything until the shock wears off. We'll take a look at what she says and maybe interview her again tomorrow just to be sure we have everything.'

'Someone's with her now. Do you want me to wait here?' asked Denise, her eyes red-rimmed and sunken with fatigue as she nodded towards the door behind which Graham White awaited his fate.

'I tell you what,' said Luke, recognising he'd need to pull rank to force her to take a break. 'Check with the medical team whether he's likely to come round and when he's going to surgery. If there's no chance of speaking to him beforehand, we'll put somebody else in here, and you go get some breakfast inside you and a couple of hours kip.'

Denise looked relieved.

'I'll be at the scene if you need me,' said Luke, pleased she'd seen sense.

SEVEN

The bus was late that morning, making Eden realise, not for the first time, that having a car in Cornwall was a necessity rather than a luxury. It was nine forty-five by the time she arrived at the office. She could see the police tape blocking off the end of the street where St. George's Road met Station Hill, but having come from the other end of town, she was able to get access through the back door with relatively little trouble. She knew after the horrific events the evening before, the fact it happened on her doorstep and, most importantly, there was a murder enquiry in the offing, this wasn't going to be a normal day. The crime scene investigators and heavy police presence in what was generally a quiet part of town would put pay to that. What she hadn't expected was to find Agnes sitting in reception, a blanket around her shoulders, whilst two police officers sat either side of her taking notes.

'What's going on?' Eden asked Molly, her trainee, who was manning the fort. Molly came out from behind the reception desk and took her to one side.

'Agnes has had a terrible shock. She found a man chained to the bandstand in Victoria Gardens this morning.'

Eden let out an involuntary guffaw at the thought of her prudish secretary finding a young buck, stark bollock naked, chained to the railings as part of some elaborate stag night shenanigans.

Molly, reading her mind, put her right.

'No, nothing like that, the man had been assaulted. He's been taken to hospital. He has burns to his feet and hands. They were chained, and whoever did it had dressed him up as a Guy. They even put a Guy Fawkes mask over his face. They think he's been there all night. The officer said his injuries are life-changing.'

The horror of the scene came into sharp focus.

'Agnes discovered him on her way to work. God knows when he would have been found otherwise.'

Eden cast an eye in the direction of her secretary. She looked dazed, her skin the colour of raw pastry, as her trembling hand reached to take a sip of water from the glass on the table next to her.

'When was this?'

'About eight this morning. She had to cut through the park because of the police cordon.'

'Oh my god, how awful.'

'If it's okay with you, I'll take her home when they've finished interviewing her. I don't think she should drive in the state she's in.'

'No, of course not,' said Eden, 'and stay with her for a while. She's on her own at home and will be glad of the company.'

'Okay, if you're sure you don't need me?'

'I'm sure.'

Eden watched Molly walk across to Agnes and touch her on the shoulder. It was a kind, tender gesture, and Eden felt pleased she'd managed to bag the young trainee, who seemed to have wisdom and sensitivity well beyond her years.

Eden followed her over. 'Feel free to use my office if you would prefer some privacy,' she offered.

'Thanks, but I think we've just about finished here,' replied the young officer, helping Agnes to her feet.

Agnes removed the blanket from around her shoulders, folded it and handed it back.

'Please let me know how that poor man is getting on, won't you? I don't mind when you ring, day or night. I won't be able to sleep until I know he's alright,' Agnes said, her voice splintering as she walked the officers to the door before rejoining Eden and Molly. She was unusually subdued. Generally, she loved to be at the epicentre of a drama.

'I'm so sorry, Agnes. How are you feeling?' Eden asked.

'Not a hundred per cent, if I'm honest. I'll be alright when I've had time to process it. I'm just not sure I'm fit to work today.'

'I don't expect you to. In fact, I won't hear of it. Molly is going to run you home and stay with you for a while, and don't even think of coming in tomorrow.'

'No, I'll be in tomorrow. Work will keep my mind off it.'

Eden didn't argue, guessing everyone had their own coping mechanisms.

After Agnes and Molly left, she headed behind the desk to pull up her appointments for the day on the computer. She had one out-of-office in the afternoon with an old client of hers. A septuagenarian called Gloria Le Grice who had been caught shoplifting from Boots. The woman was claiming temporary memory loss on account of stress caused as a result of her cat Boris going missing four days prior to the incident. It might have been a defence Eden would have run had her client not been stopped three months earlier outside Waitrose with three boxes of Tampax shoved down the front of her gilet. That time the cat had been called Maggie and had been run over on the morning of the offence. Her pitiful pleas and intermittent wails of grief had got her off with a caution, but there are only so many cats you can lose without people thinking not only are you a thief but also unfit to own a pet. Unlike her feline friends, Gloria didn't have any more lives left. The random nature of the items stolen on the first occasion had lent credibility to her defence. This time she'd stolen six packs of tights and four lipsticks. Though her age was still in her favour, Eden was pretty sure the minimum she'd get away with was a fine.

Her only other appointment in the diary was for eleven thirty that morning. A new client, Mr Retallick. A local, she guessed, with a name like that.

There was nothing in the note saying what kind of advice he needed, so she'd have to wait and see. It wasn't a bad thing. She preferred to clear the backlog rather than spend the morning preparing for the interview. As there was no one in reception, she decided she'd lock the door and put a note on it asking people to ring the bell. That way she could work in her office at the back of the building and not worry if someone wandered into reception without her knowing. She could get a couple of hours in before the new client arrived.

The morning went quickly without the distractions of ringing phones and Agnes popping in and out, and she felt pleased with herself at eleven fifteen when she shut the last of her files and could take a quick break. She carried her coffee through to reception to check the answerphone for messages.

The first was from the magistrate's court advising Gloria's case, listed for next Tuesday afternoon, had been brought forward to earlier in the day. The rest were clients wanting an update or an appointment. She was just about to ring a couple of them back when the bell rang, causing her to jump and spill coffee all over Agnes's desk. She rushed to the door and opened it, immediately turning her back on the visitor in her eagerness to return to the spillage, which was now running off the desk like a waterfall onto the carpet.

'Mr Retallick, would you lock the door behind you? I'm on my own here today, so I need to keep it locked.'

She heard the door shut and the key turn. She grabbed a box of tissues from the shelf beneath the desk, kept for the inevitable outpours of emotion that came with the job. Solicitors' reception rooms were not the jolliest of places. They were on a par with dentist waiting rooms and vasectomy clinics.

The man stayed silent as she dabbed away at the pool of coffee.

'Please take a seat. I'll be with you shortly.'

She managed to mop up most of the liquid and was relieved the leather cover of Agnes's precious diary hadn't taken a direct hit. Her secretary insisted on keeping her own paper record of appointments, court hearings and telephone contacts even though the computer was right in front of her and could bring up information at the touch of a key.

She threw the sodden tissues into the bin and turned to face her client, who she noticed had not sat down but was standing at the window watching the police activity in the street.

He was tall, about six foot two and thin, not skinny but spare. His hair was dark, pulled back in a Beckhamesque topknot. He wore a suit, which was unusual these days. A few of her elderly clients dressed up to see their solicitor, but most of the young ones didn't.

'What's going on out there?' he said without turning.

Eden hesitated. 'There was an incident last night during the lantern parade.'

He was silent for a second, engrossed by the activity outside.

'Mr Retallick?' Eden said to his back. 'I believe you have an appointment with me. I'm Eden Gray.'

The client spun around, and for a second, she was lost for words, instinctively shuffling back a step or two before offering her hand. He returned only a fleeting handshake as if it pained him.

Her own discomfort stemmed from a different part of his anatomy. His face was perfectly proportioned and chiselled as if carved from a block of stone. He would have been extraordinarily handsome but for the scar, marbled and shiny, puckering his left cheek. It trailed like candle wax down his neck to just below his collar. A corruption of beauty that drew the eye like a magnet. She tried to calm herself, but despite every effort, her mind kept drifting back to Luke's description of the man's face the evening before.

Retallick's scar signalled he was a victim too; that he had survived something terrible. She knew it was untenable to be squeamish when faced with another's disability, but still had to forcibly pull herself together.

'We're through here.'

The man followed her down the corridor into her office.

'Please, take a seat, Mr Retallick.'

'Kit, please call me Kit.'

Eden grabbed a blue counsel's notebook from her drawer and began to scribble.

'Kit, is that short for Christopher?'

'Yes, but no one ever calls me Christopher. Although I suppose that's not strictly true, they called me Christopher during my trial.'

'Your trial?'

'I'm just out of prison, on licence. I served fifteen years.'

'Do you mind me asking what for?'

'Arson.'

Eden's stomach roiled as she remembered the man the night before, writhing on the ground, Luke using the curtains to extinguish the flames burning his back. She looked up.

Kit Retallick was leaning back in his seat, his right foot resting on the knee of the other leg, his hands steepled, index fingers pressed against his lips. He was staring at her with the retina-burning intensity of a panther ready to pounce.

'What exactly did you want to see me about?' she asked, lowering her pen, worried he might see the tremble in her hands if she held on to it any longer.

'I want you to prove I was wrongly convicted. That I'm innocent.'

She felt a wave of relief, not because she believed him or no longer felt vulnerable alone with a convicted arsonist but because she could not help him and would be able to usher him out of there quickly. She dealt with live cases, not old miscarriages of justice. He'd need to contact a help group or the media or one of the universities that used such cases as training exercises for their students studying criminal evidence or jurisprudence.

'I'm afraid I'm not the right person to help you. I might be able to give you some contacts, but they will need access to your records.'

'I was hoping you would have my case file.'

'Me?'

'You took over Douglas Bassett's practice, didn't you?' he said, looking around the room.

The question was rhetorical. He'd clearly already done his research and knew she had. Eden noticed how self-contained he seemed, how much better he was dealing with this than her as if he'd been planning this conversation.

He reached down and touched the edge of the desk, running his finger along its contours as if searching for something.

'This is his desk.' He looked up. 'He was my solicitor. The one who handled my case.'

The panic was immediate and real now. She'd been in this business long enough to know an ex-prisoner with a grudge against his lawyer never made good company, and as Douglas Bassett wasn't around anymore, maybe the man intended to take out this particular grievance on the next best thing, which was her.

'I'm afraid your file may have been destroyed. We don't keep them indefinitely.'

'Oh, he will have kept this one, trust me.'

She didn't know how to reply but knew she had to get him

out of there, and the only way was to play along with him as best she could.

'Well, our closed files are off-site in storage. I can have a look for you, but I can't make any promises your file will be there.'

'So, you'll help me then?'

His expression softened, the scowl knitting his brow for the last minute or so, drifting away like thistledown.

'I didn't say that. I can give you your files if I have them, but as I said, it's not what I do. I will help you find someone to look at your case if I can.'

'But you're not ruling it out.'

She didn't answer. He seemed satisfied, for now at least, as he stood to leave.

'Aren't you going to ask me for my mobile and e-mail address? Otherwise, how are you going to contact me?'

Swallowing hard, she picked up her pen and wrote as he gave her his details.

'I'm stopping at the pub across the road tonight, but I'll be staying here after that if you need me.'

He pushed a note across the table. Eden glanced at the address before slipping it between the pages of her pad.

'Thank you, Miss Gray,' he said, buttoning his jacket. 'I'll see myself out.'

She followed him to the end of the corridor and watched him cross reception, unable to breathe until she'd locked the door behind him.

Through the window, she watched him walk up the street towards the pub. Tall and upright, he had a confident, easy gait. Head held high, he made no attempt to hide his scars. She was certain any passer-by would assume they were a badge of honour, the result of daring-do on a foreign battlefield. Certain he was gone, she walked slowly back to her office, pausing to inspect the place he'd rubbed with his finger.

At first, she couldn't see anything, but as she began to walk away, she saw it. Carved into the wood, engrained with years of dirt and polish so they were barely visible, were the initials KR.

EIGHT

Molly arrived back at the office just as Eden was slipping on her coat to leave.

'Can you man the fort until five? I'm off to see Gloria Le Grice. How's Agnes doing?'

The girl's dark eyes welled with concern.

'By the time I left, she had more colour in her cheeks, and she practically shoved me out the door when I offered to stay longer, but I'm not sure you can expect to get over a shock like that quickly.'

'No,' agreed Eden.

Eden's secretary was made of hardy stuff. To those who didn't know the woman well, she could appear offhand to the point of rudeness, but Eden knew better. Under the bluff and bluster, she was as vulnerable as the next person. More so in many ways.

'If I have time, I'll call in to tell her not to come in tomorrow. She's more likely to take notice if I do it in person rather than over the phone.'

'Don't you need to pick up Flora from school?'

'No, Mum and Dad are in charge of the school run this afternoon, thank god. I don't know how anyone with kids gets anything done. Luke was probably up all night after…' she chose her words carefully, 'the incident at the parade last night and it doesn't look like he's going to get much respite after what happened in Victoria Gardens.'

'Do you think the two might be linked?'

Eden shrugged. She didn't want to say too much until she'd had the chance to speak to Luke.

'Will you be okay here on your own?'

'Yes, of course. I'll bring my files out here so I can man the phones and deal with any clients who wander in. I've got plenty to catch up on from this morning.'

Eden thought of her own unsettling meeting with Kit Retallick and how vulnerable she had felt alone in the building.

'Best keep the door locked. The police are still out there in the street, and this kind of thing can attract unsavoury types who might wander in, hoping to get a front seat. Just take messages and lock up when you leave.'

Eden couldn't shake the image of the young man, his scar branching across his cheeks. She paused.

'Could you do me a favour? Can you check the database on Agnes's computer for a closed file? The client's name is Christopher Retallick.'

'What matter type?'

'Crime, arson. It's an old file, at least fifteen years old, probably older, given it would have taken time for the case to go to trial. It might have been destroyed, but if you could check, that would be great.'

When she had taken over the practice, as well as the office in town, Eden had taken on four lock-ups full of old files. It was the bane of every solicitor's life, having to keep every scrap of paper for a minimum of six years after a case ended. Their insurers demanded it. Some of the swanky up-country firms had gone paperless, but to most small rural practitioners like her who couldn't afford the admin staff to scan every single bit of mail, it was a pipe dream. She'd filled a fifth lock-up since she'd taken over. They were sited on an industrial estate just outside Truro in a storage facility providing coded security and CCTV twenty-four-seven. Every January, a company would turn up with a purpose-built van to shred all the files that were to be destroyed. It was a monumental task she had scrupulously scheduled every year since taking over in the hope of reducing storage costs. The file might still be there. Retallick had said as much. Then again, it hadn't been *what* he'd said but more, *how* he'd said it and that it had been in the context of a potentially mismanaged case. Eden had never worked with Douglas, but she had seen his files, and he was meticulous. He never cut corners or relied on the *you scratch my back and I'll scratch yours* ethos pervading the mindset of some small-town solicitors, which could lead to compromise for an easy life. Douglas was a fighter and a competent advocate. Every client she had inherited had nothing but praise for him.

'If I find it, do you want me to go and get the file?' asked Molly, always quick to offer more than asked.

The industrial estate with its chain-link fences was a creepy place when deserted. Once you stepped into the windowless units, it was creepier still. It was no place to be on your own, and the light was already fading.

'No, it can wait until morning. Note the file number and which unit it's in and we'll go together tomorrow. There are likely to be several boxes, if they're there at all. There's more room in my boot than yours.'

'Fair enough,' said Molly breezily. 'See you tomorrow then.'

NINE

Eden ventured slowly up the pot-holed drive, convinced she'd taken a wrong turn even though the name on the signpost matched the one she'd tapped into her sat nav from Gloria's file. 'Rosemellyn.' Yellow rose in Cornish.

The three-storey Victorian villa cast its gothic shadow across a rambling beast of a garden on the prowl. Trees overhung a pond clogged with weeds, and moss and lichen clung to the granite pavers. If you had to guess 'who lived in a house like this?' a light-fingered pensioner would not be the first person to come to mind.

She imagined the property must be subdivided into flats, but there was no such indication at the top of the steps, no name board or buzzers. She lifted the brass knocker and waited, half expecting the door to be opened by one of the Addams family.

It was answered so quickly Eden wondered if her client had been watching her approach along the drive. Gloria stood resplendent in a crimson kimono, a halo of wispy white hair stiff with hairspray framing an over-rouged face.

'Oh, it's you,' she said disappointedly, pulling the kimono up around a long stalk of neck.

'I'm sorry, are you expecting someone else? I can call back another time if it's inconvenient?'

'You're here now. You might as well come in,' she said, peering past Eden's shoulder down the drive with fugitive's eyes before bustling her inside and closing the door.

Eden followed her through the hallway towards the back of the house, noticing not for the first time what excellent posture the woman had for someone her age. No dowager's hump or arthritic hips here. She wondered whether Gloria had once been a dancer or a gymnast.

The yellowing anaglypta had not fared so well. Where it wasn't peeling, it was pinpricked with mould. There was a sour miasma of tobacco smoke and cat's piss. The thick epidermis of dust coating the carpet confirming neglect.

Eden sneezed.

'Bless you,' Gloria said, leading the way into a cramped sitting room occupied by at least six cats in various states of sleepy disinterest.

She motioned Eden to sit on the one unoccupied seat whilst she took up position on the sofa next to a lumpy ginger moggy snoozing on a pile of newspapers. To Gloria's left was a small round coffee table on which sat two cups and saucers, a teapot and a cake stand stacked with a variety of cream cakes. To her right, balanced on the arm of the sofa, was an equally stacked ashtray of cigarette butts.

Eden was starving and, in normal circumstances, would have been only too happy to take up the offer of a chocolate eclair, but not today and not here. The room was suffocatingly warm. A three-bar electric fire incongruously set in the gigantic marble fireplace had clearly been on for some time. Eden was sweating, and she imagined it was taking its toll on the cream horns too. She felt queasy and was relieved when Gloria didn't offer her refreshments; the spread clearly meant for someone else.

'Is this going to take long?' asked Gloria, moving the cake stand a half turn anti-clockwise before reaching into her kimono pocket and pulling out a pack of cigarettes.

'No, not long at all. I've come to chat about the case and to tell you the hearing on Tuesday has been brought forward an hour.'

'Oh, I don't think we need to worry about that, darling. The last time, the magistrates were very understanding. I'm so forgetful and COVID was difficult for me. Like all the other social butterflies who have had their wings clipped, I've had mental health issues coming out my ears,' she said, blowing a plume of blue smoke in Eden's direction.

What an image that conjures, thought Eden coughing.

'I think that's what happened that day,' continued Gloria, 'I was overwhelmed by the whole shopping experience having been isolating for so long and then dear Boris,' she reached out and touched the brindled tail of the sleeping feline, 'we miss him so much don't we, Tony? There were so many people I panicked. I had to get out of there and forgot to pay. I had no intention of stealing. I had the money in my purse,' she sniffed.

Eden examined the room. It was larger than she'd thought initially, the oversized furniture swallowing the space. One alcove was partially separated off with a panelled screen painted with cotton wool clouds and chubby-legged cherubs. From her seat, Eden could see that behind it were boxes of electrical goods. Food mixers, dry fryers, luxury foot spas. It worried her. What were they doing here? Perhaps her client did have problems, after all, an addiction to online shopping. The items were all too big to have inadvertently found their way into her nylon tote, so how did Gloria afford all this stuff? She had provided her income details for the court and had pleaded poverty every time they'd met, yet the goods must amount to several thousand pounds worth. She had to say something.

Eden gestured towards the boxes. 'Gloria, I hope you don't mind me asking, but where did all this stuff come from? You gave me your income details, but those items must have cost a packet?'

Gloria immediately jumped up and adjusted the screen.

'Oh, they're not mine, darling. I'm storing them for a very good friend.'

'A friend?'

'Don't sound so surprised. Being elderly doesn't preclude you from having friends, you know,' she said indignantly.

'No, of course not.'

'The boxes get dropped off by a charming young man every couple of weeks and picked up by him as and when my friend needs new stock.'

'Isn't it inconvenient for you to have all this stuff sitting here?' *Inconvenient and a fire hazard,* Eden thought.

'Not at all, my friend is also my landlord. I get a discount on the rent, and he pays me twenty pounds in cash every time he picks stuff up. I've got plenty of room these days. I'm rattling about in this place. Some of the rooms are damp, and it could ruin the packaging, so they have to stay in this room with me and the babies.' She reached out to smooth the cat's lolling head. 'Say hello to Miss Gray, Tony,' she cooed, lifting one of his floppy paws to wave in Eden's direction.

Alarm bells were ringing, but Eden decided to leave it there for now.

'So, you're all alone in this place?'

'Yes.'

That the woman didn't care to indulge her with an explanation surprised her. Gloria was a sharer. Not wanting to rub salt into what might be the wound of abandonment, Eden centred her attention back on the case.

'I think you need to prepare yourself for a conviction.'

'You don't mean incarceration, do you, darling? What would happen to the babies if they threw me in the pokey?'

'No, not prison but a fine, and you will have a criminal record. I realise it's not going to affect you the way it might others. You don't need to worry about your job like some would, but there is a high likelihood it will be in the local paper. The court reporters will spot a story behind this, and you might end up with unwanted attention.'

'The newspapers… will they take photographs?' she said, reaching up to touch her crispy hair. 'They won't come here, will they?'

The woman looked worried.

'No, I don't think it will warrant that, but I wanted you to be prepared,' said Eden, 'and to make sure you didn't want to change your plea.'

Eden hated saying the words. She always backed her clients, but Gloria had been caught red-handed and had form. She was concerned if she went in the witness box, she'd tie herself in knots or over-embellish and look like a liar. Usually, in such circumstances, she would suggest not giving evidence and depriving the prosecution of the chance to cross-examine. But, in this case, Gloria's eccentricity was the only thing likely to get her off. She had no medical evidence to back her lack of intent, no diagnosis of early-onset dementia. If she was prepared to accept culpability, Eden knew she'd be in a better position to put forward mitigating circumstances without her having to say a thing. She could strike a bargain with the CPS.

Gloria's eyes widened. 'Why would I do that? I am completely innocent.'

Eden knew from experience it was hard to make people believe in an unpalatable truth.

'But you were caught with the goods on you.'

'I know, but I have absolutely no recollection of how they came to be there. It's a complete blur,' said Gloria, blinking rapidly to emphasise the point.

Eden lifted her hands in a gesture of acceptance.

'Okay, if you're sure?'

'Absolutely. I'm an innocent woman, a victim of ageism. A sacrifice to the cult of youth. I didn't march at Aldermaston for this. Us women didn't camp out at Greenham to be thrown on the scrap heap.'

Eden had no idea where this was going, and the thought of her adopting this rhetoric in the witness box made her heart sink even further. Gloria may well have marched with the thousands of others in the sixties, but it wouldn't get her off a theft charge. Furthermore, she was pretty sure she'd never camped out at Greenham, and she should know because her mother, true to form, had. According to her father, she'd returned with a *friend* called Tomi, a sulky woman in dungarees and Doc Martens who stayed for two weeks and ousted him from the marital bedroom before leaving as quickly as she'd arrived. Her father had told her afterwards it was a phase her mother was going through and that Tomi had moved out to join an anti-motorway protest. She had been last seen on the ten o'clock news chained to a sycamore, and her mother's whirlwind dalliance with sapphism had never reared its head again.

'I'll get my office to call you about timings ahead of the hearing next week.'

Gloria was on her feet, marshalling her towards the door before she had time to slip her file back into her briefcase. No matter, she was glad to get out of the oppressive heat.

As Gloria walked her back down the hall, there was a loud thud above them.

Gloria interjected before Eden had time to question what caused it. 'Oh, that will be Boris, darling,' then thinking better of it, 'or plaster falling from one of the ceilings. It does that all the time. It's the damp, you see.'

'He's back then?'

Gloria looked deliberately confused, 'Who?'

'Boris… your cat?'

Her face relaxed. 'Oh yes… poor darling.'

Eden had thought the cat story a ruse from the beginning, and it was now confirmed. She felt the woman's hand on her back, ushering her out before she had time to say more.

Gloria stood at the door waving goodbye until she was out of sight, for all the world as if she was a valued family friend, not an exasperated solicitor at the end of her tether.

As Eden reached the junction, she had to pull into the verge for a BMW indicating left into the driveway. She waited for a second to catch a glimpse of the driver. A smartly dressed silver fox. Perhaps Gloria had a toy boy. He briefly met her gaze before putting his foot down. Eden thought of the cream cakes curdling on the cake stand and hoped for his sake he had a stronger stomach than her.

The traffic into town was nose to tail. She glanced at the clock. The meeting had taken longer than expected. She wouldn't have time to call in on Agnes now. She knew she ate early and wouldn't thank her for turning up during her mealtime. She had better call her father to check he'd remembered to pick up Flora from school, not that there was much she could do about it if he hadn't in this traffic.

'Call Dad.' The car's computer worked its magic. Her father sounded as if he was in a car too.

'Hi, Dad, just checking you remembered to collect Flora.'

'Yes, we're on the way home. Say hello, Flora, so Auntie Eden knows I'm not a senile old fool.'

'Hi, Auntie Eden.'

'Hi, Flora. I didn't think you'd forgotten, Dad.'

'But thought you'd give me a kindly nudge just in case. We've got Flora overnight, so I'll be taking her in tomorrow as well. Luke rang to say he was tied up with an investigation into the accident at the Lantern Parade and something to do with Agnes. Is that right?'

'Yes, I can't say too much, not with little ears flapping.'

'No, no, of course not.'

'I'll be around tomorrow evening as usual. I'll bring a bottle of wine.'

Friday had become a bit of a routine since her father had taken a vegetarian cookery course six months ago. Every Friday, he cooked something new from his ever-increasing repertoire and tested it out on her. Her mother's culinary efforts were not only limited by her strict vegan diet but also her complete lack of skill.

That her food was truly terrible didn't seem to bother her, neither did it stop her entertaining. You could always tell which of her guests had eaten her food before by the tentative way they brought their forks to their lips as if it were a dare. The fare she produced was usually green but sometimes greyish brown and often unidentifiable as food at all. A chef prone to extremes, her meals were either completely tasteless (a skill in itself) or made your eyes water. The latter usually occurred after she'd raided the spice racks at Waitrose or listened to a cookery segment on Woman's Hour. She never took down the recipe or bothered with measuring the ingredients. After all, that would take all the fun out of it. She'd throw a bit of everything into the pot so that her vegetarian curries tasted not only of all those lovely warming eastern spices you would expect but often a little Rosemary or a dash of soy sauce for good measure. All were added with gay abandon, a lucky bag approach she never tasted because she didn't enjoy eating. 'Once I plate it up, it's no longer mine. I'm done with it,' she'd say. All in all, she approached cooking with the same mindset Jackson Pollock approached painting. It was the creative impulse and not the end result that mattered. With her father in charge of the menu now, Friday dinner had, by some miracle, become something to enjoy rather than endure.

'I'll pick Flora up from school if you like and we'll come over together. I'll try and touch base with Luke. Even he has to stop to eat.'

There was a long pause. 'No need for that. Mum was going to ring you later, but I might as well spill the beans now. Your sister is coming home. She's arriving on the train from Paddington tomorrow. I'll pick her up, then we'll collect Flora from school together.'

'Thea? I thought she wasn't due a visit until Christmas?'

'Oh, it's not a visit. She's back for good, apparently.'

'For good… are you sure? What about Ravi and the gallery?'

'Tell you what, love, traffic's a bit busy. I need to concentrate. Your mother will fill you in later, I'm sure.'

With that, he cut her off.

Eden felt a wave of dread, the same dread she always felt when Thea's name was mentioned. She loved her sister, but she always brought chaos with her.

***

Her phone rang just as she settled down to a bowl of tomato soup and an episode of 'Ozark' she'd recorded. It was her mother. At least she'd been warned this time. Her mother's phone calls were generally random. She'd call whenever a thought entered her head with little regard for whether Eden was in a meeting or in court. Her ambiguous relationship with food also meant mealtimes were of little consequence.

'Hi, Mum.' Eden coughed, trying to clear the lump of crusty loaf she had just popped into her mouth.

'Are you eating?' It sounded like an accusation.

'Yes, I just sat down to a bowl of soup. Can I call you back?'

'It won't take long. I'm calling to let you know Thea's home tomorrow. Your father said he might have mentioned it.'

Eden imagined the grilling her poor dad had got when he'd let slip that he'd stolen her thunder.

'She's had a falling out with Ravi and decided she can't put up with it any longer.'

'Put up with what?'

'The oppression. A man telling her what to do.'

Ravi was an innocuous, laidback bear of a man. Eden had never heard him raise his voice. She couldn't imagine her sister being under his heel.

'He's smothering her creativity. They've been putting together a new website for the gallery, and she's been struggling to bring things together.'

Eden reached for another piece of bread.

'He suggested they bring in a web designer. Can you imagine? Like a slap in the face after all the work Thea's done.'

'Perhaps he was trying to help. I imagine building a website is a technical process. It's hardly her skillset.'

'Trust you to take his side. You always take the man's part. I've noticed you do that whenever your father and I disagree. You always rush to back him up.'

'I was just saying. Ravi's motives may not have been all bad.'

'Well, anyway, she's coming home, and I want you to show some sympathy. Her self-confidence is in tatters, poor darling, and I don't want you upsetting her with loads of questions. I know it's what you do for a living, but there's a time and place. So, promise me no interrogation tomorrow when you come over.'

Eden's annoyance, like the lump of bread stuck in the back of her throat, was difficult to swallow. 'Fine,' she snapped. 'Now can I finish my dinner?'

'Is it tinned? There is bound to be sugar if it's out of a tin. They put spoonfuls of sweetener in to disguise the taste of the additives. You should make your own. We grow plenty of veg in the garden. You only have to ask.'

Eden sighed. 'Goodbye, Mum.' The soup was cold. Eden lifted the bowl and drank it down in one, leaving an orangey moustache she wiped away with her sleeve. It tasted tomatoey and sweet… and delicious.

TEN

Kit woke early with a start, his body clock wound by years of institutional living.

Next came the usual thirty seconds of dread before he opened his eyes and remembered he was no longer incarcerated, at least not physically.

It sometimes took longer if he'd had a drink the evening before or a restless night's sleep. On those mornings, his senses deceived him, and the fetid stench of stale sweat, urine and industrial-strength bleach burned his nostrils. He'd struggle to force his eyes open as his innards knotted, waiting for the metallic clank of cell doors, the relentless din of prison life, day and night, so you could hardly hear yourself think.

If the noise didn't drive you mad, the monotony and bowel-loosening fear would.

He'd learnt early on that all prisons were about rules and terror.

The first place he'd been taken to for assessment was different, of course. He'd been a kid. The emphasis was on spilling your guts in the hope the dive to the bottom of the slurry pit of trauma and abuse propelling you to offend would cure you. The therapists, psychologists and social workers all worked from a well-thumbed script he'd learnt off pat. He'd been glad to be free of those life scavengers. He'd been ripped apart and put back together so many times by them he'd forgotten the truth or bits of it. The stuff he knew for certain he'd kept to himself. To tell it might have attracted too much attention. It might have catapulted him into a case study. Worse still, he might have become brain fodder for some student's thesis. Then he'd never get out; valuable lab rats never did, not alive.

It was best to stick to the police profile. That way, you could predict your outcome.

In prison, rehabilitation was the name of the game, after shame and repentance, of course. It always amused him for all the left-wing rhetoric, the language of the do-gooders was the language of the confessional, sin, damnation, redemption and resurrection. Without the admission of guilt, there was no release on licence.

Lying in this warm, comfortable bed with its freshly laundered sheets, floral curtains at the window and holiday posters on the walls, he knew to the world out there, and by his own admission, he was a guilty man. The trouble was, he wasn't guilty. He had never been guilty, not of what he was accused of, and now it was time to set things straight. He'd played the game, toed the line and embraced his redemption, and it had, as predicted, got him released. Now he was out and it was time to turn the tables, prove the bastards had got it wrong. What could they do to him? You could only die once.

He was encouraged by how the meeting with Eden Gray had gone, although she had been different than he'd expected. Not the way she'd looked. He'd seen photographs of her on her website and thought her stunning, and he hadn't been disappointed. Not that he had much idea what passed for attractive these days. The blokes in prison seemed to be obsessed with girls with trout pouts and breasts so big it amazed him they didn't topple over. Everything about Eden Gray was natural, even the long copper-coloured hair he imagined most women would die for. It was the way she'd behaved that threw him. He'd expected her to be more assertive, less reserved. He'd done his homework. She had a reputation for being feisty and relentless. The kind of lawyer who liked to win and wasn't too concerned whose feathers she ruffled in the process. She was also known to have a soft spot for the underdog, and he was certainly that.

She had seemed nervous. Then again, he couldn't read too much into it. She hadn't been forewarned about why he was there, and there was the scar, of course. He had learnt the hard way never to underestimate its effect on people. They were generally either disgusted or, worse still, morbidly fascinated by it, like Rob Davey's girlfriend in the pub.

Eden, to her credit, had been neither. Of course, she might have been distracted by the kerfuffle going on outside. The police and the CSI boys. Having that lot camped outside your office had to be a worry. It wouldn't exactly attract passing trade.

There were mumblings when he went down to breakfast about the tragedy the night of the parade. He didn't engage but overheard the woman at the desk saying a man had died.

The police tape was still there when he headed up the hill to the station. He listened to his inner voice telling him to keep his head down. It had served him well during his years inside. He had good instincts. It wouldn't do to antagonise people or draw attention to himself.

Part of him didn't know why he was doing this. Only fools returned to the scene of their crime. Then again, when it came down to it, this wasn't the scene of his, and he didn't really have a choice. He needed to look at it without the cataracts of grief and disbelief he'd had back then. He had to be prepared for any questions Miss Gray might ask about the place.

He'd disguised himself as best he could. A beany pulled down over his ears and a scarf to cover his scar.

The train journey to Penzance was uneventful. He was the only one in his carriage, but there was a moment when he thought he recognised a woman queuing with him for the bus to Morvah. He was relieved when she looked straight through him. Perhaps his memory was playing tricks, or the confrontation with Rob Davey in the pub had sent his paranoia soaring. Much as he hoped it was the case, he couldn't bank on it. Gossip and tragedy were common coinage in this corner of the county. Here, they still spoke of mining disasters that decimated villages centuries before, of men flushed from the mineshafts out to sea. Fifteen years was recent history here.

He sat at the back of the bus, galvanising his nerve, his legs heavy and uncertain as he disembarked, and the bus rumbled away behind him. He took his time climbing the stone style to the side of the church. He would have vaulted it as a kid. Now there was nothing to hurry him, no one to beat him if he was late.

This was the less trodden path, not the coastal route popular with tourists marked on all the maps. This one eeled through heathland down to the beach. If he had taken the other way, he would have met someone for sure. A dog walker or a jogger, maybe, but mid-week at this time of year, he didn't expect to meet a single soul here.

Despite his leisurely pace, he felt hot in the winter sunshine. November had been unusually mild, and the odd solitary bee still hovered to loot the last of the nectar. He loosened his scarf, letting it surf the coppery bracken, waist-high in places, until it caught on the prickly gorse.

He had always felt more at home out of doors than inside. It had been the worst of the many horrors prison held for him. The total disconnection with nature. The seasons blurred within the confines of concrete walls. He had been hemmed in and vulnerable for most of his adult life, but as a child, the granite keystones of the farmhouse, despite every effort, had never been able to hold him in.

He had first climbed out of his bedroom window when he was twelve years old, shortly after his mum moved in with Ray and started working nights in a nursing home in the village. Ray was often out in the evenings, busy on the farm in the summer or down the pub in winter, so he'd been left in the care of his elder sister, Tamar. At fifteen, she had managed well enough. She'd made sure he got to bed at the right time and poured him a bowl of cereal before he did, but after that, she never thought to check he'd stayed put.

He'd hated the farm when his mother was absent almost as much as he hated Ray for bringing them there. According to Ray, it was hundreds of years old and had been in his family for generations. It was cold and uninviting at the best of times, but without his mother's presence, it felt like the enemy. The house they'd had in Truro before she'd met Ray was on an estate and had magnolia paintwork and big windows to let in the light. The farm's thick granite walls and multi-paned windows barred the sunshine even on the brightest of days, and it was never warm, not in the way their old house was with its central heating and wall-to-wall carpets. The slate floors downstairs were icy. No one dared pad about barefoot there.

The bathroom was dingy. The chipped enamel bore orange stains that wouldn't budge no matter how much Mum scrubbed at them. You never got to have a proper bath where the soap suds slopped over the top. The old Rayburn only heated a few inches of water, so you still felt the cold cast iron on your ass cheeks.

Nothing was new, not the furniture or the curtains, not even the crockery. The crazed white plates chipped when Mum washed them, and the forks made your tongue fizz where the silver plate had worn off. Two orange melamine bowls he and Tamar ate cereal from seemed to be the only concession to colour.

They did have a decent television. It was one of the few things Ray had let them bring with them, along with the microwave and the VHS. Their dad had insisted they buy the

TV when he'd sent home his first pay cheque from the rigs off Aberdeen. It was the one and only time he'd been as generous. Very soon, the cheques became as sporadic as the visits home and eventually, both stopped altogether. When his mum filed for divorce, his dad hadn't objected. He'd hated him for that, so much so he'd always told anyone who asked that he was dead, sometimes saying he'd died in the Piper Alpha explosion even though it gave the man a heroic end he didn't deserve.

They had lived happily without a dad despite money being tight. His gran had helped out where she could. She'd bought the school uniforms, cooked them Sunday roast, and looked after them in the holidays so his mum could work as a barmaid at the Royal Hotel in Truro, where she'd met Ray one afternoon after the Wednesday livestock market.

He realised now his mum must have been lonely. Ray filled the gap his father had left and was solvent to boot. He wasn't bad-looking, had never been married and owned his own farm. He brought her flowers and chocolates and was nice to him and Tamar to begin with, but once he and his mum were married, Ray's only contribution to the union was a temper that held them all captive.

His sister escaped through books and her music, reading at night under the covers with her earphones in. She had a torch Kit longed to get his hands on, not to read by but so he could get out in the dark. Not that the want of a flashlight stopped him. Even in winter, the night was never truly black, not once you got used to it and if the moon was out, the scintillating light turned the patchwork of fields silver and the sea to mercury. On such nights, he would layer his clothes over his pyjamas and lie amongst the tall grass, listening for the owl that nested in the top barn to begin her nightly sweep for food. If she didn't fly, he'd cup his hands and blow between the thumbs into the small echo chamber, mimicking her call so she would fly out to defend her patch. Over time, he learned to judge the position of the creatures in the fields by sound alone. The bark of the vixen and the high-pitched scream of the rabbit she'd chosen for dinner.

In the summer, when the light didn't die until ten or even eleven at night, he would wait until the orange ball had sunk into the sea before leaving the house, crouching down behind the low Cornish hedges, tracing the Jack-n-Jills. The ground would be warm, the vanilla-scented gorse fluorescent yellow in the twilight. He'd clamber down the cliff path to watch the bats swoop in and out of the caves, catching insects trapped in the clefts. He'd sit for hours listening to waves as loud as avalanches crash against the rocks until his senses overloaded. Then, he'd lie back, close his eyes and breathe in nature's salty essence, letting it rest in the pit of his stomach until everything bad drifted away and he felt safe again.

As he got older, he would explore farther afield and lie on the stone slab they called the Giant's Grave, hoping to hear his mighty voice rise from the burial chamber beneath. The fields hereabouts were full of standing stones. Tilting like drunken guests at a wedding, they occasionally toppled or were misplaced, the smaller ones turning up later in someone's garden.

Back then, he hadn't known their history. He'd heard only legends and folklore, like how mothers passed their children through the one they called Men-a-Tol, known to the locals as the Crick Stone. He had only learnt about their Neolithic origins and the pre-Celtic tribes who raised them whilst in prison studying for his anthropology degree. He had chosen the course in the hope the past would inform his future, that it would give him the key to understand why people behaved the way they did. Why he was where he was and why those who had put him there had been prepared to lie. He had been offered psychology but had rejected the option on the basis there must be more to man's evil than mother fixation and sexual perversion. Both seemed to place women at their core and didn't ring true because of it. He had never believed women were the problem. He had been loved and nurtured by his grandmother, his mum and his sister but had known only two kinds of men growing up, shits and sharks. Both his father and Ray had been inadequate, and this had formed the basis of his thesis. As far as he could tell from his studies from Atilla the Hun to Hitler, inadequate men with chips on their shoulders had caused most of the world's sorrows. If he had one phrase to put on a t-shirt that could save mankind from pain, it would be;

'BEWARE INADEQUATES. THEY HAVE TOO MUCH TO PROVE.'

Rounding the corner, he could make out the blackened skeleton of Tregardock Farm. Like the standing stones, it was a reminder. Something happened here, and the dead linger where there is unfinished business. He'd met arsonists in prison who mistook him for a soul mate and had confided they liked returning to the scene of devastation on rainy days when the charred timbers released the scent of smoke. He was certain it wouldn't be the case after all these years, but nevertheless, he was grateful for dry weather. What had once been the farmhouse was a shell, a scar on the horizon. He leant against the hedge, his legs stubbornly refusing to carry him further. He hadn't expected this. The police had shown him dozens of photographs in the days following the fire, but they were mostly close-ups taken at odd angles, and the debris, police tape and people milling around in white onesies made the whole thing look unreal, like a scene from a film.

Now he could see that the roof was completely gone, as if a giant bird had plucked it from the granite walls and carried it off. Where windows had once glinted, blackened sockets now stared blindly across the barbed wire circling the yard. He felt a bead of sweat trickle down his forehead and reached up to tug off his hat. Scrunching it into his coat pocket, he took a breath, let go of the wall and carried on up the lane, eyes concentrating on his boots to avoid looking up at the ruin. He was finding the memories of that night more difficult to avoid.

It had been like any other Saturday. He'd spent the day doing chores around the farm and for once Ray had said he'd done a good job and let him watch the football on telly while he'd gone off to buy screws for the repairs on the old piggery. Tamar and Mum had gone to Plymouth on the train to shop for a dress for Tamar's leaver's prom in two weeks. His sister had saved her wages from the newsagents, and Mum had managed to squirrel away the money for the shoes and was going to pay for Tamar to get her nails done on the day. It was a big thing, and all his sister and her giggly mates ever seemed to talk about.

The two of them had come off the bus later that afternoon all smiles, loaded down with carrier bags. Ray had mumbled something about wasting money when they'd come in, but they'd ignored him, and as usual, straight after tea, he'd gone down the pub. His mum was on late duty at the nursing home and had hired a video from the shop for them to watch while Ray was out, but they'd never got to see it. Ray had come home in a foul mood, having only had one pint because a coach party of girls on a hen do had turned up at the pub. He'd stomped back into the kitchen carrying two four-packs of lagers from the off licence, saying 'if he wanted to listen to the cackle of hens he'd sit in the coop round the back of the barn'.

Their disappointment on his return had been difficult to hide.

They knew he'd settle on the sofa, commandeering the TV for the rest of the evening and that the video would stay firmly in its case.

His mother had put on a brave face.

'I tell you what, let's go upstairs so Tamar can try on her dress. Let's have us a fashion show.'

They'd gone up to Tamar's room and waited while she changed in the bathroom before parading around in the short silver dress she'd got from Topshop. He'd never seen her look like that before, her shoulder blades beneath the silvery straps like the buds of angel's wings as she oozed glamour.

'Like a Bond girl with those legs,' Mum said as Tamar walked about the bedroom, trying to balance on her high heels. They'd laughed until they cried when she'd tripped and landed on her backside, Mum joking that she had better get a few lessons before she tried to dance in those things, or some poor boy would be going home with broken toes.

The hilarity was short-lived. Ray heard the bang when Tamar toppled and rushed upstairs, not out of concern but because he could never bear to hear them having fun. He'd stood in the doorway, itching for an excuse to have a go.

'What the fuck is going on up here?'

'Nothing, Tamar is trying on her prom dress, that's all.'

Mum had tripped over her excuses just like Tamar had tripped in her new heels, her confidence evaporating.

Ray looked Tamar up and down as if she was something he'd trodden on in the yard, then turned on his mother. His face twisted, spittle gathering in the corners of his mouth. "What the hell were you thinking letting her buy that?' She'll be a bloody laughing stock. You needn't bother teaching her to dance. It won't be dancing them boys will be after. They'll be like rats up a drainpipe when they see the little tart in that getup.'

Tamar's cheeks had scorched scarlet. Eyes blazing, she'd turned on Ray.

'Well, you should know all about tarts. You spend enough time with one of the best.'

'What the hell are you on about?'

'Shona down the pub, that's what I'm on about. I've heard she's not averse to being paid for what she gives for free to you.'

The barmaid at the Red Lion, where Ray drank away most of the farm's profits, was the woman Ray used to see before he met Mum, Tamar had told him. Shona was married and years younger than Mum, and they'd guessed it hadn't been anything more than sex, but the whole village knew and when they'd first arrived, the woman had sought Tamar out in the newsagents and questioned her about Mum and Ray. Ray had steered clear of her for a while, but according to Tamar, the pair had started getting friendly again, and one of her friends had seen them together in Ray's van after hours.

He'd watched his mum, her face stitched with disbelief, waiting for her to say something, to at least ask Ray if it was true. But she didn't say a thing until Ray moved forward as if to hit Tamar, his right fist working at his side. He had been certain the bully was going to thump his sister.

Then a miracle had happened. Mum had squared up to him.

'You touch her, you lay one finger on my girl, and I swear to God, I'll kill you. One day, when you least expect it, I'll take a scythe and cut you down, and what's more, I'll make sure it looks like an accident. Not that anyone will care if it is or isn't because they'll be too busy dancing on your bloody grave.'

They'd held their breaths, waiting for the customary thwack that might break their mother's nose this time, but Ray had seemed taken aback. Mum was the peacemaker, the one always biting her lip.

'Do what the hell you want, the lot of you, but don't expect me to keep the little cow under my roof if she lands up pregnant. She'll be out on her ear, and the rest of you can get out too if you don't like it.' He'd spun on his heels and thundered down the stairs.

Tamar had been seething. She'd discarded the dress for jeans and a sweatshirt and headed out. Kit had raced after her.

'Go back, Kit,' she'd shouted over her shoulder. 'I hate that fucker so much. Why the hell did Mum choose him of all people and bring us to this shithole?'

He'd had no answers to the question he'd asked himself a hundred times before.

'If I was bigger, I'd have thumped him, you know. I wouldn't care whether he thumped me back or not,' he'd said.

Tamar's sobs were punctuated with a snort of laughter.

'You could have at least kicked him in the balls.'

He had laughed then, too.

'Look, I'll be okay. Only a few more months and I'll be out of here, and once I'm in university, I'll get a job and a flat, and as soon as you're sixteen, you can come and live with me.' She'd held him by his shoulders. 'Now promise me when you go back there, you won't give Ray an excuse to knock seven bells out of you.'

'I won't say anything, but where are you going?'

'I'm meeting someone. I won't be home tonight. I'm staying over.'

'Where?' he'd asked.

She'd tapped the side of her nose. 'With someone who's got our backs. Go home and keep out of Ray's way. Lock yourself in your room and pretend you're asleep, and remember this isn't forever.'

But it was forever. It was the last time he saw her.

He shook his head, ridding himself of his reveries, letting anger fill the spaces left. It spilt from his lips in a yell that would have shaken anyone who heard it if there had been anyone there but him to hear.

ELEVEN

Molly was already there when Eden arrived at the office.

'How did you get on yesterday afternoon?'

'Okay, it was quiet, only a couple of calls. I managed to finish the brief to counsel on the Robinson's boundary dispute.'

'Good, why don't you e-mail it to me and I'll look it over before it goes?'

'Oh yes, another thing. I found the archived file you were after, Christopher Retallick. It's in storage. I've got the number, but it's not an arson case. He was convicted of manslaughter.'

'Manslaughter? He didn't mention anyone had died.'

Eden had half hoped the files had been destroyed when she'd been led to believe it was an arson case. The stakes had just risen considerably. Now she'd have to retrieve them and hand them over to the client, explaining she couldn't help. This was too big for her to take on.

'There are loads of files listed for the matter. We'll need boxes to carry them back here.'

'We might as well go now,' said Eden, wanting to get this over with as soon as possible. 'The diary is empty this morning.' Eden brought the car around to the back of the office so Molly could load the boxes into the boot.

'Why do we need the files?' Molly asked, sliding into the passenger seat.

'The client has recently been released from prison on licence. Now he's out, he wants to challenge his conviction.'

Molly's face lit up. 'Do you think he's got a chance? I mean, do you think we can help him?'

'I know absolutely nothing about the case other than it was

arson. That is until you told me differently. My predecessor, Douglas Bassett, was his defence lawyer. If it turns out he did a bad job defending Retallick, we could be conflicted out in any event. We took over his practice, including all potential negligence claims within the limitation dates. If Douglas made a hash of the case, I'll have to alert our insurers to a potential claim.'

'But a miscarriage of justice on the evidence doesn't mean Mr Bassett did anything wrong. It could simply be all the evidence wasn't available at the time. Or maybe the police withheld it, or a witness lied. Then we could act, couldn't we?'

Her trainee was itching to get her hands on this, and she couldn't blame her. This kind of opportunity didn't come along often, but she couldn't let her get her hopes up. Aside from the scope for conflict, there was the matter of costs. She had no idea how Retallick intended to fund this review. Legal aid would only be available if he found solid new evidence to back his innocence. Until then, he'd be self-funding, and she had no idea if he had the money. A bigger firm eager to tap the kudos a case like this might deliver if successful might be willing to handle it pro bono. She couldn't afford to do that. This was reason enough not to get involved. Plus, the man made her feel uncomfortable.

Although she wasn't a novice at this game and had represented her fair share of unsavoury criminal clients over the years, there was something brooding and dangerous about Retallick that made her nervous, and she wasn't sure she was prepared to expose Molly to him. She was responsible for the well-being of her trainee during work hours and took the responsibility seriously. Cold cases were funny, unpredictable animals. They could take over your life. The idea of putting things right, clearing someone's name and getting justice against the odds was intoxicating. It was easy to get swept away, thinking you might find the key to a quashed conviction only to crash back down to earth with a bang when you failed.

The euphoria was followed by spiralling regret and the particular kind of guilt linked with professional responsibility. The worry that someone else could have done better. The crashing sense of failure niggled every criminal lawyer who had lost a case. With time, as with all things, you got used to it and moved on. It was a rough kind of justice, but the only one they had, and let's face it, there were far worse systems out there. Until they invented an algorithm to predict innocence or guilt, they were stuck with it. Young lawyers who hadn't learnt to control their emotions combusted easily. They invested too much of themselves in the outcome. The only saving grace in this case was that Kit Retallick was not behind bars. He had served his sentence as a guilty man. As long as he didn't re-offend whilst on licence, he was free - innocent or guilty.

Eden could feel the anticipation rising from Molly like kettle steam. She decided to shelve her concerns for the time being until she'd had a look at the files and could tell what they were dealing with. 'Did Agnes ring in this morning?' she asked, changing the conversation.

'Yes, she's coming in later. She said something about Luke coming around to talk to her this morning, but she was adamant she'd be in after lunch.'

'I hope you told her I wasn't expecting her to come back until she was good and ready. It hardly seems worth coming in this afternoon, given it's Friday.'

'I don't think she was planning to at first, but when I told her we were going to collect some old files from storage, she asked which ones. When I told her the name, she said she was coming in. She seemed a bit flustered by it, to tell you the truth, so I didn't press her.'

'She would have been here when Douglas handled the case.

It would have been a big thing for him, given the charge and the boy was so young. It could be she recognised the name and was curious, or perhaps she thought she could help if we needed a bit of background info?'

'Maybe,' said Molly, although she didn't sound convinced.

The industrial estate where the storage units were was a short drive to the other side of town. Luckily, they were able to park right outside.

'Going by the number, the files should be in the second unit towards the back,' said Molly.

Eden tapped in the code while Molly lifted the boxes from the boot. The units were racked floor to ceiling, four rows a container, six shelves a row, each file stacked sequentially by year and in the order they were opened. Eden insisted the removal from storage of any file was not only recorded on the database but also in a log book hanging from a hook at the end of the first row. Details of the client's name, number, and date of removal, plus the name of the person taking the file, had to be noted and signed out, and a similar entry had to be made when it was returned. It was important. The content of each was confidential, whether it was a criminal case, divorce, or house purchase; every file held information the client would not want broadcasting. Security was crucial, as were the tight lips of those who had access.

They carried the boxes towards the back of the room to where Kit Retallick's files were housed, according to the records.

'What's the number again?'

'1392/05, twelve correspondence files plus eight lever arch files of documents,' said Molly. 'They should be on the third shelf of the second row.' Molly grabbed the stubby step ladder to scan the shelf just above her eye level for the files. '1389, 1390, 1391.' She paused to look down at Eden.

'The next is 1393. 1392 to 1395 are missing, as are all the

documents. They should be here, but they're not.'

'Are you sure?'

Molly shuffled through the files again, mumbling the numbers. 'No, they're not here.'

'That's odd. Someone must have signed them out. I'll take a look in the log book. You're positive they haven't been destroyed?'

'Not according to the record,' said Molly, climbing down from the ladder to join her boss.

Eden walked to the entrance to check the log book.

'Here… I've found a record of them coming into storage in 2007 at the end of the trial, but there's no signature or date indicating they've been signed out. It doesn't make sense. They were clearly in this container once. Where the hell are they?'

'Perhaps Mr Bassett had a different system,' suggested Molly, picking up on Eden's concern.

'No, I adopted his system, or rather Agnes made me adopt it and every other time I've needed to retrieve files, they've always been where they should be.'

'Maybe someone misfiled it then?'

'It could happen with one file, I suppose. It would be easy to slip a single file out of sequence, but not as many as this. No, the record is wrong, and I'm not sure where to start. I really haven't got time to hang around here looking for them all day. I need to get back to the office.'

'I don't mind staying to look if you can spare me?' said Molly. 'I can hunt around here and in the other containers if you like?'

Eden paused.

'No, it would be like looking for a needle in a haystack.'

'Let's get back. Agnes may be able to shed some light on where they are. Failing which, I'll just have to tell Retallick we can't find them.'

TWELVE

Agnes sat in the chair by the window, contemplating the constellation of age spots quietly growing into a universe across the backs of her hands. If only she hadn't argued with that young policeman and done what he'd asked in the first place, she might have found the man earlier. Minutes mattered in medical emergencies. If she had known some first aid she might have been able to help him while she waited for the paramedics to arrive. She hadn't even had a bottle of water from which to give him a sip. Everyone carries a bottle of water these days. It was as if they expected dehydration loitering around every corner. She regularly chided Molly for buying water when there was a perfectly good tap in the office, but at least Molly would have been able to pull that hideous mask off and give the man a drink. What had she had to offer him? All she'd had was a packet of ginger nuts. She'd always prided herself in being a useful member of society, yet when push came to shove, she'd frozen.

The call from Molly earlier saying she and Eden were looking for the Retallick files had been the final straw. It hadn't crossed her mind when a Mr Retallick booked the appointment and wouldn't say what it was about that it was Christopher Retallick calling. Though not prefaced with the Tre, Pol, Pens associated with Cornish surnames, Retallick was common enough. The husky masculine voice had been polite, educated. When she thought of Christopher Retallick she thought of a sullen, foul-mouthed teenager glowering through a greasy fringe, the left side of his face wadded with bandages. Had she known he was out and it was him, she would have made excuses and told him Eden was too busy to take on any new clients. That dreadful case had almost killed Douglas. He had lived it day and night for months, and when he lost it, he had spiralled into a deep depression that he never fully recovered from as far as she was concerned. That boy had been a monster, and she had no reason to believe the man would be any different.

She knew they wouldn't find the files in the storage containers. Douglas had taken them before Eden took over the firm. She knew exactly where they were and they could stay there and rot as far as she was concerned.

By the time Luke Parish arrived with Denise Charlton to go through her statement, anxiety had her firmly by the throat. It was a sensation Agnes was not used to. They said troubles came in threes, but two was more than enough for her. Finding that poor man and the knowledge Christopher Retallick was out of prison and back in Cornwall had knocked her off kilter. She found herself unable to remember the contents of the statement she made the day before, let alone anything new. Try as she might to recall the details, she couldn't. It was as if the page had been wiped clean. The thought of the man's suffering and the idea she might hold the key to identifying the person who had caused it and couldn't come up with the goods was mortifying. When DS Charlton told her that his feet were to be amputated, she felt nauseous as a recollection of the smell momentarily came back, a smell so awful she had no words to describe it, so said nothing.

When Luke's mobile rang, she knew it was bad news. He had taken the call in the hall, leaving her with Denise. They had met before and she felt comfortable with her, almost as comfortable as she did with Luke, who was always in and out of the office with his little girl Flora.

Denise always struck her as dedicated and super-efficient. She admired her for that. She often wondered whether if she had been born thirty years later, she might have joined the police force or maybe the civil service. She would have loved a career.

There was no mistaking Luke's expression when he came back into the room.

'He's dead, isn't he?' she said.

'I'm afraid so. The surgery went well, but he suffered a post-operative cardiac arrest. We need to go, I'm afraid. I know it's a long shot, but if you could write down anything that comes to you, whether you think it's important or not. You never know it might help.'

Agnes nodded, unable to speak as she got up to see them out.

They were halfway down the path when she ran after them.

'What was his name? I don't even know his name?'

'White. His name was Graham White.'

Agnes swayed a little, and Denise had to help her back up the path.

'You go, I'm fine,' she said as she steadied herself against the front door.

She was not fine at all. She knew only too well where she'd heard the name Graham White before.

THIRTEEN

Luke called everyone in. The mood in the incident room was sombre and would worsen when he announced all leave was cancelled for the foreseeable future.

'We all know why we're here. We've got two victims, both murdered on the same night and no suspect.'

'When you say suspect, guv, are you saying you fancy the same perp for both murders?' said DC Nathan Hawkins.

'I am. The facts are too similar for this to be a coincidence, although we'll keep an open mind until we have hard evidence to support the theory. The CSIs have finished, but the forensics aren't in yet. Both sites have their difficulties. The first has the obvious problem of too much material. The place was packed with dozens of people that night, all brushing past each other, all leaving their mark. Then the panic caused by the victim running through the crowd meant valuable evidence may well have been contaminated or destroyed altogether. The park where White was found was quieter, and there was less chance of contamination, but White wasn't discovered until the next morning, and it rained heavily overnight. The crime scene was also littered with all sorts of drug paraphernalia, which we assume was there before the crime was committed but which has to be examined, nevertheless. Until we have a suspect, we have no one to test against DNA or fingerprints collected at the scene. We'll be relying on the killer being already in the system.'

'What about witnesses, sir? Surely with all those people around, someone must have seen something.'

The question came from DC Rosie Jenkins, the newest member of the team.

'You would think so, wouldn't you? But so far, we have no witnesses to the attacks, which means either no one in that crowd saw anything suspicious, which I find hard to believe, or for some reason, they're unwilling to come forward. We can't rule out some might be feeling guilty they didn't help Vincent.'

Luke remembered the crowds scattering as Paul Vincent ran down the road screaming for help.

'Maybe it's not so much they didn't see anything but rather they didn't know what they were seeing,' offered Denise.

'Come again?' said Luke.

'I mean when you witness something unusual, it registers because it stands out. Say you see a stray dog running down the middle of the motorway, it registers, but if you saw the same dog run past you in the park or on the beach where it's commonplace, you might not even notice.'

'You mean they were desensitised?'

'Exactly. Those watching may have dismissed the event leading up to this as part of what was going on with the parade.'

Luke remembered how he himself had thought there was nothing wrong for a split second. He had the benefit of a mind tuned to trouble. Denise was right. People may well have thought this was part of the show.

'So, what's the plan, boss?' chipped in Nathan.

'We'll start with the database. Anyone with a history of fire starting, violence vandalism or cruelty to animals warranting prosecution, but use your discretion. I'm not interested in farmers with animal welfare issues or brawling louts. I'm talking about the really nasty stuff involving behaviour that equates to torture. These men weren't just killed, they were tortured first.'

'I know the toxicology results aren't back yet, but did the hospital think the men had been drugged?' asked Nathan.

'They did.'

'Then should we also be looking at anyone with form for

dealing or possession?'

Luke's heart sank. He needed to be narrowing the options, not expanding them.

'Not at the moment. According to the hospital, it's likely the drug administered to the victims was ketamine. We all know how widely available that is.'

'Have we considered this has all the hallmarks of an OCG reprisal?' Rosie said.

The idea these men had been murdered in such a horrific and public manner by someone with organised crime connections was something Luke had not even considered, and he felt foolish. It wasn't as if he didn't have first-hand experience of cases involving known OCGs. In fact, he had received his promotion on the back of a successful joint task force operation with the National Crime Agency, but these murders didn't feel like an OCG job to him. The profile of the two victims didn't fit. Neither did the MO. Those bastards took the trouble to bury the bodies or, in these parts, threw them down old mineshafts or dumped them at sea. They didn't leave them in public parks to be discovered by middle-aged secretaries on the way to work. Nevertheless, they couldn't rule anything out, and he wasn't about to admit he hadn't thought of it.

'It's a possibility. Let's look at each victim's bank statements. Have they received or paid out large sums of money recently? Scrutinise their social media and check if there's anything dodgy on their computers or phones. We need to know whether they've entered chatrooms or paid for porn. You all know the form. Could they have got on the wrong side of someone with OCG connections? Can I leave that with you, Rosie? Start with police and AML checks on both men. If they're on some other agencies list, we need to know.'

The girl's face flushed with pleasure.

The task ahead was monumental. Luke anticipated he'd need

help and had contacted the chief constable to ask for additional financial resources and more men, but he had yet to hear back. He knew this would be an uphill struggle without something to centre this investigation, a witness or a potential suspect. He needed to shake free of this overwhelming despondency. He had to stay upbeat, or they'd fail before they'd begun.

'Okay, let's get on with it,' he said, rubbing his hands together as if he was relishing the task.

He could hear Denise continuing with the brief behind him as he walked into his room.

'The names of both victims will be released to the public shortly,' she said. 'We're keeping some of the details to ourselves for the present to avoid hoax calls and false confessions. Bear that in mind when you speak to anyone who rings in about the victims or the crime. If something sounds right, we take it seriously at this stage. Dismiss no one, not even the usual nutters. If the caller was in the vicinity that night and took any footage of the parade, make sure you take a look at it. You never know, they might have got a shot of our victim or his killer.'

'It's a lot of work for a small team. We're never gonna get any downtime with this lot. Some of us have plans.'

'Then cancel them,' Denise said, her voice as sharp as the look she shot Nathan Hawken before relenting a little. Nathan had a new baby and no doubt his wife was expecting him to do his bit.

'I know you've all got your personal pressures, and I can tell you we've requested help on this, which, given the crimes, we can expect to get pretty promptly. In the meantime, we do everything we can to get the twisted bastard who did this under lock and key. If that interferes with date night or Saturday afternoon footy, too bad. You'll be waving goodbye to your private lives for a while. Get used to it.'

FOURTEEN

Eden and Molly were poring over Molly's brief to counsel when Agnes walked in. Eden immediately skirted around the desk to greet her.

'How are you holding up? I really didn't expect to see you until Monday, you know?'

'I had to come in. I need to speak with you, and it won't wait.'

Eden noticed Agnes's coat was buttoned incorrectly so that it sat skew-whiff. It was unlike her. She was always immaculately turned out. A little frumpish, perhaps, but smart, nonetheless. As she led the way along the corridor to her office, it crossed Eden's mind her secretary might be about to produce a sick note advising she'd been signed off for stress, or worse still, that she was handing in her notice. The thought horrified her. When she had first bought Douglas Bassett's law practice, Agnes had been difficult at best and downright hostile on some issues. She had blocked many changes Eden considered crucial, and when they had been forced on her, she'd done her level best to sabotage them. In the end, Eden had taken her aside and had one of those frank conversations that either broke or cemented a relationship. The woman had looked at her with gimlet eyes, waiting for the cracks to appear, but Eden had held her ground, and whilst they'd had their moments, they had not locked horns since.

Truth be told, she had not held the upper hand back then. She had been petrified of losing the woman before she herself had got to grips with everything. Now it was different. Now she would genuinely miss her if she were to leave. They would never be friends. There was the age difference, and they had absolutely nothing in common, but they had developed an excellent working relationship, galvanised by Molly's arrival. Her trainee's propensity for patience, good humour and an overwhelming eagerness to please had melted even Agnes's heart. The trio made a good team.

'Molly, can you bring a couple of teas through, please?'

Agnes all but collapsed in the chair when they reached Eden's office.

'What was it you wanted to talk about?' Eden asked, her concerns multiplying.

'The files.'

'You mean the Retallick files?' Eden knew Molly had spoken to Agnes about the missing files, but she couldn't understand why her normally unflappable secretary was getting flustered over a bit of shoddy admin. It was hardly the end of the world. Even Agnes with her exacting standards was allowed to slip up sometimes. 'There's really no rush about the files. They can wait until next week,' she reassured. 'After the shock you've had, a few missing files are the last thing you should be worrying about.'

Molly arrived with the tea. Agnes took the cup, her hand shaking, her eyes glassy with tears as she placed it on the desk. Molly hovered at her shoulder. Eden gave a sideways glance towards the door and Molly took the hint and left.

'He died… the man I found. Luke told me this morning when he called around.'

Eden felt a new wave of disbelief.

'He died of a heart attack after they… they amputated his feet.'

'Agnes, I'm so sorry.' Eden reached for a box of tissues, but Agnes waved them away, pulling a crisp white handkerchief from her cardigan sleeve.

'His name was Graham White.'

Eden nodded, although the name had no significance for her.

'I thought you should know.'

'Thank you, but you really needn't have come in to tell me. I'm sure Luke would have let me know in due course. Please, Agnes, I can see you're very distressed by this whole thing. I would feel much better if you forgot about work and went home.'

'I can't, not yet; this is too important.'

'What is?'

'The files.'

Agnes twisted her cup in its saucer. 'Douglas took them.'

Eden couldn't hide her surprise.

'Where did he take them?'

'He took them home, boxes of them.'

'Why?'

'I don't know, unfinished business… concern they might be destroyed before he had a chance to go through them thoroughly. He always believed the boy was innocent, you see. I didn't. I thought he did it. We had words about it more than once, but Douglas was adamant there was something off with the evidence.'

'What do you mean 'off'?'

'He never said. I suppose because I was so convinced Christopher Retallick was guilty, he didn't confide in me. Something bothered him about the case. He avoided criminal cases after that.'

'So, where are they now?'

'He left a note for me before he died asking me to collect them when he passed. I did as he asked and put them in the basement.'

'Our basement here in the office?'

'Yes, at the very back, under a tarpaulin. I'm sorry, I should have told you they were there. It's not my business to interfere, but I felt Douglas would not have kept them unless they were important and felt guilty for not supporting him at the time.'

'It's okay, Agnes, there's no harm done. At least they've not been destroyed.'

'Perhaps it would be better if they had been, especially now, with all that's going on. Poor Mr White.'

'Graham White, what's he got to do with the Retallick files?'

'He was Christopher Retallick's teacher. Graham White gave evidence against him at his trial.'

Words rolled around Eden's mouth like boiled sweets before she spat them free.

'Agnes, are you suggesting the murder of Graham White is linked to the Retallick case?'

'It's too much of a coincidence him being back in Cornwall and Graham White being dead.'

'But it's a giant leap to allege Kit Retallick had anything to do with this atrocity. The allegation alone could have serious implications for him as someone released on licence. Don't get me wrong, if you have hard evidence he did this, you should say so, but if not… you would be depriving one of our clients of his liberty, not to mention jeopardising the integrity of this firm.'

'But we don't act for him yet. You haven't even seen the files.'

'This isn't America. Money hasn't got to change hands here for us to owe a duty of confidentiality.'

Eden didn't know the ins and outs of the case. She had no clue of the circumstances, but she did know Retallick had been a kid and kids did stupid things. It didn't mean he'd carried that recklessness with him to adulthood, or worse still, he was capable of a cold, calculated act of torture. Whoever set fire to Graham White was evil. Much as Retallick had unnerved her, she could not imagine him doing that. Then again, she didn't know him.

Agnes took a sip of her tea. 'It was his whole family the last time. Mother, sister and his stepfather,' she said.

Eden held her stance despite the chill icing through her. 'Agnes, stop and think. You have to ask yourself why a man who is on a mission to prove he is innocent of past crimes would wish to risk incarceration again so soon after his release. It doesn't make sense.'

Despite her protestations, Eden knew you only had to read the papers to know reoffending of the worst possible kind happened all the time. Clever recidivists, adept at fooling parole boards, reoffended within weeks, if not days of release. Drug dealers, child molesters, sex offenders, even drunk drivers. It happened all the time, but despite her unease about Retallick, there was something about his determination that led Eden to believe he was not one of those men.

'The way the minds of the likes of him work will never make sense,' retorted Agnes, her voice quivering. 'Who could imagine someone could set fire to a fellow human being? But trust me, it happened. I saw the aftermath with my own eyes. I try not to judge, as you know, but I always thought that boy was capable of anything… anything. He killed his own flesh and blood. I had to come and tell you because I'm afraid for you and Molly. I wanted to warn you to have nothing to do with the man. I couldn't bear it if anything happened to you two because I kept these feelings to myself. I just couldn't bear it.'

Agnes, her face red and puffy, began to cry again.

Eden, worried, reached across to touch her hand.

Over the years, she had developed the knack of fading Agnes out as if turning down the dial of a radio so that by the time her secretary finished rambling, she was listening in her head to the shipping forecast, which was usually infinitely more interesting.

This wasn't the case today. Finding White had changed Agnes, and she deserved to be heard.

'I think you need to take some time for yourself. I'll retrieve the files and hand them back to Retallick. You needn't worry about me and Molly. I won't risk either of us or the firm, I promise. I want you to take a couple of weeks off. When did you last take a holiday?'

'I can't remember.'

'There you go then. It'll do you good to get away.'

Agnes looked dumbfounded, as if Eden had suggested she take a rocket to the moon.

'I wouldn't know where to go.'

Eden's heart was in her mouth. She was not a particularly sociable person. She'd always left that to Thea but could call on half a dozen close friends in times of need. It was clear Agnes was not so lucky. She racked her brain for suggestions, remembering hearing Agnes talk of her neighbour, a retired journalist whom she used to talk about a lot but hasn't mentioned lately. Patsy... Polly, something like that.

'What about your neighbour, the journalist, Patsy, is it? She's single, isn't she and used to travel? Perhaps she might like a trip somewhere. A city-break abroad maybe?'

If anything, Agnes seemed even more downcast by the suggestion, and it didn't take long for Eden to find out why.

'Pinkie,' Agnes said, her lip trembling. 'Her name is Pinkie. She sold up and moved on. She lives on Bodmin Moor now. She met a man on holiday, and they've moved in together.'

Eden didn't know what to say.

'I could ring my sister, I suppose,' muttered Agnes. 'She lives in Exeter. Her husband died a couple of years ago, but she has her grandchildren close by, and they seem to keep her busy. Too busy for a woman her age, in my opinion, but I could call her.'

They left the conversation hanging, Eden pleased she had at

least managed to get her secretary off the subject of Kit Retallick for the moment.

As soon as Agnes left, Eden locked the door.

She glanced across the room at Molly. She was becoming a fixture behind that reception desk. She needed to break it to her that she would be there for the next couple of weeks while Agnes took her forced vacation.

'Are those your good clothes?' Eden asked.

Molly's eyes widened. Eden realised the girl thought she was being pulled up for not being smart enough for front of house.

'We need to go into the basement, and I didn't want you ruining anything decent. To say it's a bit dusty is an underestimation.'

The girl's face relaxed and Eden saw the glint of excitement. 'Is that where the files are?'

'According to Agnes, that's where she stored them after Douglas Bassett died.'

As far as her trainee knew, the basement housed only old unclaimed deeds, accounting records and law books long superseded by new volumes. With this new revelation, it had suddenly become a treasure trove to be plundered.

'It's a bit of a story, but the crux of it is that Douglas thought there was something not quite right about the case and took the files with him when I took over. Maybe he intended to revisit them to see if he'd missed something. Who knows? I know his health deteriorated quite quickly after he retired, and maybe he wasn't up to a review, but the files were important enough for him to ask Agnes to bring them back after he died. He obviously didn't want them destroyed in a house clearance.'

'So, there could be something important in them,' said Molly, wide-eyed and eager.

'I honestly can't say, but there are other issues I won't go into now. Suffice to say it's clear this whole thing is very upsetting for Agnes. She has bad memories about this case and a particular dislike for Kit Retallick. If it comes down to choosing between her and him, she's going to win hands down, I'm afraid. At the moment, we just need to locate the files and hand them back to the client.'

Disappointment scudded across Molly's face.

'Come on,' chirped Eden, trying to lighten the mood. 'No time like the present.'

'I've never been in the basement. What's it like?'

'You've seen those horror films where the victim feels her way down the stairs into a dark space under the house, you know, the ones where the light doesn't work and the boiler grumbles ominously. The kind where you instinctively know there's something lurking below the stairs ready to grab the victim's ankle and can't figure out why the hell she doesn't know it too. Well… our basement's not quite as bad, but it's not a place to loiter.'

Molly laughed nervously.

The basement door was at the end of the building to the left of Eden's office.

'Here goes,' said Eden, wondering whether the key would turn or if it hadn't been used for so long she might need a squirt of WD40 to oil the lock.

'This feels like an episode of Scooby-doo,' joked Molly.

'Well, let's hope you're channelling your inner Velma,' said Eden. 'I never trusted Daphne to get anyone out of a scrape.'

Eden knew her forced jollity masked her nervousness. Her stomach was clenching not because of the thought of spider's webs and mice but what might be in those files and, more importantly, the decision whether to open the boxes or deliver them to Kit Retallick intact without even a sneaky peek. She did not relish telling him she couldn't help. She had found him a difficult person to say no to. He had a persistence and intensity that drew you in. His femoral desire for truth would infect her if she found something that pointed to his innocence. She would be required to share the burden he, for the moment, shouldered alone, and the thought of the responsibility made her feel physically sick.

After a couple of attempts, she managed to jiggle the door open. Molly stood behind her, peering over her shoulder into the darkness.

'Don't worry, there's a light switch.'

Molly exhaled.

Eden yanked the string to her right and the strip light buzzed for a full thirty seconds before it came to life and then flickered, bathing the basement in a hesitant strobing light.

Eden had only been down there once before when Douglas showed her around the building with her surveyor. She remembered he had mentioned the dodgy light fittings then, and unsurprisingly, they hadn't cured themselves. Their replacement had become secondary to the possibility of asbestos in the ceiling, which thankfully had turned out to be a false alarm. Had it not been, its removal would have swallowed up most of her renovation budget for the year. After the all-clear she had locked the door and tried to forget about what lay below her feet as she traversed the floors of the office. She was suddenly filled with the awful dread that comes when you know you have to do something, and it's going to be a complete pain in the backside.

Eden took the short flight of stairs carefully, not trusting the rickety handrail. *This is a health and safety nightmare*, she thought, wondering whether she should don her employer's hat and send Molly back. At the bottom, she turned to face her trainee, who was still teetering on the top step.

'Are you sure you want to help? I can manage on my own, and it is filthy down here.'

'I'm sure,' Molly shouted back before heading down the

stairs after her.

The space was exactly as Eden remembered it. A large rectangular room stacked to the gunnels with old filing cabinets, drawers off their hinges, stacks of bank boxes marked up in thick black lettering with decades-old paperwork.

TRAVEL RECEIPTS 1975 to 77.

LAW SOCIETY GAZETTES 1988 to 91.

To her left were ancient square computer screens and keyboards, along with a couple of electric typewriters. Propped up against them was a projector, and resting against the wall were two stained glass windows in rotten frames, obviously removed from somewhere in the building when double glazing was installed. To the right was an old cast iron safe that must weigh a ton and would have taken a gargantuan effort to install.

Lodged in one corner was an overflowing box of empty handbags, suggesting either Douglas was a kleptomaniac or they had been collected over the years from nursing homes or hospital wards, the last remnants of life. The trouble was that once the cash had been accounted for, the briefcase full of sepia photos or the handbag containing a few fluffy mint imperials or false teeth wrapped in a tissue were rarely thought worth collecting by the dearly departed's relatives. Enquiries as to where they should be sent were met with grave-stony silence. Most family solicitors had a stash like this one that they would keep for a while and then send to infill like the rest of life's detritus.

Eden had always found it difficult to be ruthless about other people's history, maybe because she was adopted and knew little of her own. From the look of it, Douglas shared her sentiments.

Thankfully, the route to the back of the basement, where Agnes said the files were stored, was clear. Eden noticed with relief that the atmosphere was musty rather than dank, without any hint of rodent pee or mould.

'It's quite cosy, really,' said Molly.

'I wouldn't go that far,' said Eden, but in truth she was pleasantly surprised. The ceiling was higher than she remembered, and despite the rubbish, the room felt spacious. At the far end, there was a table, upturned chairs stacked on top and in the corner, a cast iron fireplace. It crossed Eden's mind that this room might have been the scullery or the kitchen. Beside the table, she spotted the tarpaulin Agnes had spoken of. She tugged it free to reveal twelve numbered boxes. Resting on top was a clipboard listing the contents of each box along with schedules of indictments, witness statements, expert reports and court orders. It was clear from the meticulous organisation Agnes had a hand here, and the boxes would be in good shape. Eden lifted the chairs from the table and heaved the first heavy box on top. She turned to Molly.

'We'll need a trolley for these so we can at least get them to the bottom of the stairs.'

She looked at her watch. It was gone five o'clock. She needed to get home and change before Luke arrived to take her to her parents, that is, if he was still able to spare the time. She should probably check. With two murders on his books, the thought of dinner with Thea might be a distraction he could do without.

She took her phone from her back pocket. No reception.

'I need to make a call. I'll be back in a sec,' she said.

Molly was engrossed, flipping through the schedules.

'No probs, I'm fine.'

Eden headed back upstairs and called Luke. Expecting him to be busy, she intended to leave a message, but he answered straight away.

'Hi, what's up?'

'Just checking you're still okay to pick me up this evening. Agnes told me about Graham White.'

Luke gave a deep sigh. 'Yeah, poor sod.'

'I thought you might be too busy to spare the time this evening.'

'I am, but I need to show willing. I don't want that sister of yours thinking I'm running scared because she's back. I fought too long and hard to get custody to lose it without a fight. I'm not going back to the way it was before. I can't afford to be an absent father right now, no matter what else is going on, at least not until I know exactly what Thea's planning.'

Eden felt like jumping for joy. At last, Luke had got his priorities right. Eden loved her sister, but she was not capable of caring for Flora. She had proved it time and time again. They had given her the benefit of the doubt one too many times, and Luke had been forced to step in when Thea had left their child with friends and eloped to Scotland with Ravi. It had been a watershed moment for them all.

'Good, see you at six thirty then.'

Molly was still engrossed when she returned to the basement. She had opened the first box and was poring over the paperwork.

'I've got to go, I'm afraid. I'm at my parents for dinner tonight. We can pick this up tomorrow.'

'You go ahead, I'll clear up here. I was planning to stay late anyway. I need to e-mail that brief.'

'Okay.'

Eden had an inkling the basement light would flicker on for a bit yet.

***

Once home, Eden went through the motions of showering and changing into something uncontroversial and plain. It had crossed her mind on the drive back that it might not have been such a sensible decision for Luke and her to arrive at her parents' together. She'd been given strict instructions by her mother not to antagonise Thea, and it had only been a year ago that her sister had accused her of sleeping with her ex.

It had been nonsense, of course, and had only come about because a local journalist had caught Luke on camera leaving her flat in the early morning hours. They had been on opposing sides of a particularly juicy case at the time that had attracted a rabid variety of media attention. Luke had, in fact, been dropping off Flora after driving half the night to collect her from Thea's less-than-pleased babysitters. But when did Thea opt for the rational explanation when there was drama to be had? She wondered whether she should call Luke again and confide her worries but decided against it. The man was busy.

It annoyed her she was already thinking of making compromises for Thea's sake. She had done it all her life and was starting to worry it was a habit she'd never shake.

By the time Luke arrived to pick her up, she had changed no less than three times, eventually opting for the skinny jeans and faded 'Surfers Against Sewage' sweatshirt she'd put on at first.

Luke looked equally flustered as she sidled into the passenger seat.

'So, what can we expect?' he asked.

'You're asking me? I gave up trying to predict the unfathomable years ago,' replied Eden, thinking he meant Thea.

'I meant to eat.'

'Not sure. Vegetarian, of course. One of Dad's specials.'

'Good, I'm starving and I'm out of Pepto-Bismol.'

Eden laughed. 'I hope you're not criticising my mother's cooking. That's a capital offence for a son-in-law.'

'An ex-son-in-law... no, actually, not even that. I prefer to think of myself as a culinary victim. Your mother's done things to my tastebuds they'll never recover from.'

'Harsh but true,' Eden laughed.

He was right. He and Thea had never tied the knot officially, and Flora was the only good thing that came out of their disastrous relationship.

'Agnes said Graham White suffered a cardiac arrest after the amputation?'

'Yes. I would have preferred not to tell Agnes, but she guessed as soon as I walked back into the room after taking the call. She's not herself, you know,' he said, glancing at Eden. 'I would have bet money on her remembering more details about the crime scene, but I drew a complete blank with her this morning. Her statement is basic, to say the least.'

'I know what you mean. I thought she'd be full of it, but she's obviously been badly shaken by the whole thing. I've told her to take some leave.'

'It would have been a shock for anyone. She shouldn't feel guilty about the way she's feeling,' said Luke.

'Hopefully she'll get away for a few days.'

'A change of scenery is probably the best thing. I did ask her to write down anything she thought of, but I'm not holding my breath.'

Eden thought of Agnes's suspicions about Kit Retallick and about the link between him and Graham White. She felt her cheeks burn.

'Are you busy? Will you be able to manage without her?'

'Molly can stand in for her while she's on leave. It'll mean extra work for me as she'll be tied to the office, but we'll manage.'

They were approaching her parents' house now. Eden had put on extra layers. Her mother and father rarely put the heating on until mid-December. The house was in darkness other than a glimmer of light from the kitchen window. She hoped her parents weren't using the current energy crisis as an excuse to go fully retro.

Eden had got used to the lectures on burning fossil fuels over the years, but she drew the line at going to the loo by candlelight.

She gave Luke a sideways glance as he pulled into the driveway. He looked nervous, and who could blame him? The last time he and Thea had met had been at a mediation appointment to deal with Flora's custody. An appointment that had gone better than expected for him, largely down to the cash Eden had given her sister in order to oil the wheels of the negotiations. Luke knew nothing of this, of course, and might be worried Thea had felt pressurised and resentful at losing the battle.

'Come on,' she said, trying to sound encouraging but convincing no one, least of all herself. 'I'll be your wingman, and if things get messy, you can always cut the evening short with an imaginary text from Denise.'

This was a light-hearted dig at Luke, who had asked her to come with him and Flora to Hall for Cornwall to see the panto a fortnight before, only to abandon them halfway through because work called.

'I did apologise at the time,' he said.

'I'm only joking. I know it wasn't an excuse.'

The kitchen was empty, which accounted for the blackout. She could hear voices coming from the dining room at the other end of the house. Castro, the family mutt, was lying on the mat looking longingly at his empty bowl. He raised a doggy eyebrow in their direction but didn't consider them interesting enough to shuffle out of their way as they stepped over his twitching tail.

Thea, Flora and her parents were already seated at the table, in the centre of which sat a large dish of Moussaka with a bowl of couscous and a Greek salad to the side. Thea, who was pouring Flora a glass of water, looked up.

'Sorry… are we late?' asked Eden, trying to judge the mood of the room.

'No, no, just serving up,' replied her father, rising to give her a hug. 'I hope you two are hungry.'

'It smells good,' said Eden. 'Is this a new recipe, Dad? Have we moved to a different culinary continent?'

'Nothing to do with me. Thea did the honours this evening.'

'Isn't she clever, putting a meal together when she only arrived this afternoon on the train?' her mother gushed, reaching across to squeeze Thea's arm. She made it sound like the achievement was roughly on par with single-handedly building the Acropolis.

Eden had never known her sister to cook a thing in her life or do anything domestic, come to that.

'Well, that's you redundant, Dad.'

Her father seemed crestfallen.

'Help yourself to grape juice,' he said.

Damn it, thought Eden, she'd forgotten to bring the wine.

Eden's mother served grape juice as if it was one step away from Beaujolais, assuming as a non-drinker, it contained the primary ingredient. She had no idea it was like serving raw egg whites with ice cream and calling it Baked Alaska.

Eden stuck with water.

Following the telephone conversation with her mother the evening before, she had expected to find her sister curled up on the sofa with a hot water bottle and a box of tissues licking her wounds, but this was a very different Thea. Glowing with vitality, her fine blonde hair pulled back from her face to accentuate her delicate features, she looked relaxed and beautiful. She wore a cream silk shirt, and Eden noticed she had skimmed her lids with coppery shadow that made her eyes look even bluer than usual. Eden felt decidedly dowdy.

'You look really well,' she complimented.

'Thanks. I've decided it's high time I put my house in order. I haven't treated my mind, or my body for that matter, with the respect it deserves, but things have changed. From now on you're going to see a better, healthier me.'

If this was true, Eden was pleased to hear it, but they had been here before. These fresh starts usually came after a binge, during which Thea stopped taking her meds and sought inspiration in booze and other equally damaging substances. She would hit rock bottom and then discover some new wonder therapy. The last time she had signed up for a course called, 'Seven Ways in Seven Days to Get What You Want.'

Thea had jacked it in on day three, predictably, undecided about what she actually wanted. A raised eyebrow from Luke told Eden he was probably as sceptical as she was.

'Have you found the people who set fire to the man at the parade, Daddy?' asked Flora.

The question came from nowhere. Eden thought her niece was quiet when they arrived. She assumed it was because the child had years of experience navigating Thea's moods and probably sensed her usual effervescent greeting of her father would trigger a sulky accusation from Thea that she loved him more than her. Now, she wondered if she had been quietly dwelling on the previous night's events and whether she should have talked them through with her rather than marshalled her off to bed. Then again, where do you find the words to explain an unfathomable horror to a seven-year-old without scaring her?

'Everyone at school was talking about it. Naomi in my class was right there in the crowd when the man ran past her on fire.' There was excitement in the child's voice.

'Flora,' Luke snapped, 'that's enough. It's not something we should talk about at the dinner table.'

'But she said his whole back was on fire and he was screaming, but nobody could touch him cos they would have caught on fire too. Naomi's dad took a photo on his phone.'

Luke slammed his fist down on the table and shouted, 'I said enough. A man lost his life. This is not some film or a video game to be gawked at. This was real. Someone set fire to a man and killed him.'

Flora's bottom lip began to tremble. She pushed her chair back and ran from the room.

'Now look what you've done,' Thea shrieked. 'Why do you always have to be the fucking policeman?'

Here we go, thought Eden, putting down her knife and fork.

'Now, now,' said Eden's father. 'Can we please just all calm down?'

'She's a seven-year-old child, not one of your bloody plods to order about,' spat Thea, her sulphurous words hanging in the air as she flounced out of the room.

Luke pushed his plate away. Eden glanced at her mother, who she could tell was itching to launch a lemon-lipped attack on Luke in defence of Thea. Eden decided to get in first.

'I agree with Luke. Flora needs to understand the enormity of what she saw last night. It was horrific and Luke has had to deal with another case in much the same vein today. Two men have died… been murdered in a barbaric way. What does it look like if the chief investigating officer's child is gossiping about it with her friends? She's young, I know, but she's old enough to know better than that.'

Luke stared straight at her; his temper shaved away by a sliding smile she was pretty sure no one else but her noticed. He pulled his phone from his pocket. 'I'm sorry, that was my DS. I'm afraid I'm going to have to leave. Thanks again for the invite.'

'I'll come with you,' said Eden. 'It will save Dad dropping me home.'

'Well…' huffed her mother, clearly outraged at her mutinous child.

Thea was in the kitchen, Flora's face buried in her shoulder.

'That's it… off you run. Have a nice evening,' said Thea, the words barbed with innuendo.

Luke opened his mouth to object, but Eden threw him a warning, and he thought better of it and instead addressed Flora.

'Night, love. I'll pick you up tomorrow morning. I love you, Flo.'

Flora looked up through wet lashes. 'Goodnight, Daddy.'

'Fuck. I walked right into that,' said Luke as they pulled away.

'Flora will be fine. You're her dad. One cross word can't erase the time you've put into your relationship.'

'Thanks for backing me up in there.'

Eden wondered if it would have been better had she not interfered.

A thick mist curtained the fields and shrouded the car in grey drizzle as they drove along the lanes to Eden's house. The silence stretched between them, neither knowing how to fill it, their thoughts too big to share.

It was barely eight o'clock when they pulled up outside the beach house. They'd managed to maintain peace with Thea for less than an hour before war had broken out.

'Are you hungry?' she asked, turning in her seat to face Luke.

'Starving,' he said, slipping his hands from the steering wheel and slumping in his seat, clearly deflated by the evening's events.

Neither had managed to eat much food before the row had begun.

'I can do you cheese on toast if you like and there's beer in the fridge.'

'What, no grape juice?' Luke quipped.

'Come on,' she said, knowing he would follow. She could read him like a book. The room felt cosy. Then again anywhere would feel cosy after the sub-arctic conditions at her parents' house. Eden banked up the fire, took off her jacket and headed for the kitchen to pop the bread in the toaster.

'Do you want Worcester sauce on yours?' she shouted.

'Have you got pickle?'

'Afraid not, but I can run to ketchup.'

'That'll do.'

She brought the cheese on toast and two beers in on a tray.

Watching Luke attack the food, she wondered whether she should have called out for a takeaway.

'Can I get you some more?'

'No, that hit the spot,' he said, taking a gulp from his bottle. 'Not up to Thea's standards, of course, but passable.' he said, mimicking her mother.

Eden couldn't help but laugh at the conspiratorial mickey-take. It lent perspective to the argument with Thea, and if her sister intended to stay, there would be more than enough times in the coming months when she'd be the topic of conversation. Tonight, she wanted to forget about her.

'How's the investigation going?'

'It's not. We begin questioning those with form for anything remotely like this tomorrow. Remote being the operative word. Denise has been trawling through incidents of anti-social behaviour reported over the last few months, especially those that include fire starting or threats of violence, but I don't hold out much hope. Without witnesses or statements from the victim, it's going to be an uphill struggle. Neither family have a clue why these men were targeted, and as yet, we've found no connection between them.'

Eden thought about Kit Retallick. 'Do you think maybe the link is the festival?'

'Denise asked the same thing. I think she was hoping it was the beginning and end of it, as I am, too. If not, we're in trouble. We haven't got the manpower for this and since I lost Ross, I've been chasing my tail as it is.'

Ross Trenear was one of Eden's surfing buddies, had been

for years. She had never got to the bottom of why he'd resigned, but she wasn't surprised. He had never struck her as police material. He was a typical surfer. A rule bender, dancing to the beat of his own drum. His father had been a policeman in Penzance for years and she imagined he joined the force to please him.

'Do you think he might come back if asked?' she said.

'No chance. I think he was relieved to have an excuse to hand in his notice. He's kept his pension and now he's back with his wife, helping out in the family pub. Although he did ring me a couple of months back to ask what he'd need to get a licence as a private detective.'

'Do you think he's seriously considering it?'

Eden used private detectives as process servers and to rake over the lives of key witnesses in criminal cases. None of the local ones were particularly good and the prospect of Ross becoming available gave her an unexpected boost.

'Reading between the lines, he's a bit bored working behind the bar. I think it would be an excuse to get out and about rather than something he's passionate about. Don't get me wrong, I think he'd be damn good at it. There was never anything wrong with his investigative skills, even if his methods were a little unconventional, and he's kept all his contacts.'

Eden thought of the files in her basement. She knew she'd have to make a decision soon whether or not to take Retallick's case. Molly was more than keen to use her investigative skills in the hope of discovering a miscarriage of justice, but the help of a seasoned professional with knowledge of how the system worked wouldn't go amiss.

She was getting ahead of herself. She hadn't yet been able to shake off her concerns about the young man, concerns that had only deepened since Agnes told her about the connection between him and Graham White. She knew it was a connection

Luke, in the frame of mind he was in, would leap on. However, she had no intention of telling him. She could hardly do the exact thing she'd warned Agnes against.

'Well, I'd better be getting home,' said Luke, breaking her train of thought. 'Thanks again for supper.'

'You're welcome,' she said, seeing him to the door, 'and don't worry about Thea. I'll speak to her and smooth things over. Her bark is worse than her bite.'

It wasn't strictly true. Her sister's bite could be rabid, but she felt the man needed a bit of positive thinking to get him past this.

'Thanks,' he said, raising his hand as a gusting wind practically pushed him down the path.

'Another stormy night,' he said, 'time to batten down the hatches.'

FIFTEEN

Agnes sat by the window, coat on, waiting for her taxi to arrive.

She wished now she had taken the bus. She had a train to catch, and if the car was late, she'd have to wait hours for the next one to Exeter. They weren't so regular at weekends.

Her sister was expecting her. She'd rung her the afternoon before after speaking to Eden to ask if she could go and stay for a few days, and to her surprise, Margie had been delighted at the prospect of the company. That was before she'd told her about finding Graham White in Victoria Gardens. Once she'd relayed the sorry saga, her sister had seemed even keener to have her there.

Margaret, or Margie as the family called her, was fifteen years older than her, and the age gap meant they had never been close. By the time she was six or seven, Margie had moved out to get married to Neil and, within a few years, had kids of her own.

As far as she knew, she'd had a full and happy life with Neil until he died. It always seemed that way every time she visited with her children. Mother always said Margie had hit the jackpot when she married Neil. She'd made him sound like Richard Branson rather than the manager of the local MFI.

It had always struck Agnes strange she was an aunt whilst still a child herself. The children in school thought it even stranger. Some even accused her of lying. Something she never did unless Mother specifically instructed her to. Had she known how they'd react, she would never have told them in the first place. They didn't need a further excuse to ridicule her. She hadn't enjoyed Margie's visits after that and had increasingly resented her nieces for the life they led. They always came armed with tales of broadened horizons. Riding lessons, school skiing trips, A-levels and eventually university, whereas her life had become one of ever-decreasing circles, with her mother at the epicentre. Like a tragic heroine in a Victorian novel, she'd become her mother's companion, then her carer, whilst her sister and her nieces lived the life of Riley. Over the years, despite every effort to be glad for them, she had become tight-lipped and resentful.

She had only rung Margie because she had been desperate. Eden had pressed her to get away. The fact she had been met with open arms scuppered all her excuses not to go.

She looked at her watch. The taxi was two minutes late. Thank goodness she had allowed plenty of time. It wasn't far, but she didn't want to rush. She was flustered enough. She hadn't known what to pack and was wondering whether she should have bought something casual to wear around the house. She'd packed only smart clothes, the sort she wore to work, but now she thought about it, she imagined, given her sister's age, most of their time would be spent around the house.

She rummaged in her bag, checking yet again she had a spare hanky and that her purse was tucked safely away. She had the fare in her coat pocket. At least she didn't have to worry about a taxi at the other end. Her sister was picking her up from the station. She couldn't quite believe Margie was still driving at her age, but when she queried it, she'd said she wouldn't be without her little car, that it gave her independence. She herself hadn't learnt to drive until Mother died. Mother had said it would be the death of her if she had to worry about her having an accident whenever she left the house. She'd gone on about the expense, what with the petrol and the insurance, not to mention the servicing and how hard it would be without a man around to check the oil and the tyre pressure. In the end, Agnes had left it until she'd passed away. She was glad she'd taken the plunge but still didn't have the confidence to drive on the motorway.

She looked at her watch again, almost five minutes late now. She wondered whether she should ring and check the booking. They'd better not say the driver had been and gone and that she hadn't been there. Her eyes had never left the window. Of course, in Exeter they had Uber. Here, they had to rely on a couple of firms. No competition, that was the problem.

She decided she'd wait on the doorstep. That way, they'd have no excuses. She lifted her handbag from the table. Her case was already by the door. She'd bought a new one in the end. The one upstairs on top of the wardrobe didn't have wheels or a retractable handle and was full of old jumpers and coats she kept meaning to take to the charity shop. She'd bought the case in Wilkos on her way home from the office after speaking to Eden. They sold everything there. She'd been amazed at how light it was when she lifted it.

She pulled the door shut behind her. It looked like it might rain.

A red Mazda pulled up, and a scruffy, balding man got out to open the boot for her case.

'I was just about to ring your boss,' she said, 'you're late.'

The man shrugged. She wasn't sure whether he didn't care about being reported or the fact he was unreliable. It was the sort of shrug that meant he didn't give a damn about much.

His collar was frayed, and as she shuffled into the passenger seat, she was hit with the smell of stale sweat and tobacco smoke. If the driver thought the pine-scented air freshener in the shape of a Christmas tree dangling from the mirror would do the job, he was sadly mistaken. The only way to get rid of that kind of whiff was a good boil wash.

'The office said you're on the eight o'clock. You'll be there in plenty of time.'

How did he know whether she'd be in good time or not?

Maybe she'd arranged to meet a friend or fancied a cup of tea in the café on the platform before she set off. She certainly didn't relish a mad dash forcing her to sit sweaty and dishevelled all the way to Exeter. She bit her lip.

She handed over the exact money when they arrived at the station. She didn't believe in tipping for the sake of it, and when the driver pinged the boot open and made no attempt to lift her case out for her, she was glad she'd made the right choice.

For the first time ever, she'd booked her ticket online. As she headed for the glass doors, she wondered if she needed to show it on arrival or whether it would be checked at the other end or by the conductor on the train. There was no one to ask. The kiosk was unmanned. The barrier onto the platform was raised and signed 'Out of Order.' She waited, wondering whether to go through. Then, seeing the platform on the other side was already quite full, she decided to press on, wishing she'd thought to reserve a seat.

She paused by the newsagents to put her phone back in her bag, wondering if she had time to buy a newspaper. There might be some new information about the police investigation into Graham White's death. She pulled out her purse, unzipping it to rummage for change. It was only when she looked up she saw the newsstand, the headline blazoned in capital letters.

VICTIM OF FESTIVAL TRAGEDY NAMED AS LOCAL CHARITY WORKER PAUL VINCENT

She heard the coins clatter and roll around her feet. A fellow traveller bent to help her retrieve them as she stood, rooted to the spot. As the woman placed the coins in her hand, she heard herself whisper, 'Thank you,' but it was as if she wasn't there, as if she was floating above herself.

'Are you alright?' the woman asked, leading her to a nearby bench.

She heard a voice announce the arrival of her train, the

distant sound of its approach and sensed the light dim as it filled the space opposite, screeching to a halt.

'I'm sorry, I need to catch that train. Are you sure you're okay?' said the woman, looking around for someone who might step in as a good Samaritan.

Agnes nodded, watching her race along the platform, up the steps across the bridge, and onto the train. She was powerless to follow, unable to lift her leaden legs and move from the seat.

It was not until the train pulled away that she was able to shake off her stupor, zip the coins back into her purse, and lift her phone to dial 999.

SIXTEEN

Eden unlocked the door, expecting to hear the steady beep, beep, beep of the office alarm until she tapped in the code to disarm it, but there was silence. It hadn't been set. Molly had probably forgotten. It was generally Agnes's job, the last thing she did before she left every evening, but Agnes hadn't been there yesterday, and Molly had worked late. The lights in reception were on, which was odd. She would have expected her trainee to have turned those off at the very least. Molly must know the price of energy bills. She'd have to have a word with her. She flipped the switch. She was about to head for her office when she heard the floorboards in the room above creak. Her body tensed.

'Molly, is that you?'

There was no response. Tentatively, she walked towards the staircase, pausing to listen on the bottom step. She heard the noise again. Not footsteps this time, so much as a shuffling around. She sensed someone was there, and if it wasn't Molly, who the hell was it?

She took the first and then second step and listened again but could hear nothing now except the rumble of a bus passing outside. Maybe she'd imagined it. The old building had a habit of groaning. The sash windows rattled in high winds, and the central heating pipes echoed with a clunk every time the boiler started up. Agnes told her it was nothing to worry about, that old buildings, unlike old people, became more mobile with every passing year. She was being ridiculous. The events of the last couple of days had unnerved her. She was about to turn away when a massive thump, as if someone had either fallen or thrown something onto the floor, made her jump. She pulled her phone from her back pocket, wondering whether she should call Luke. The trouble was, he could be anywhere, and to be honest, this hardly justified calling the police, not without knowing for sure there was somebody there.

She shouted again. 'I can hear you. You should come down right now. I have the police on the line and I'm videoing this.'

All sorts of thoughts were racing through her head. Had someone noticed the alarm wasn't flashing outside and broken in? It wouldn't be the first time. There had been an incident in the first month she'd taken over the firm before the alarm had been fitted. Someone got wind that she had builders in and broke in through the back door to steal their gear. The power tools had been insured, and the wake-up call had forced her to consider security issues. However, lack of funds meant not everywhere had been burglar-proofed. The skylight on the landing was secured with a simple padlock. She suddenly thought of Molly. What if she had been here when whoever they were had broken in? She had to climb the staircase in case Molly was in trouble.

One by one, she took the narrow stairs, phone in hand, camera on. At the top, she was faced with a scene of what could only be described as organised chaos. Files littered the desk where Flora had sat to draw a picture for Thea on the evening of the parade. Yet more files and empty boxes were stacked around the room, and, kneeling amid papers piled like mountain ranges across the width of the floor, and with her back to her, was Molly.

Eden let out the breath she had been holding since she began the climb. Then, tip-toeing her way to where Molly knelt, she tapped the girl on the shoulder.

Molly jumped like a scalded cat.

'Oh my god, you gave me a fright.'

'Likewise,' said Eden, 'I thought you were an intruder. Didn't you hear me call?'

Molly reached up and pulled out her ear pods. 'Sorry.'

Eden noticed the girl was in the same clothes she'd been wearing the day before.

'Have you been here all night?'

'Once I started, I couldn't seem to stop.'

Eden bent to lift a sheet of paper from the nearest pile littering the floor, 'And all this?'

'Case notes… witness statements, police reports.'

Her voice was shaky, with what Eden could only surmise was nervous exhaustion.

'How on earth did you manage to get the boxes up here on your own?'

'My kid brother and his drippy mate were coming into town for their usual Friday night on the lash. I paid them a tenner each to carry the boxes upstairs.'

Eden was impressed.

'I think Mr Bassett was right,' Molly said. 'I think there are gaps in the evidence and Kit Retallick may well have been wrongly convicted.'

'Look, let me take you for some breakfast,' said Eden.

'But I need to show you what I've found… I—'

'Breakfast first. This lot isn't going anywhere. We can chat over coffee, then afterwards, you can show me what you've found,' insisted Eden, lifting the girl's coat from the chair.

'Okay,' sighed Molly, rising stiffly as if she'd been crouching on the floor for some time. Notebook rolled in her hand, she followed Eden back downstairs.

***

They made their way towards Victoria Square, then took the

shortcut to the Lemon Street market through Walsingham Place. Eden always took the picturesque route through the quiet cobbled crescent. The Georgian cottages looked like dolls houses with their elaborate porticoes and pocket handkerchief gardens, although they were mostly offices nowadays.

'I love these houses,' said Molly. 'I like to envisage the people who once lived here. Imagine all those crinolined ladies, hair in ringlets, sewing tapestries by the window, hoping for a handsome suitor to knock on the door.'

Eden shivered at the claustrophobic image.

'They have a fascinating history, you know.'

Molly's father was a member of the Cornish History Society, and the girl regularly gave Eden the lowdown on the city's landmarks. The last time they'd had a conversation like this, Molly had pointed out that the funeral directors around the corner had been a plague hospital once. *There was a macabre continuity there*, Eden had thought.

'This part of town used to be called Carabee Island, some think because of the port's involvement with the slave trade. It was boggy and inhospitable. A place for thieves and layabouts, with a couple of bawdy houses and a rowdy pub known for gambling and Cornish wrestling, until that is, the Wesleyans built a church here and put pay to the fun. These houses replaced the doss houses.'

'Well, I can honestly say I will look at the place differently from now on,' said Eden, amazed at the information Molly carried around in her back pocket. Although she did wonder how this type of conversation went down with those of her own age on a Saturday night out.

'It's a lesson into how things are often not what they seem on the surface. You often have to dig deeper to find the truth,' Molly said, looking down at her feet.

And there it was, thought Eden, *the case for the defence*. She had been wondering where the impromptu history lesson was taking them. Now she knew. Back to Kit Retallick. Like all good advocates, the girl knew how to spin a story. Not the sort that went down well with vodka shots at the bar of a nightclub, but the sort that would certainly engage a jury. She had high hopes for Molly.

Lemon Street market was busy. The small boutique shops already bustling with Christmas shoppers eager to get their lists filled early. The place had its own scent, a heady, exotic mix of freshly ground coffee and expensive candles: tonka bean and myrrh. Eden, who had done no Christmas shopping yet, made a mental note to visit the kiosk on the corner, which sold craft beers and designer spirits, in the hope of finding something for Luke. Men were always so difficult to buy for. She supposed she should count herself lucky she only had two of them to consider, the other being her father. Yet, surprisingly, the thought made her sad rather than relieved as she thought of her ex-husband and the lengths she had gone to buy him the perfect gift when they were together, much good it did her. It hadn't stopped the divorce, an unexpected present no amount of clever packaging on his part could make pretty.

Despite the shoppers, the two-storey open-plan space felt more like a conservatory than a market, with its giant palms soaring to the vaulted ceiling. They headed upstairs to the balconied gallery and café. Eden often went there to work when she needed to get out of the office for a couple of hours. Sometimes, solitude slowed her thought processes, finally grinding them to a halt. During such times, noise sparked the old grey matter. They grabbed a seat next to the window where they couldn't easily be overheard, although the festive music and the hubbub rising from below were enough to drown them out in any event.

'What are you two doing here on a Saturday,' asked the

waitress as she gave the table a wipe. 'Don't tell me you lawyers are so hard up you've got to work weekends these days.'

Eden was used to Verna's lawyer jibes and never took offence, knowing it was part of the woman's makeup to take a poke at her regulars. She took comfort in the knowledge she was even more abrasive with holidaymakers, who she seemed to regard as an inconvenience, despite her livelihood depending on their custom.

'Not quite,' said Eden, 'but never say never.'

'So, what can I get you? The boss has put on a special Christmas tipsy hot chocolate with marshmallows whipped cream, cinnamon sprinkles and a candy crisp straw to suck it up with,' said the woman with more than a little disdain in her tone.

'Where does the tipsy bit come in?' asked Molly

'That'll be the bottle of vodka I keep under the counter to take a swig from every time some idiot asks for one,' Verna replied, a self-satisfied smirk twitching her top lip.

'I think we'll give that one a miss,' smiled Eden, 'we wouldn't want to contribute to your spiralling dipsomania, would we? The usual, please, and two bacon and cheese paninis.'

Molly had already pulled her notebook from her pocket. Eden could see she was itching to tell her what she'd discovered. She waited until Verna had slouched back to her counter before she began.

'There's so much that's not quite right about the case, and Bassett knew it. Those yellow Post-its all over the papers are his. He's gone through every scrap of evidence, witness testimony and the judgement highlighting his misgivings. He's flagged up all the errors and discrepancies in the evidence as if he knew one day someone would be revisiting the case. They are all dated and made post-trial. He was working on this right up to the week before he died. That's how important it was to him.'

'When you say errors and discrepancies, what do you mean

exactly?'

'Where do I start?'

'How about the prosecution's case? The police evidence?' offered Eden.

Molly's face flushed with delight at the thought her boss was engaging with the process. 'Okay, so the fire was reported at one am by an anonymous caller from the phone box in the village.'

'When you say anonymous, did they trace the person who made the call?'

'Molly beamed. 'No, they never did. Despite an appeal on the local news, no one came forward. Remember, this is one in the morning, and the farm is out of the way. Who would be passing at that unearthly hour to see it from a distance? There has to be a chance they started it.'

'That's a bit of an evidential leap.'

'But if they weren't involved, why not call from their own home or from a mobile? Why make the call from a phone box and then not come forward?'

Eden couldn't fault the girl's logic. 'Did they question Retallick about the phone call?'

'Of course, but he denied making it and they didn't find his fingerprints on the door handle of the phone box or the receiver.'

Their coffees and paninis arrived, and they paused to tuck in, but Molly's hunger was outweighed by her eagerness to talk, and after a couple of bites, she put hers down.

'Okay, said Eden, 'I get that there's a possibility the person who made the call may have started the fire, but we mustn't get ahead of ourselves.'

'But… surely it should have been raised by the defence at trial. It could have put reasonable doubt in the jury's mind,' said Molly.

'Maybe, but it's not enough. Let's, for argument's sake, take the caller's word for what they saw. They spot the fire at one am, by which time it's engulfed the farmhouse sufficiently for the smoke or flames to be seen from the village. It has to have been set when the family is asleep, or otherwise, they would have raised the alarm themselves and got out of the building. So, let's assume it was set between ten and midnight.'

Molly flipped through her notes.

'The fire team said as little as an hour before and that it probably took hold before anyone in the house knew anything about it. The shed to the rear of the farmhouse was filled with accelerants, diesel and liquid fertilisers, all highly combustible, which meant it would have gone up quickly.'

'So, we have to pose the question, if Retallick wasn't the culprit, why wasn't he a victim? Why wasn't a fourteen-year-old boy at home in bed at one o'clock in the morning? Where the hell was he?'

Molly's eyebrows knitted into a frown.

'He was found asleep in the other barn in the top field above the house. He'd been drinking. There was an empty bottle of cider beside him.'

Eden thought of Kit Retallick's scars.

'I've met the man, he's badly scarred. How did that happen unless he was in the house or mistimed his exit after setting the fire?'

'There were no injuries when they found him,' said Molly triumphantly. 'They came after they woke him. He broke free from the police and tried to enter the house to save his family. He was stopped, but not before he'd been hit by debris and suffered an injury to his face. Why would he do that if he set the fire in the first place?'

'I don't know… maybe to cover his tracks?' said Eden.

Molly looked shocked. 'That's what the police argued. Are you sure you're not working undercover for the CPS?'

'Know your enemy. Poachers make the best gamekeepers remember. In this case, though, I think it unlikely. It's a sophisticated tactic for an inebriated fourteen-year-old to employ.'

'Exactly what I thought,' said Molly, looking more hopeful.

'So why was he the prime suspect from the get-go? There has to be more?'

'The police had the family down as dysfunctional. The farm belonged to Kit's stepfather. His mother, Kit and his elder sister lived there, but neither of the children got on with Ray Polglaze, according to the social worker who gave evidence at the trial.

Eden felt a hollowing in the pit of her stomach as she thought of Paul Vincent.

There was evidence Kit was being hit by his stepfather. It was obviously not a particularly stable or happy home. Although everyone agreed, Kit got on well with his mum and sister Tamar.'

'Apparently not well enough.'

'If he did it,' Molly bristled.

'If he did it,' Eden conceded, 'and 'I'm not sure a bad relationship with his stepfather is enough to make him the prime suspect here. Granted there's proximity and opportunity, but it would be hard to find a teenager who doesn't have disagreements with their parents at some time or other. Few, if any, settle the argument by setting fire to their home, especially when it holds others you love.'

Molly took another bite of her panini before meeting Eden's eye.

'So…' Eden enquired, sensing there was more the girl wasn't telling, 'why the rush to charge him?'

'They found matches and an empty can of kerosene in the barn.'

'Ahh…'

'And…' Molly paused as if trying to frame the next piece of information without it nailing down Retallick's coffin. 'He'd been cautioned three months before after setting fire to the contents of a skip in the school playground. He said it was an accident, but the authorities were not convinced. They found a can of lighter fuel, which suggested it had been started deliberately. The fire was spotted early on, so no damage was done, but it resulted in a trip to the school psychologists and social services becoming involved.'

'Are their reports to hand?'

'Yes, but they are inconclusive.'

'What about character witnesses?'

'His gran and the woman from the local newsagents where his sister worked part-time spoke up for him. His gran's evidence was easily set aside as biased and ill-informed as she lived a good distance away, and regular visits had ceased since her daughter married Ray, who she clearly had no time for. The newsagent spoke about the mutual affection between the brother and sister and how she didn't believe Kit would have wilfully harmed her. She said the children were close but that the home environment was tense. She was derogatory about the stepfather, who she called a drunk and a bully. The problem was, on cross-examination, everything she said played into the prosecution's troubled kid scenario.'

'Teachers?'

'The headmaster gave evidence for the prosecution.'

Eden knew that much from her conversation with Agnes and her secretary's theory that Retallick was out for revenge.

'And what do Douglas's notes say?'

'Plenty,' said Molly.

They were interrupted by the buzz of Eden's phone. Eden was about to reject the call, but seeing the number, decided against it.

'Hello, Miss Gray.'

She recognised the gruff baritone of Jake Fairchild, the custody officer from the local station.

'I'm not on duty this weekend, Jake,' she said.

'I know, but it's a client of yours. He's been pulled in for interview, and he's asked for you to attend.'

'A client of mine?' Eden said, trawling through her list of potential idiots who might have been dragged in for a drunk and disorderly on Friday night and had woken up in the cells this morning with her name on their sticky lips. No one came to mind.

Fairchild helped her out. 'A young man on licence called Christopher Retallick.'

Eden's stomach flipped. She knew what was coming but felt compelled to ask the question nevertheless. It didn't do to let the police know you'd had suspicions about your client before they had.

'What's he being questioned about?' she asked.

'The murder of the two men killed this week, Paul Vincent and Graham White.'

Eden's chest was pounding. 'I'll be there right away. I don't want him interviewed until I'm there.' She didn't know why she said that to Fairchild. The man knew the job inside and out. He was not one for underhand tactics. He'd be insulted by the comment and she had the sense to backtrack. 'Not that you would allow it, of course, Jake.'

'Don't worry, the lad's a seasoned professional. There's no way he's going to be giving anything away until you get here. I take it we'll be seeing you in a bit then?'

Eden ended the call. She wanted to ask more, Agnes being in the forefront of her mind. Perhaps she was not giving the police credit where it was due, and they had linked Retallick to the two men without any help from her secretary, but her gut told her they hadn't.

'I'm sorry, Molly. I'm going to have to love you and leave you. I'm wanted at the station. One of my clients is in custody, about to be interviewed,' she said.

She didn't want to elaborate. The girl would only want to come. Things were complicated enough. 'Here,' she said, handing Molly a twenty-pound note, 'you settle up when you've finished, then go home and get some sleep.'

'I'll make sure I tidy the room upstairs before I leave.'

'Forget it, leave it as it is. We can use it as our base for this case. Let's call it our incident room.'

Molly's face glowed with pleasure.

'You mean we're going to run with it?'

'More of a sedate walk, like your crinolined ladies,' Eden replied.

If the police were trying to link Kit Retallick to the murders of those two men, she had little choice. This was no longer just a cold case.

SEVENTEEN

Kit paced the interview room, waiting for Eden to arrive. He'd exercised his right to a solicitor, and there was little more to be done until she turned up. He was relieved she'd agreed to come. She could have decided not to take his case or to help him deal with this latest shit storm. Plenty would have jumped ship.

He'd listened to his fellow inmates shout the odds about their briefs in prison. Not many had a good word to say about them. Only the drug dealers and fraudsters with deep pockets, able to afford the hefty price tags attached to the best, held them in high esteem. He'd known enough to keep his mouth shut when they bragged about their legal muscle, never daring to ask the question on everyone's lips.

'If they're so bloody brilliant, what the hell are you doing in here with the rest of us?'

He hoped Eden Gray would surprise him. He'd heard she was the exception to the rule. Bright, determined and willing to go the extra mile for a cause she believed in, but would she believe in him after this?

When he'd set off for his nan's cottage that morning, he hadn't dreamt within a couple of hours he'd be sitting here.

He'd ordered the taxi and booked out of the pub the night before so he could leave first thing before the village woke up. He knew anonymity was a nonstarter. The villagers would recognise him. His nan had been born there and had lived there until the day she'd gone into the care home. He and Tamar had spent half their childhood there.

Truro or Tri-veru in Cornish, took its name from the three rivers it was built upon. The rivers were still visible in certain parts of the city if you knew where to look, running alongside the pavements in gullies or leats. When he was little, the water used to rise up through the gratings, flooding the shops during periods of prolonged rain or high spring tides. Nowadays, the city's maritime history is most apparent when you take the two miles of riverside road out of town to Malpas. It hasn't changed much in fifteen years. Victorian warehouses had been transformed into swanky flats and offices, but beyond that, the winding flow of the river was as he remembered it.

It was a fine but bitter morning. A wispy mist hovered above a high tide. Had the tide been low, the channel would have been narrow, banked with thick mud. There had once been a dredger employed to clear the channel daily, but not anymore. Large yachts didn't venture up this far unless their skippers knew what they were doing.

The taxi had taken him past Boscawen Park with its Edwardian tea house and the tiny cricket ground, both dormant this time of year. Then, on to Sunny Corner, the strip of pebbled beach where he had swum and skimmed stones with his mates before moving away to live at the farm.

Beyond that, the road crawled high above the widening river, its steep banks hemmed with woodland, thickets of hawthorn and beech on the left and on the riverside, above the shimmering water, towering Monterrey Pines.

As they rounded the corner into the village, his heart began to pound. New houses had crept towards the village boundary. Modern three-storey affairs, a far cry from the modest two-up-two-down terraced cottage which was now his.

When the solicitor dealing with his nan's probate had told him it was valued at five hundred thousand, he'd thought he must be mistaken, but now he could see why. The village had undergone not only an expansion but a gentrification. There were dozens of cars parked along the narrow road. His nan would have had something to say about that, he was sure.

Her cottage was next to the pub, the Heron Inn. It too had been treated to a makeover, now sporting a steel and glass balcony designed to protect alfresco diners as they looked out across the picture postcard estuary. By the look of the boats bobbing on their moorings, the place had taken the fancy of the sailing fraternity and the second homeowners. No more tatty dinghies here making the place look untidy, thank you very much.

As his taxi dropped him off in the pub car park, he noticed despite all the new development, the post office and corner shop opposite were gone. He began to wonder if he had been worrying unduly and whether, other than the long-legged waders who lent their name to the pub, there were any locals left to recognise him. He paid the driver and, taking a deep breath, headed up the granite steps, key in hand.

The cottage was freezing. The kind of cold you only got when there has been no heating on for a while and you live by water, a briny dankness that nibbles at the bones. The thick granite walls kept the place cool in summer, but the idea they kept it warm in winter and saved on heating bills was wishful thinking. The single glazed sash windows put paid to that.

The cottage had been rented out after his nan went into care. It had helped pay her fees. Even so, most of her savings had gone. He still hadn't decided whether he would live there or sell up and move somewhere cheaper. He had no idea where. All he knew was he would stay in Cornwall. After fifteen years in prison, he needed space to breathe.

He headed for the kitchen, hoping to God the letting agents had kept the boiler serviced and there was still enough bottled gas left to get it going. He was relieved when the thing fired up the first time. He scanned the kitchen. The tenants had left the place tidy. He guessed it was easy to keep clean. The units had been replaced, and the jazzy orange vinyl flooring he remembered had been ripped up and the floor laid with tiles.

He put the kettle on, reaching into his carrier for the provisions he'd bought in town to keep him going until the supermarket delivery he'd ordered for later that day arrived. He opened the cupboards in search of a mug. Nothing was where it used to be. Nothing was familiar. He supposed everything had been cleared and replaced with the seaside neutral decor the holidaymakers had come to expect for the high price they paid for a week by the water. In the front room, the old electric fire had been ditched for a wood burner and the tongue and groove ceiling had been given a whitewash. The sideboard where Nan had displayed his and Tamar's school photographs had gone. In its place stood a floor-to-ceiling wall unit housing a widescreen telly.

He'd felt an overwhelming sense of loss. He had not been allowed to go to the funeral or been offered counselling. He guessed a grandmother was not considered sufficiently close to warrant it. She was old and her death was not unexpected, and after all, in their books. He'd murdered his nearest and dearest. Hardly what you'd call family-minded. He had shed his tears alone after lights out.

He wasn't sure what solace he had expected from this place. He knew time didn't stand still outside the way it did behind bars. He supposed he'd hoped to find comfort here, to somehow feel his nan's presence. Yet in these unfamiliar surroundings, he felt even more bereft, as if the happy times before Ray, before everything turned bad, had been erased. The feeling came with the terrible realisation he was starting out all over again and was utterly alone.

The kettle whistled, and he returned to the kitchen to pour his tea. He had taken only one sip when he heard the banging of fists upon the door.

EIGHTEEN

Eden pulled her coat around her as she headed across town to the station. She wasn't dressed for work. It was Saturday morning, after all. She had expected to be moving boxes, not defending a client in the cells. Her trainers were caked in sand, and her jeans had paint spots on them, and that wasn't the worst of it. Under her coat, she wore a t-shirt with the words 'Surfers Do It Standing Up' emblazoned across it.

Her hair blew across her face as she fought the funnelling wind blasting through the alleyway into Lemon Street. She hadn't bothered to wash it that morning, and it was now a mass of unruly auburn curls, the way it always was when she didn't straighten it into submission. She paused, balancing her bag on her knee to rummage for a scrunchy to tie it back with, but didn't find one. She wasn't sure she even had a pen on her. She felt flustered, and flustered was never a good look for a lawyer.

Jake Fairchild was at the desk when she walked through the station door. She could tell by the smirk on his face that she looked like, as Agnes would put it, *she'd been dragged through a hedge backwards*.

'Ms Gray, looking very… casual today and why not, eh…it's the weekend after all. I suppose we should count ourselves lucky you're not in your wet suit, dripping all over our lovely shiny floor.'

Eden heard a definite guffaw from the young officer shuffling paperwork behind the custody sergeant.

Eden's obsession with surfing was no secret. She knew (although she was not supposed to) that Fairchild and his fellow officers regularly warned each other of her presence in the building with a shout of 'surf's up.'

She pushed her unruly hair from her eyes, trying to avoid her jacket riding up and exposing her t-shirt in the process.

'Your client's in interview room two.'

'Who's the conducting officer?'

'Denise Charlton,' replied Jake, pushing the record in front of her to sign in.

'And who's watching?'

'Take a wild guess,' said Jake, a huge grin creasing his chubby face, like a school boy who'd put a worm down the back of your blouse and was waiting for you to feel it wriggle.

He meant Luke, of course. Who else would it be? He'd be watching from behind the two-way mirror. She could imagine him, pensive, arms folded, watching for telltale pointers of innocence or guilt, an unwillingness to meet the eye, scanning the room for inspiration to questions you didn't want to answer. Looking to the left when you answered truthfully. Looking to the right when you lied. All bollocks as far as Eden was concerned. Did the police really believe hardened criminals didn't watch true crime dramas on Netflix? Experience had taught her it was nigh-on impossible to know what went on behind the face of a practised liar. Shakespeare had it right. 'There's no art to find the mind's construction in the face.'

Denise Charlton strode purposefully around the corner.

'Eden, good to see you.'

Eden knew the greeting was genuine.

Whilst not exactly friends, Eden and Denise trusted and liked each other. They had been through a lot together. A couple of years before, Denise had come through for her in more ways than one during a particularly difficult case, which had found her at the centre of a media witch hunt. Luke was lucky to have Denise on his team. She was ambitious, committed and adept at winkling out the truth in interviews. Eden guessed it was why

Luke had deferred to her in this instance. She was always one step ahead with her questions and more inventive than most. She knew how to throw a curve ball and had a habit of interrupting suspects mid-sentence, so they lost their thread. If they were lying, this was often enough to trip them up or frustrate them. They'd lose their temper and give away their secrets. She got under their skin.

As long as you weren't on the other side of the table, she was a joy to watch. It wasn't always the case. Police interviews were often clunky, inelegant affairs, not at all like they were on the telly. Countless times, Eden had been forced to listen to pure drivel from disinterested, under-briefed officers eager to clock off or dodge the paperwork.

Of course, they weren't the only ones in the justice system who failed to perform. Once things got to court, many of her own colleagues stumbled over their words, shuffled their papers and lost their places. They asked pointless questions leading nowhere and leading questions that raised objections. They unwittingly confused the jury rather than help their case. As a spectacle, it was all very disappointing, and Eden wondered sometimes whether it was fair to require unsuspecting citizens to sit through weeks of boring mediocrity when they were expecting Atticus Finch and Judge Judy.

Denise Charlton, unlike all those jobsworths, was at the top of her game. Unlike her, she would have prepared well.

All Eden could do in response was utilise the advantage she had from her inside knowledge. She was pretty sure this whole thing had been triggered by a tip-off from Agnes.

She knew Luke had no evidence. He'd told her as much. Both his victims had died without giving statements and no one else had come forward with information. There were no witnesses and no forensics yet. True, her client was in the city when the murders happened, and if Agnes was correct, both victims had a connection with him, but this was Cornwall. If you could get a conviction on connections alone, the jails would be full. If you drew a chart on a whiteboard aiming to link individuals, you would be hard-pressed not to find a connection with another face through marriage or acquaintance. Anyone who had lived here for generations could probably join the dots to every local in the county. Connection was not enough. Luke needed more. There was added pressure here because her client was on licence. The slightest misdemeanour could see him back inside. He'd had a taste of freedom and wouldn't want to go back. Who in their right mind would? It was another stick to beat him with, metaphorically, of course.

'Your client hasn't been arrested,' said Denise, interrupting Eden's train of thought.

'So he can leave at any time?' said Eden.

'Technically, yes, but you know he's on licence. It makes sense for him to cooperate and clear this up as soon as possible.'

For you maybe, thought Eden. 'Can I speak to him alone before the interview?'

'Of course,' said Denise, 'ten minutes enough for you?'

'That'll be fine... I wonder, could I borrow a pen?'

'Jake, have you got a spare pen Eden can borrow,' asked Denise.

Jake Fairchild pulled a biro from the pot holder on the desk and handed it to Eden with a flourish.

'There you are. Mind you don't walk off with it, or we might have to arrest you,' he said.

'Oh, ha bloody ha,' said Eden, smiling back.

***

Kit got up from his seat as she entered the room.

'Thanks for coming,' he said, holding out his hand.

'Please sit,' said Eden, taking her pad from her handbag. 'I take it you've been told why you're here?'

'Not really. They said they wanted to talk to me about an investigation into attacks on two men in Truro. I thought it might be because I was staying in the pub last Wednesday and they thought I might have seen something.'

'They didn't tell you the names of these men or the nature of the offences against them?'

'No, should they have?' he said, his expression blank.

Had they arrested him, they would have had to give him the details, but for the moment, he was just assisting them with their enquiries. Eden guessed it served their purpose to spring the names on him in interview. To ambush him.

'Haven't you listened to the local news?'

'No, I've been busy arranging the move to my nan's…' He corrected himself, 'my cottage.'

'You've not watched any television or listened to the radio?'

Eden found that very hard to believe. The death of the two men was all anyone was talking about.

'No, there was only a small set in my room at the pub and I'm not that into TV anyway. I don't do social media, remember? I've been inside. I've not got the phone bug everybody else seems to have. I prefer to read.'

'Do the names Paul Vincent and Graham White mean anything to you?'

Eden knew the answer, of course. The question was whether he would admit to the connection.

Kit's face blanched as he slumped back into his seat.

'Graham White was my headmaster. Vincent was my social worker; rather, he was supposed to be my social worker. They both gave evidence at my hearing. Are you saying they're the ones who've been attacked?'

'They are the men who have been *murdered,* both set alight.'

Kit raked his fingers through his hair and leaned forward, his eyes staring down at the tabletop before lifting to meet hers.

'And they think I did this?'

'I think they're aware of your connection with the men, and because of your previous conviction, you are on their radar. In the circumstances, you are bound to be their prime suspect. The fact you're recently released will seem too much of a coincidence to ignore.'

'But I didn't do it. I have no idea about any of it,' he said, rubbing the back of his neck.

'You don't need to defend yourself to me; that's my job.'

'But I need you to believe me. How can I expect you to clear me of killing my family if you think I've done this?'

It was a question she'd asked herself.

'How were they killed exactly?' asked Kit.

'I know some details primarily because I witnessed the aftermath of one of the attacks, but if you don't mind, I'm not going to tell you. It's in your best interest not to know. I can, however, advise you they were both attacked last Wednesday evening. Have you got an alibi for that evening?'

The self-assurance the man had displayed in her office was gone, replaced now with a slump-shouldered reticence Eden found equally unnerving. She guessed he was too jaded from years of incarceration to react with indignation. He knew better. He knew it was possible to become the primary suspect in an investigation with very little evidence and, moreover, for someone like him with a record and on licence, even the most circumstantial of evidence could be fatal.

The eyes she had found so intimidating swam with fear. He looked as if he might burst into tears.

'Look, they have no evidence, forensic or otherwise. What they have is circumstantial. If you can show you were elsewhere, they don't even have enough to arrest you, let alone charge you.

They believe the attack on Paul Vincent was planned and that he was abducted and held last Wednesday afternoon.'

'I was on the train from London,' he said, straightening in his chair.

'Have you got the ticket?'

Kit reached for his wallet and shuffled through the contents. 'It's not here,' he panicked.

'Calm down. Did you buy the ticket online?'

'Yes.'

'Is there anyone who could corroborate you were on the train? Someone you sat next to or had a conversation with?'

'Not really.'

'There will be CCTV, and I assume you booked into the pub that evening?

'Yes, and I did speak to someone there. The girl behind the bar who booked me in and an old school friend.'

'Good… that's good, Kit. DS Charlton will be in to interview you soon. I suggest in this instance you give a no-comment interview. Let her do the work.'

'But should I admit to knowing the men if they ask?'

Before Eden had the time to answer, Denise Charlton entered the room.

Eden vacated the seat opposite and took up position next to her client.

Denise took her seat. She looked relaxed, perhaps even a little cocky, and why wouldn't she? She had a tip-off from the soundest of sources and now, within days of the crimes, had the prime suspect in her sights.

'Mr Retallick, I'm DS Denise Charlton. Is it okay to call you Christopher?'

'Kit, I prefer Kit.'

'I will be recording our interview, but of course at this stage, you are here to assist us with our enquiries as a volunteer and can leave at any time.'

'My client understands,' said Eden.

Denise's eyes did not leave Kit's face as she turned on the recorder and began the preliminaries.

'Interview commencing Saturday 5th of December 2022 at 12.11 pm. Present Mr Christopher Retallick, his solicitor Eden Gray and Detective Sergeant Denise Charlton.' Then came the caution.

'Firstly, Kit, it is my duty to caution you.'

'I thought you said I'm not under arrest, so why are you cautioning me?'

Eden reached across and touched her client's arm. She needed to calm him down, although it had been clear to her the minute she received the call from the station, Kit was only a step away from arrest. He'd been told he could call a lawyer and that he could leave at any time and now was being cautioned. The truth was if he got up to leave, he was likely to be arrested and the custody clock would start ticking.

'For the sake of clarity, you are confirming my client is here voluntarily?'

'At the moment,' Denise said with a flicker of annoyance. Eden didn't take the bait, and her client had the good sense not to do so either. Denise proceeded with the caution. Eden could feel the tension sparking off Kit like static.

'Can you tell me where you were last Wednesday, that is, Wednesday the 28th of November?'

'No comment.'

Denise sat forward in her seat, a defiant glint in her eye.

'Is it that you don't remember, or are you not prepared to say where you were?'

'Neither,' interjected Eden. 'It means he doesn't wish to comment.'

Denise slid two photographs across the table. 'Do you know

either of these men?'

Kit looked at Eden for reassurance.

'No comment.'

'Look, Kit, we know you know them. This is your old headmaster, Graham White,' she said, pointing to the man on the left, 'and this is Paul Vincent, your original social worker. They may or may not look a little bit older than when you last saw them.'

Eden raised her eyebrows at the clear inference Kit may have met with them recently, presumably to kill them.

'No comment.'

Denise changed tack. 'How are you settling into your new routine, Kit? I expect it might be difficult to get back into the swing of life outside… so many things must have passed you by: technology, social media. I suppose had you not been convicted, a good-looking chap like you would probably be dating by now or even married with kids of your own.'

'Are you taking the piss?' snapped Kit, nostrils flaring.

Eden could tell Denise was pleased she'd rattled her suspect.

'No, of course not. I'm just saying you've got plenty to be resentful about. Those two men were instrumental in snatching away your formative years, all the firsts… first pint, first car, first kiss.'

'You think I've never been kissed? That just goes to show how little you lot know about life inside. I didn't miss out on my first fuck either, in case you're interested. No doesn't mean no to the men in there. It doesn't matter how loudly you scream it or how much you fight.'

That took the smirk off Denise's face.

'I don't think my client needs a lesson in loss, detective,' said Eden. 'He could write a book on it. But you might as well know we hope he'll be compensated for at least some of it when his conviction gets quashed. Now, if this little trip down memory lane is finished, myself and Mr Retallick would like to leave. That is unless you have evidence to keep him here.'

Eden frowned at the two-way mirror, knowing Luke was watching.

Denise said nothing.

NINETEEN

'Where's your car?' asked Eden.

'The police brought me here. I never got to pass my test.'

Eden realised it had been a stupid question. He'd told her he'd arrived on the train, and it wasn't as if driving lessons were on the prison curriculum. It would be like handing convicted criminals the means to a more effective getaway.

'Come on,' said Eden, 'I'll give you a lift.'

Kit looked relieved. They walked to her car, neither of them in the mood for idle chit-chat. Kit's hands were shaking as he struggled to release the seat belt and pull it across his chest. She'd noticed the raised scars spidering the back of his right hand during the interview. Defensive wounds suffered when he tried to protect himself from falling debris on the night of the fire. She hadn't noticed the vertical red lines on the inside of his wrists, though, until now. She wondered whether they had been self-inflicted before or after his transfer to prison from young offenders. Both would have been hell for someone like him. He'd have found it impossible to insulate himself from the unwanted violence he'd suggested in the interview. His crime and his scars meant keeping a low profile was a nonstarter.

'You did well in there.'

'They're going to get me for this, aren't they?'

His voice cracked with a barely suppressed sob.

They were approaching Boscawen Park. Eden pulled into the gravelled car park by the river, undid her seatbelt, and turned to face him. As she suspected, his eyes brimmed with tears. Not wanting to embarrass him, she concentrated her attention on a cormorant perched on a rock midstream, drying his feathers.

'I can't go back to prison, I can't, I'd rather die.'

'Kit, no one is going to pin this on you if you're innocent.' She gave him a tight smile, trying hard to conceal her worry.

He choked back a laugh, though tears were now streaming down his marred face.

'Not like last time, you mean. Be honest. *If you're innocent,* you said, if. What the hell chance do I have if my own solicitor doesn't believe me?'

Eden swallowed hard. It would be trite to explain to him as a lawyer, she didn't look for innocence or guilt, just evidence. Her job was to scrutinise the prosecution's case, find its flaws, and if all went to plan, get an acquittal on the back of them. But this man didn't need a lecture on criminal defence, he needed reassurance.

'I don't think you're guilty, Kit. I have no idea who killed those two men, but I'm sure it wasn't you, and I am determined to defend you from those who say it was.'

She didn't add her belief was based on good old-fashioned logic rather than blind faith.

Kit wiped his eyes with his sleeve. 'Thank you.'

'Don't thank me yet. You can thank me once I've proved it to the rest of the world. In the meantime, I need you to stay strong and keep your head down.'

'How am I supposed to do that? I refuse to lock myself away. I'm done with hiding.'

'I appreciate that, I really do, but I'm not sure going back to Malpas is your best option.'

'I'm not being driven out. I'll look guilty if I leave now like I'm running away.'

'You can't leave the county because the police won't allow it and your licence conditions require you to report to them in any event. As long as you do that, no one can accuse you of running away. Look, leave it with me. I'll have a think about what's best.'

'When do I need to see you again?'

'Let's meet on Monday afternoon, say at two. My assistant Molly is already on the case. She's started to fill me in on the details, but I need to get to grips with your files myself. The key to all of this is proving you're innocent of the original crime.'

She reached across and touched his arm. This time, he didn't pull away.

'Are you ready to go home?'

Kit nodded.

As she watched him climb the steps to his grandmother's cottage, she wondered whether he was up to this. He would need a will of iron. It would be difficult enough if he had the support of friends and family to sustain him, but he had no one. She was concerned he was a risk, not to Jo Public but to himself. She imagined him at seventeen entering the adult system and the horrors that occurred. Now he had to deal with the isolation of release. The longer he was alone, the more likely he was to finish what he'd started the day he'd taken a razor to his wrists.

TWENTY

Back in the office, Eden picked up the notes Molly had left for her and dialled Ross Trenear's number. He didn't pick up, and she wondered if it was because he didn't recognise her office number and rang him on her mobile.

'Eden?'

He sounded breathless as if he'd been running. Perhaps he was at the gym or had just come out of the water. She could hear glass bottles rattling in their crates and the screech of seagulls. She remembered Luke had told her Ross was working at the family pub in St. Ives these days.

His voice lifted. 'How's it going, mate? If you're looking for a surfing buddy to play hooky with, you're out of luck. Karenza's picking up Livvy from college, so I'm here on my own. Otherwise, you know me, I'd be there like a shot.'

'Actually, it's not a social call.'

'Oh?'

'A little bird told me you're thinking of getting your PI licence.'

'Oh, it did, did it, and was this little bird a six-foot-tall DCI?'

She hesitated, afraid she'd dropped Luke in it.

'I'm sorry. I didn't know it was a secret.'

'Not so much a secret as a bone of contention.'

'Between who?'

'Who do you think? Me and Karenza, of course. She's not too keen on the idea. She thinks it's my way of returning to the job without the benefits of a decent salary. She wasn't that keen when I had the badge and the regular pay cheque, let's face it.'

'Have you decided against it?'

She couldn't keep the disappointment from her voice.

'I didn't say that. Let's say we've reached a compromise. I've got the licence and am all set up. Karenza's agreed I can take cases out of season when the pub is less busy, as long as I treat it as a nine til five. No late-night stuff. That way I'm around to help out in the bar in the evenings. I think she thinks I'll hate it anyway and will give up if she doesn't object too much.'

'How come?'

'She thinks I'll get fed up hanging around street corners taking snaps of adulterous husbands and bogus personal injury claimants.'

'I have to say, I think you'd hate that too.'

'I suppose I'm hoping there will be other investigations I can get my teeth into. I know how the force is stretched. It hasn't got the resources to investigate half the stuff that gets reported, you know that. I don't know, maybe I'm being naïve in thinking I might be able to help out.'

Eden covered the phone with her palm and punched the air.

'So, how do you feel about lending me a hand with a cold case investigation? It's one of Douglas Bassett's old cases. I've already got the files, and I'm guessing anything I don't have is in the public domain. I need some help scrutinising the police handling of the case and the crime took place in your neck of the woods.'

'Really, what's the case?'

'Arson that turned to manslaughter. A farmhouse in Morvah. The convicted man's family died.'

'Who's the client?'

'The kid… well, the man now, convicted of it and out on licence. He's asked me to look at his case. He says he's innocent.'

'Don't they all.'

'I knew you'd say that, and it's good you're sceptical. That's why I want you on the team. Who better than you to give the police perspective? Molly, my trainee, is handling the case with me, but she's still wet behind the ears. She's already convinced he's innocent. We'll need some objectivity in the mix.'

'And what about you? Do you think he's innocent too?'

She had to think about her response. 'I think there's something amiss and a lot at stake.'

'I thought you said he was out on licence. He's home and dry as long as he keeps his nose clean. Why rake up the past? Or is he another one looking for compensation?'

'I don't think so. I think he genuinely wants to clear his name. There is an additional problem.' Eden took a deep breath. 'He's a suspect in a murder case.'

Ross was silent on the other end of the phone.

'The recent fire attacks? Bloody hell, Eden.'

'I know, I know. But there is no direct evidence linking him to the deaths, other than his past history.'

She didn't want to reveal Kit's connection to the two men so brutally attacked. Not yet, anyway.

'Who's SIO on this one?' asked Ross.

'Luke. He has my client down for it.'

'Does he now?'

She could tell by the change in his tone she'd just made this whole thing a lot more interesting for him by adding an element of competition with his old boss.

'Does he know you're calling me?'

'No.'

'Okay, I'll take a look at the case, but I'm not promising anything. If I think Luke's right, I'm out of there. I'm not like you lawyers. I won't defend the indefensible, and I won't assist anyone else to either.'

'I understand. Just take a look at the evidence. If you don't want any part of it, I'll pay you for the work you do and we'll call it quits.'

'Okay.'

'Can you pop over on Monday?'

'The earliest I can do is Tuesday.'

'Fine, I'm in the magistrates' court in the morning. We could meet there and go for a coffee. Say at eleven thirty?'

'The magistrates, eh? Just like old times.'

TWENTY-ONE

Eden surfed when she got home. Talking to Ross had put her in the mood. The raw November wind rendered the sea warmer than the beach. Nevertheless, its icy sting shocked her tired body back to life, and the hot shower afterwards relaxed her as she focused on getting ready to look through Molly's notes.

She was waiting for the kettle to boil when she heard banging on the door. She wasn't expecting anyone and wondered for a minute if it was Thea still in a rage about the other evening. That was all she needed, or maybe it was someone wanting directions. Tourists asked all the time in the summer, especially if she had the door open, but generally not out of season. She contemplated pretending she was out. Whoever it was would go away if she waited for a minute or two, but to her dismay, they didn't. The banging continued, and she gave in and answered the door.

It was Luke, his face like thunder as he barged past her into the house.

'What the hell do you think you're doing?'

'I think it's me who should be asking you that, don't you?'

'Why are you defending Christopher Retallick?'

Eden pressed past him into the kitchen where the kettle had just boiled.

Luke was hot on her heels.

'The man is dangerous.'

'I hardly think so,' Eden said, popping a teabag into her mug. 'Do you want one?'

'No, I bloody don't. You know he killed his whole family when he was a kid and now, he's killed again.'

'You have no proof of that,' said Eden.

'Come on, I don't believe in coincidences and neither do you.'

'I'd prefer it if you didn't tell me what I do or don't believe in.'

'What's the chances of two men he's connected with - more than connected - two people who gave evidence against him at his trial, being murdered the day he arrives back in the county?'

'I don't know, I'm not a mathematician, and what's more, I don't care. I don't deal in likelihoods. Run an algorithm on the police computer system if you like. I'm sure it will tell you, but I don't choose to gamble with other people's lives. I'm interested in certainties, and unless you have evidence proving Kit Retallick, beyond all reasonable doubt, killed those two men, which, by the way, I'm sure you haven't, I suggest you think again before barging into my home and reading me the riot act.'

Luke plonked himself down hard onto the sofa.

'Agnes tipped you off, didn't she?' continued Eden. 'She gave you Retallick's name. She filled you in on the connection between him and the two victims and now like all those idle jobsworths you claim to despise, you want to take the easy route. Now you have him as your prime suspect, you've stopped looking for anyone else. I thought you were better than that.'

'Don't be ridiculous. Agnes did what you should have done the minute she confided in you, and if I was so keen to wind this up quickly without a proper investigation, how come your client's not back behind bars?'

'You know she's biased, don't you? Douglas Bassett handled the boy's case. It practically broke him. I've told you before how Agnes felt about Douglas. Whether she'd admit it or not, she held a torch for him for years and is extremely defensive of him, both professionally and personally. She dislikes Retallick. In fact, she won't have a good word said about him. She thought he was guilty the first time around and believes he's guilty of these latest murders too. Nothing's going to shake her on that. Even Douglas couldn't persuade her. He thought the boy was innocent and was clearly worried he'd handled the case badly or missed something, but no, Agnes knows better. Agnes *always* knows better. You know how obstinate she can be. She called you to stop me from taking this case. She thought her call would result in his licence being revoked. It's her way of putting me back in my place.'

'God, the vanity of you. Listen to yourself,' sniped Luke, his expression tight. 'These crimes are horrific, monstrous, and you're protecting the man who perpetrated them. I admire Agnes for going against your wishes and calling this in.'

'I can't talk to you when you're in this mood,' Eden shouted back. 'You should know I will defend my client if these allegations go further, and I intend to investigate his conviction and get it quashed. Until then, I will sleep at night knowing I'm doing my job. I suggest if you want to do the same, you get out there and look for your killer.'

Luke shot up from his seat, his face red, nostrils flaring as he tried to contain the rage bubbling to the surface. He headed for the door.

Their friendship went back a long way. It had survived his split with Thea and many near misses since. They had managed to maintain it despite being on opposite sides of the justice system. She could not countenance anything jeopardising her relationship with Flora. If she lost Luke's friendship, she might lose her beloved niece forever, and she couldn't bear that.

She followed him. She would not apologise. Why the hell should she? But she had to pull back from the vitriol. 'Look, I hope this case isn't going to drive a wedge between us. I know you want to catch the person who did these terrible things. If we're going to do battle, let's both bring our best game, knowing we'll shake hands at the end of it no matter who wins or loses. You know how I feel about Flora and… you too, of course.'

Eden's eyes pricked with tears.

Luke began to walk away down the path towards his car before changing his mind and heading back the way he'd come. Eden could tell by the curl of his lip he'd not finished with her yet.

'You talk about bringing our best game,' he said, his finger jabbing at the air in front of her face. 'Murder isn't a game, Eden. Or if it is, the losers are the poor bloody victims. Do me the courtesy of listening to someone who knows a thing or two about victims. They almost never see the train coming. Watch your back. Don't take chances with Retallick. He's lived his entire adult life in prison and that changes a person. Don't begin to think you know him. Guilty or innocent, he's damaged goods.'

She didn't answer back. She had let ego colour her judgement. Point scoring was risky. Like the child's game where you extract body parts without setting off the buzzer. Touch too many nerves and you risk killing the patient.

As she closed the door, she was glad she hadn't mentioned Ross. She might have been left with a corpse to bury.

***

Eden called Molly. 'I know it's Sunday tomorrow, and you'd be well within your rights to tell me to take a flying jump, but I wondered if you'd be up for meeting me to go over the Retallick files?'

'Yes,' the answer ricocheted back without the slightest hesitation.

'Good, then let's meet at the office at ten thirty. We need to break the back of this as soon as possible. There has been a development I need to fill you in on.'

'Not bad news, I hope.'

'Nothing to worry about, not yet at least. Let's just say proving Kit Retallick's innocence has become more pressing than we first thought.'

She sensed the net was closing in on their client but didn't intend to divulge Agnes's role in casting it. They needed to stay focused and not get bogged down in the rights and wrongs of her secretary's actions.

'I'll be there,' said Molly.

TWENTY-TWO

Eden was the first to arrive on Sunday morning. She'd stopped off at the supermarket to buy them sandwiches and a box of doughnuts. There would be no time to pop to the café today. They'd need to eat as they worked if they were going to get through the files before her meeting with Ross on Tuesday. He'd sounded busy. She didn't want to waste his time or her money come to that. She needed solid leads to give him something he could get his teeth into.

She intended to look through Kit's statement before she saw him. She would not take it with her to the meeting and had no intention of reminding him of its contents. Once he re-read it, he'd find it difficult not to refer to it. It would gnaw its way into his subconscious, like being shown a photograph of the suspect before being asked to pick him out in a line-up; unsafe.

She knew it had been a long time since the night of the fire, but she bet there had not been a day since that he hadn't thought about it. But what exactly did he *remember*? He was little more than a child when he lost everything. Children had a way of burying traumatic memories. It was the only way they could survive them. They didn't have the intellect to rationalise or departmentalise; instead, they developed selective amnesia to insulate themselves from an unfathomable truth. She had been involved in cases of historic sexual abuse where allegations were made decades after the event. The victims were always challenged with the same question. Why hadn't they reported the abuse at the time? Told their parents, teachers or the police? Time and time again, she had heard psychologists explain they had only recently recalled these terrible traumas. Until the point when the memory was triggered, it lay like a sleeping shark at the bottom of an unfathomable ocean.

Was there something Kit had forgotten, a buried memory she needed to hook from the depths of his subconscious? Something that, if Douglas Bassett had known about it, would have changed everything?

She was in the upstairs office trying to compute the enormity of the task ahead of them when she heard Molly on the stairs.

The girl beamed when she saw her.

'Good work,' Eden said, handing her back her notebook.

Molly blushed. 'You think we have something then?'

Eden didn't want to burst the girl's bubble. She had spent the previous evening reading Molly's notes. Her trainee had done the best she could in the short time she'd had thus far, but they contained only the briefest of insights into the case. She had picked up snippets of information about Kit's background and listed things she found at first glance to be amiss, and she was right to do so, but what those meant in terms of reversing Kit's conviction remained to be seen. She had to be realistic. Douglas Bassett had known this case like the back of his hand. It was his files they were scrutinising. He had trawled through them with a fine-toothed comb, trying to piece together enough evidence to get the conviction overturned and had failed. All those yellow Post-its, enticing as they looked, were not golden tickets to success.

'I think there are anomalies that need explaining, but no answers at present,' she replied, sighing at the mountain of files cluttering the office floor.

Molly followed her gaze. 'Where do we start?' she asked.

'I think we need a system,' said Eden.

Molly was a fan of systems. She liked to work in a methodical, regimented way. She, like Douglas Bassett, was a fan of indexes and colour co-ordinated notes. Eden, on the other hand, relied on her instincts. She liked to get a feel for the case and fill in the gaps once she had the broader picture firmly fixed in her mind. They were the dream team when everything worked well. In a cold case like this, Molly's meticulous attention to detail would be invaluable.

'There is something you need to know before we start,' said Eden.

Molly frowned. 'Is this the something you mentioned on the phone?'

'It is. The call I received yesterday at the café was about Kit. He'd been asked to attend the station to answer questions about the murders of the two men who died last week. He wanted me there.'

Molly's eyes widened. 'They think he killed them?'

'They haven't arrested him. He attended voluntarily, but he is certainly their prime suspect. In fact, I think he's their only suspect.'

'I suppose he is an obvious choice. His record singles him out for attention.'

'It's more than that. He has a connection with both victims. I'm assuming you haven't had time to get to the transcripts of the trial yet, so you probably don't recognise the names. Both men were witnesses for the prosecution. Paul Vincent was Kit's social worker and Graham White, the man Agnes discovered in Victoria Gardens, his headmaster. Unlike the police, who seem to think no one else could possibly have done this, I'm keeping an open mind about Retallick. That said, if we intend to rule him out, we need another suspect. One thing is certain, though. Whoever tortured and killed those two men has something to do with this case.' Eden gestured towards the files. 'Somewhere amongst this lot has to be a clue to who it is. As in all criminal cases, we have to look for motive, and the best place to look for motive is to examine the victims.'

Eden expected Molly to react in the same way she herself had when she had heard about the connection from Agnes, with a mixture of shock and disbelief. Instead, the girl fell to her knees and began rummaging through one of the many boxes of papers stacked on the floor.

'What are you looking for?' asked Eden.

'The headmaster, Graham White. He was the responsible adult who attended Kit's first interview with the police the morning after the fire. I saw something yesterday. I didn't make a note of it because I wasn't sure of its relevance.'

Eden joined her on the floor. 'Are you sure? I would have thought in the absence of his mother, they would have called his father or maybe his grandmother?'

'The father was on an oil rig in the North Sea. I know about it because the grandmother filed a complaint. She said no one had let her know Kit was in custody. She heard about her daughter and her granddaughter's death from Tamer's employer, who ran the newsagents in the village. The police had made no attempt to contact her. I know it's here somewhere. Here it is... her complaint.'

Molly pulled out a clear plastic wallet containing a photocopy of a handwritten letter. It confirmed Kit's grandmother had been kept in the dark. If that wasn't bad enough, if the information in her complaint was correct, the very person seconded to protect and assist her grandson during his interrogation had not only failed to do so but had later given evidence at the trial against the boy. It was unheard of. The man would have been privy to the police case from the get-go. He had no reason to question it. If it was persuasive enough, he would have been convinced of the boy's guilt. His evidence as a witness for the prosecution had to be tainted by prejudice and unsound. She could not believe Bassett would not have picked this up. He'd surely been there at the boy's first interview.

'Why didn't Douglas object?'

'He's not mentioned. I don't think he was there. The boy spent the night in the hospital because of the wound to his face. The police didn't interview him at the station. He was interviewed in his hospital bed with the headmaster in attendance. It was not under caution, and there's only the briefest of records of what was said. He was cautioned a few days later after his arrest. By then, Mr Basset was on the case and a social worker, someone linked to the hospital, had been appointed as Kit's responsible adult.'

'We need to find White's witness statement.'

'Witness statements for the prosecution are in boxes three and four to the left of the door.'

Eden picked her way across the room and retrieved the boxes, plonking the first of them on the desk before lifting its lid. It contained three large arch-lever files.

It wasn't hard to find White's statement. It was brief, running to only two pages. It gave background as to Kit's arrival at his school mid-term. It conceded the report that followed him from his previous school had been fairly standard. He had a good attendance record and had reached all of his academic goals without additional tuition. It confirmed for the first three months this pattern was maintained. However, after that, Kit had become disruptive and uncooperative. White said he did not respond to authority. He failed to complete his homework, played truant and did not attend his scheduled detentions following these breaches. He was suspended twice. Once for the fire incident Molly had told her about and the second time for refusing to change out of his uniform for games. White said he had numerous complaints from parents and teachers about the boy's disruptive influence within the classroom and that despite contacting his mother and stepfather, neither had attended meetings when requested to do so, although Kit's elder sister

Tamar had turned up at the school when the police were called following the skip incident.

Eden handed the statement to Molly. 'We need to find the transcript of his evidence at the trial.'

Molly headed towards a pile of files in the corner of the room. Each marked with a large red sticker.

'Red for the prosecution witnesses. Blue for the defence. The transcripts have the evidence in chief and the cross-examination.'

The girl had obviously researched far more than her notes indicated. Whilst this looked like chaos to Eden, Molly knew where to lay her hand on everything.

Molly retrieved and unclipped Graham White's evidence in chief.

'I'll make us a coffee,' offered Molly, leaving her to it.

'Thanks,' smiled Eden, pleased the girl had picked up on the fact she didn't like to read with someone looking over her shoulder.

As expected, the prosecution's barrister had drawn White on much of the contents of his statement. In particular, he had asked for his opinion as to the rehabilitation he believed Retallick required to set him back on the right course. The defence barrister, to Eden's surprise, only objected once during White's diatribe and only then on the basis that the teacher was not appearing as an expert in child psychology. There was no cross-examination to speak of and certainly no reference to White having been prejudiced during his attendance at the hospital. What the hell were the defence team playing at? It was as if they were going through the motions, believing the police had a slam dunk case and they were doing the kid a favour by getting him the help he deserved.

Kit's grandmother, bless her heart, had played into the prosecution's hands, admitting the boy was troubled and had changed since the family moved in with Ray. Tamar's employer came across as an elderly do-gooder, privy only to the gossip she gleaned in the village or rare snippets from Tamar when working in the newsagents. Their cross-examination was condescending and dismissive.

After they'd eaten their sandwiches, Eden and Molly tackled Paul Vincent's statement. He had not appeared in the capacity of an expert either. Another psychologist had taken on that role. Vincent was called because of his dealings with the boy following his referral after the fire at the school. He said he had visited the family on numerous occasions during the subsequent weeks. His evidence portrayed Kit as a teenager with severe behavioural problems, frustrated with his circumstances and unwilling to engage in any conversations about his home life. He had not been willing to confirm the social worker's suspicions of abuse or to undergo a physical examination after turning up at school with bruising to his upper arms. The boy had explained away these injuries as having occurred whilst helping his stepfather with the animals on the farm. He said, notwithstanding many hours of interviews on several separate occasions, the boy remained sullen, unresponsive and defensive.

Again, the defence's cross-examination was minimal. Eden understood this to some extent. The man was bringing nothing new to the party and certainly had no direct evidence of the crime itself. She was beginning to suspect the defence team were, from the outset, hedging their bets. Perhaps they thought the evidence given by the two men would evoke pity in the jury or at least give the judge something he could take into consideration by way of mitigation when sentencing the juvenile. The trouble was, neither tactic worked. The jury had not been able to see beyond the horrors of the crime, and the judge had thought the best way to deal with the boy was to protect the public by removing him from the equation.

Finally, they read through the transcript of the chief prosecution witness, the investigating officer who attended the fire and found Kit in the barn. DI Brett Noble. It was a compelling contemporariness statement of what the detective witnessed first-hand that night and, without doubt in Eden's mind, the evidence that convicted Kit.

She could imagine the jury hanging on Noble's every word as he painted the horrendous scene. He was articulate and persuasive. By the end of his testimony, she was pretty sure the jury would have been ready to lock Kit up and throw away the key.

'It's bad, isn't it?' said Molly.

Eden had never been good at poker.

'I'm afraid so.'

Eden photocopied the statements of White, Vincent and Noble and, thanking Molly for her time, called it a day.

She hoped to God Kit had something to throw into the sorry mix to make her feel differently because, without it, she feared the worst. Not only would he fail to quash his conviction, he may well find himself before another jury. This time on a double murder charge.

TWENTY-THREE

Eden had a long evening ahead of her. Her objective was to familiarise herself with Kit's evidence. He hadn't testified at his trial. Douglas had had the good sense not to call him, no doubt recognising the dangers of the boy suffering a meltdown under cross-examination. His evidence was confined to the interview he gave at the station three days after leaving hospital. This interrogation, unlike the one with Graham White in attendance, had been under caution.

She expected it to be intense. It had been carried out on tape rather than video, so she had no way of gauging the reaction of those present other than by the tone of their voices. The written transcript of the interview was likely to be even less helpful.

She poured herself a large glass of wine, slipped the tape into the cassette player and pressed play.

It felt strange listening to a recording from so long ago. Her thoughts inevitably drifted back to what she might have been doing at the time. She'd have been in London, having just finished her law degree, looking forward to the summer vacation before starting the Legal Practice Course and work. She had spent months attending hideously pressurised recruitment fairs held by the major law firms. She'd been ready to do anything, including working for a pittance to get a training contract with the promise of a practising certificate. It seemed like a lifetime ago now, back when everything was still rosy in the garden of Eden.

Life had moved on for her, but there was no moving on for Kit. He wouldn't be able to shake off his past until he cleared his name. She listened to the mandatory introductions.

Present were DI Noble, Douglas Bassett and Kit's newly appointed appropriate adult, a Miss Devlin, employed by social services.

Eden took notes as the interview began in earnest.

Noble's accent was hard to place, but it was not local. She guessed Thames Estuary.

'How's the face healing?' he asked, sounding concerned.

Kit's reply was little more than a mumble: 'Fine.'

The Cornish burr, now long gone, was pronounced, and Eden couldn't tell if his reticence was borne of anxiety or teenage belligerence.

'Christopher, I want to talk to you about the night of the fire, but before we begin, I'd like to say how sorry I am for your loss. I cannot imagine how it feels to carry that much guilt at such a young age.'

'Now hang on a minute,' Douglas Bassett interrupted.

'I meant the guilt you clearly feel about not being able to save your family. I can quote your own words on that very night.'

Papers shuffling.

'No… no. I didn't mean it. I need to put it right. I need to save them… Mum and Tamar. I need to save them.'

He was a clever operator, this DI Noble. He knew not to rush in all guns blazing with his accusations. His tone gentle, his concern sounded genuine. If the jury were looking for the good cop in the room, they'd found him.

Still no response from Kit. No denial.

Noble, undeterred, changed tack. 'I'm going to take you through the evening's events. First of all, I'd like to know if you often sleep in the barn?'

'Sometimes.'

'When you say sometimes, what do you mean? Once… twice a week or more like once a month?'

'Maybe once a month, but only in the summer. It's too cold

in the winter.'

'Did your mother and stepfather know you slept there?'

'No.'

'So, it was something you kept secret?'

'I just didn't say anything about it. It wasn't a secret.'

'Well, you didn't tell anyone. That sounds like a secret to me.'

'My client has answered the question,' Douglas interjected.

'Fair enough,' said Noble, once again the voice of reason.

'Can I just ask why you slept there so often?'

'I felt like it.'

'It wasn't when you had a row with your stepfather or because he'd hit you?'

Again, nothing from Kit.

Noble continued. 'Because everyone would understand you'd be afraid to stay in the house if a bully like Ray Polglaze was violent towards you. You had every right to take yourself out of the situation. No one should have to put up with that, and after all, he wasn't your father. Was that it? Was the barn the place you escaped to when things got unbearable at home?'

'I suppose,' Kit replied.

Eden wondered why Douglas had allowed this line of questioning to continue unchecked. Maybe he hoped it would evoke sympathy for the boy; not spotting Noble was slowly but surely building his motive.

'Is that why you kept alcohol in the barn?'

'My client doesn't need to answer that question.'

'Don't worry, Christopher. I'm not about to charge you for underage drinking. I'm only saying I understand why you might need something to dull the pain of the beatings or to help you forget. We all need a little something now and again to help us through things.'

Kit didn't reply.

Eden made a note to ask him about the alcohol.

'Let's move on. So, you had a violent row with your stepfather, and you ran and hid in the barn, fearful for your safety. You then drank the cider you'd stashed there.'

'I didn't say he hit me.'

'Are you saying he didn't?'

Douglas finally spotted where this was going.

'Please do not put words into my client's mouth.'

'Okay, let's put aside whether Ray did or didn't rough you up. You were drunk when we found you. That is not up for debate. You were breathalysed at the scene and a subsequent blood test confirmed it.'

'Then you have your answer,' said Douglas sharply.

'You smoke, don't you, Kit? We found a lighter, tobacco and cigarette papers on you, so I assume you do. Did you ever smoke in the barn?'

'Sometimes.'

'I assume you knew that was dangerous. There was hay in there and kerosene. There are rules about not smoking in farm buildings. Weren't you worried you might accidentally start a fire?'

'I was always careful.'

Douglas again. 'There was no fire in the barn. There is no relevance here. Can we please keep to the point?'

Eden could hear the frustration in the lawyer's voice.

'You're right, of course. There was no fire in the barn, but there was a fire. We all know that. It would have done so much less harm in the barn.'

'Detective, I—,' Douglas interrupted again.

Noble cut him off.

'We've established you are a smoker, used to carrying and handling a lighter on a regular basis. Willing to take risks, some might say.'

'I said I was careful,' Kit's voice was raised, and for the first time, Eden got a glimpse of the bolshie teenager Agnes disliked so much.

'So, you've never started a fire before… even by accident… say, thrown a cigarette into a bin or a skip, causing the contents to catch light?'

Eden remembered the incident at the school.

'I didn't do that,' shouted Kit.

'My client will not answer questions on that subject.'

Douglas rightly wanted to make sure Noble didn't sneak in evidence of Kit's previous caution.

'Okay, back to the night of the fire at the farmhouse. What time did you head out to the barn?'

'Dunno about eleven, or maybe half past.'

'And what time did you fall asleep?'

'I don't remember.'

'Not right away then?'

'No.'

'Let's say you started drinking, had a couple of cigarettes, then finally dropped off. Does that sound about right to you?'

'I suppose.'

'Well, you did, or you didn't, which was it?' For the first time, Eden heard impatience in Noble's tone.

Kit's appropriate adult spoke up.

'This was a traumatic event for Kit. It is to be expected he cannot recollect the minor details of that night. It might be months before he does. Perhaps he never will.'

Noble wasn't going to be put off.

'I'm a little confused, Christopher. If all you did was drink, smoke and fall off to sleep, how come there was kerosene on your clothes when we examined them?'

'I tried to light the lamp.'

'What lamp? We didn't find a lamp in the barn.'

'There's an old lamp… an oil lamp I use sometimes to read

by. I don't know why you didn't find it. It's always there.'

'But like I said before, there are rules about flammables being kept in farm buildings. It seems strange to me in this day and age that your stepfather kept an oil lamp in the barn.'

'There was a lamp. The place is full of old stuff. Ray never gets rid of anything.'

'Did you manage to light this lamp? Is it what you used to start the fire? Is that why we couldn't find it? Did you carry it back to the house and start the fire with it?'

'No, I told you. I don't know why you couldn't find the lamp, but that's how I got the kerosene on my clothes. I tried to fill the lamp from the big can and it went all over me.'

'Why didn't you go home to change? The stink must have been unbearable.'

'I took my shirt off.'

'You wore a shirt over the t-shirt you had on when we found you. Where is it?'

'I don't know. Still in the barn, I suppose.'

'What was it like, this shirt you say you were wearing?'

'Blue and white check.'

'Like this?'

There was the sound of plastic rustling on the tape.

'For the purposes of the tape, I'm showing Christopher a strip of check fabric found on the track between the barn and the farmhouse on the night of the fire.'

'Is this a piece of your shirt?'

There was a pause while the boy handled the bag and then passed it on to his solicitor.

'It looks like it, but where's the rest of it,' asked Kit.

'This is all we found: a long strip of fabric soaked in kerosene. If you unzip the bag, you can still smell it. Did you rip your shirt, Christopher?'

'No.'

'Well, that's a puzzle because someone did. This isn't the sort of rip you'd get if you caught your shirt on brambles or barbed wire on your way to the barn. This is the sort of rip you get when you tear something on purpose.'

'I don't know how it got ripped. It wasn't ripped when I took it off.'

'Do you know what a Molotov cocktail is?'

No reply.

'Well, let me explain. It's a homemade incendiary device. You fill a bottle with something flammable, say petrol or kerosene, then plug the neck with a piece of fabric very much like this one. Then, when you're ready, you light the end of the fabric, which acts like a wick, soaking up the kerosene. When you throw the bottle, it smashes and starts a fire. Simple but effective.'

'Detective, where exactly is this going? Interesting as your foray into the world of guerrilla warfare is, this piece of fabric was clearly not set alight, and who's to say it even came from my client's shirt?'

'Oh, I'm sorry. I didn't make myself clear. I know this piece of shirt wasn't used to start the fire because it lay amidst broken glass in a patch of kerosene-soaked grass. It's the rest of the shirt, I believe, was used along with the bottles you prepared in the barn for the job. Isn't that right, Kit? There's no trace of the rest of the shirt because it burnt in the fire. This is the only piece that's left.'

'I never did that. I never made one of those Molat… whatever you called it.' The boy was shouting now.

'But you see, Christopher, I can't get over what you said, the words I referred to earlier. If you didn't do this, why did you say them? I'll read them again for you, shall I?'

'*No… no. I didn't mean it. I need to put it right. I need to save them… Mum and Tamar. I need to save them.*'

'What were you sorry for, Kit? What did you want to put right?'

'This is ridiculous. It's an off-the-cuff comment made at a time of crisis. He was not under caution,' Douglas objected.

The lawyer was right. The statement should have been inadmissible, but Eden knew through reading the transcript of DI Noble's evidence, time and time again throughout his testimony, the detective found ways to introduce it to the jury. He was aided and abetted by the prosecution's barrister with leading questions. Eden turned to the trial transcript.

"And this reflected what the boy had told you at the hospital?' and a couple of pages later: "So to be clear, DI Noble, you felt confident the boy was telling the truth when he said he felt responsible, this being his initial reaction when you found him in the barn. Is that correct?"

Noble had been more than happy to agree that everything pointed to Kit being the culprit. It was as much as Eden could do not to throw the transcript across the room. What on earth was the defence barrister thinking? Why hadn't he objected to its introduction? Finding Kit in that barn and what he said in the aftermath of the fire had led the police to centre all of their attention on him. They had stopped looking for anyone else, fixating instead on Kit's initial reaction when woken with the incomprehensible news his entire family had burned to death.

His words of contrition were lobbed at the jury again and again. Once those words were in the mix, there was little else a jury could do but convict. It was as good as a confession. Only it wasn't one, not in the true sense of the word, and Kit's barrister should have had it excluded before it had time to take hold in the jury's mind.

She listened until the point when Kit was taken to the custody officer to be charged with increasing dismay. Turning the tape off, she headed for bed.

This was going to be an uphill struggle. Sure, the admissibility of some of the evidence was questionable and much of what remained was circumstantial, but like it or not, it had done the job. They needed something new. What's more, if she were honest, she had doubts about Kit Retallick. Luke's warning buzzed like a bad case of tinnitus. There was no doubt back then the boy was bad news. He was described in one of Vincent's reports as almost feral. Eden could cope with feral. Feral was all about resilience and survival in her book. The question for her was, did the boy have it in him to kill in the most grotesque of ways? Moreover, did that wild rage still burn in him? Was the man she'd driven home a fake?

She needed help. She had never defended an arsonist but was aware they were a rare category of criminal with particular patterns of offending. Pyromania was a recognised psychological condition. Before she went further, she needed to know what kind of man she might be dealing with. The next morning, Eden called an old school friend, Dr Cassandra Mitchel. Cassy was a psychologist and an expert in criminal pathology. If anyone could fathom what drove people to use fire as a weapon, she could.

TWENTY-FOUR

The incident room buzzed like a beehive on full alert. Murders were a novelty in Cornwall, but now, like London buses, two had arrived at once. As Luke walked into the room, the hum subsided, and all eyes fixed on him. It was a feeling he was getting used to, although when he'd first suffered it on his promotion to DCI, the pressure to perform had sat like a dead weight until he had realised his colleagues, unlike the press and his superiors, didn't expect miracles, only leadership.

Denise stood to the side of the whiteboard. It was pretty empty except for a photograph of the two victims on one side and of Kit Retallick on the other. He was their only suspect; all other inquiries having drawn a blank.

No one on their patch had a history of anything as heinous as these crimes. The closest they'd got to it was an acid attack three years before, carried out by a couple of no-marks from Manchester who had been paid five grand to put the frighteners on a dentist with a penchant for gambling. They had picked the wrong address, door-stopping and disfiguring an innocent man going about his business while his children played on the trampoline in the garden and his wife cooked Sunday lunch. The two men responsible had been caught by chance because a neighbour had snapped their numberplate on his phone as they sped away.

If these crimes had been carried out by the same callous class of criminal willing to do anything for money on instructions from outside the county, they were unlikely to catch them. It would normally have been Luke's primary concern, but he didn't intend to spend much time worrying about it because he knew he had the culprit. Retallick's scarred face stared at him from the whiteboard across the room.

'Denise, can you let the team know what we've got so far?' Luke said, resting his back against the wall. He knew he was being optimistic, calling them a team. Most were not used to working on anything like this. He'd requested backup from different stations across the county and from over the border but hadn't heard back yet.

'We know there is a link between the suspect and the two men recently murdered. Vincent and White both gave evidence at Retallick's trial, and we know they met at the school he attended on more than one occasion.'

'And the suspect's got a conviction for arson,' interrupted DC Nathan Wilton.

'He has,' agreed Denise. 'Until last week when he was released, he was serving a sentence for the manslaughter of his family. They burned to death in a fire set by him when he was fourteen.'

The room began to hum again.

'So, what are we waiting for? Let's get the little shit in and charge him,' chipped in Nathan.

Luke stepped in. 'A matter of evidence. Retallick's got an alibi for last Wednesday afternoon.'

Denise wrote the word London Paddington on the board.

'The London train arrived at Truro station at four thirty on Wednesday evening. The cameras didn't catch him at this end, but we know Retallick was on the train because we've got CCTV footage of him getting on at Paddington.'

'But these men were killed after that,' said Nathan.

'Probably,' agreed Denise, 'but we believe they were abducted earlier in the day.'

'Abducted?' DC Rosie Bray asked.

'Paul Vincent arranged to meet his wife at five for an early dinner, after which they intended to watch the parade together, but he didn't turn up. The last time she spoke to him was at three when she rang to chat through their arrangements for the evening. When she tried to ring him back an hour later to ask him to bring her a waterproof coat from home because rain was forecast, he didn't pick up. She tried several times after but got his voicemail. When he stood her up at the restaurant, she knew something was wrong. We found his phone on him at the scene, and her story pans out. We have to assume at this stage he didn't answer because he was being held against his will.'

'And White?' asked Nathan.

'Last seen by his neighbour in the flat below, leaving the building at about four. She remembers he was smartly dressed as if he might be going somewhere special. She had a good look at him because there's a streetlight right next to the flats. They were not the clothes he was wearing when he was found. His daughter has looked through his wardrobe to see what's missing. She says she's not sure about the trousers, but his best blue sports jacket, a shirt she bought him last Christmas and his bowling club tie are gone, as are a pair of size ten slip-on brown leather shoes. When we found him, he was dressed in second-hand clothes and a Guy Fawkes mask. His killer took the trouble to dress him in those clothes. It must have taken up valuable time, adding to the threat of being caught, so we have to assume it was important to him. We need to find those clothes.'

'Could Retallick have had an accomplice?' asked Rosie. 'Someone on the outside willing to do the groundwork for him?'

'It's possible. We need to check whether he had any special friends who were released prior to him or if he corresponded with anyone on the outside.'

'There's a touch of the theatricals about it, don't you think, sir?' said Rosie. 'Almost as if the killer was staging the scene. Wasn't Guy Fawkes a traitor? Maybe Retallick thought White giving evidence at his trial was an act of treachery.'

'More likely he was trying to disguise the man's identity, thinking it would take longer for someone to raise the alarm if they thought White was a down-and-out,' said Nathan.

'Or it could mean, as Rosie suggests, the killer was trying to tell us something about him or his victim,' said Denise. 'It shows careful planning.'

Luke heard a tinge of aggravation in Denise's tone as she stood up for her fellow female officer. They were the only women on the team. It was natural they would have each other's backs.

'Perhaps the killer fancied a new sports jacket,' chuckled Jake Fairchild, who was not strictly part of the investigation team but had asked if he could sit in on the briefing.

Though in bad taste, Jake's gallows humour lightened the moment, and Luke was glad of it.

'Where do the forensics point, sir?' asked Nathan.

'The toxicology reports on the two men came back this afternoon. As we suspected, both men were drugged with ketamine. It explains why neither put up much of a fight. We tested for DNA and have samples on the system from Retallick. We had hoped there would be some touch DNA present on the bodies, but there was nothing. We have to remember both men had been doused with fuel and set alight.'

'There's likely to be some splashback evidence on the killer's clothes, though,' said Nathan.

'You would have thought so, but we found none on Retallick's clothes and no inflammables in the property where he's staying. That's not to say he didn't dispose of them. We have to hope we find White's clothes and find something on them. I know it could be a fool's errand. It's likely they've been destroyed, but we don't have anything else at this stage.'

'What about giving the local media a description of the

clothes so they can ask people to look out for them?' said Rosie. 'You never know, someone might remember seeing him that evening. At the very least, it might give us a better idea of when he was killed.'

'Good idea, get on it,' agreed Luke.

'Even if we find no forensic evidence linking Retallick, surely the fact he's done this before and had links with the two men will be enough for the CPS to let us charge him?' said Nathan.

'All circumstantial. We have nothing but his past conviction and...' Luke hesitated, 'there's something you all might as well know now. Retallick has asked for his original conviction to be reviewed.'

'Officially?' asked Denise.

'Not yet, but he's engaged a local solicitor to look into it.'

He was careful not to say which local solicitor, although he assumed Denise would guess.

'Well, let's hope we get him before he's given the chance to kick the system into touch on some technicality,' said Nathan.

'We'll leave the past to the lawyers. I'm concerned we stop this from happening again. We might not have enough to charge Retallick, but we can stop him from lighting the match to anyone else. I want him watched 24/7. It shouldn't be hard. He's living at his gran's old house in Malpas. The road is a dead end. One way in, one way out. He doesn't drive, so he's reliant on buses, taxis and lifts. We can park a car in the lay-by on the outskirts of the village and we'll know when he comes and goes. I imagine the villagers are none too pleased at the prospect of having him there, so let's make sure we use them. We might be low on numbers, but we can rely on them to pick up their mobiles to tell us what he's up to. A regular presence in the village will work wonders if they think we're on their side.'

'Have the press cottoned on to him yet?' asked Rosie.

'Not yet,' said Denise, 'but it's only a matter of time. We

found out the connection because of a tip-off. I'm pretty sure others will spot it, too, and once that happens, the focus won't only be on him. They'll expect us to nail him for this.'

'I hope I don't have to remind you that if I find out anyone here has leaked anything to the press, I will make it my mission to see you're out of a job. We have kept back much of the detail to avoid false confessions, so I will know where it comes from if it gets out,' Luke warned. 'We do not want to lend ammunition to Retallick's lawyers. We keep our hands clean and our lips tight.'

There was a rumble of agreement around the room.

'Okay, we're done for now. Jake will sort out the rotas for the surveillance. Warn your families they'll be seeing a lot less of you over the coming weeks.'

He left them pondering the uphill battle ahead, hoping above hope the forensic team would come up trumps and they would have something to hang their case on.

Back in his office, he poured himself a coffee and took out his mobile. He was about to get up to close the door before tapping in Thea's number when he noticed Denise loitering outside.

'Are you okay there, Denise?'

'Can I have a quick word?'

'Of course, what's on your mind?' he said, closing the door behind her.

She looked anxious.

'It's about the detectives who'll be joining us. I know we really need more experience and all that, but I'm concerned…'

'Go on,' said Luke.

'That we… that I'll be sidelined.'

'You've nothing to worry about on that score. As far as I'm concerned, you're my right-hand man… I mean person here.'

Luke knew she was being diplomatic. It would be pot-luck

who they got. No doubt they'd be decent enough detectives. They were unlikely to send him slouches, but Denise knew from experience young male detectives could be arrogant and dismissive of their female colleagues even in this day and age, and whoever they got was unlikely to be another Ross Trenear. Ross didn't have a sexist bone in his body. He was also the sort who could turn a pile of shit into a Christmas pudding and then find the sixpence to boot. Others were great ideas men, but when it came to the hard yards, they were less enthusiastic. They routinely passed the admin to those they considered more adept, the women. The force had a long way to go before it achieved equality in the true sense. It was getting better, but Luke knew they weren't there yet.

'We need all the experience we can muster, but whoever we get will be guests here, and I'll make sure they behave accordingly, don't you worry.'

'Thanks, I appreciate it,' Denise said, wheeling away to leave before turning back. 'What about our other cases, sir? Who do we delegate those to?'

'Unfortunately, we can't ditch them or pass them on to another station, although I've told the Avon force their case will have to go on the backburner for now.'

The murders could not have come at a worse time. The lantern parade seemed a lifetime ago, but it had only been a week since Vincent and White were murdered. He had been run off his feet before that terrible night trying to keep on top of the admin and deal with a case of sex trafficking passed down from Bristol, who apparently had information that four Ukrainian sex workers had been trafficked into the county and could be being held somewhere in the region against their will. He would have liked to have helped, but a double murder trumped trafficking. A double murder trumped most things.

TWENTY-FIVE

Meeting Cassandra Mitchell for the first time, one would never guess in a million years what she did for a living. You might think fashion blogger, jewellery designer or boutique owner. Glamorously elegant with a lighthouse smile, it was hard to believe she was one of the rare breeds of individual willing to get down and dirty with those the rest of humanity confined to the realm of nightmares.

Eden had texted she wanted to talk to her about a case she had involving arson.

The text back had read, 'Where there's smoke…'

'Eden, so good to see you,' Cassy beamed as she opened the door. 'Go on through. I'll fetch the coffees.'

Eden headed into the photoshoot-ready sitting room with its vaulted ceiling and polished concrete floor. Cassy, wearing a pale grey cashmere sweater dress, followed behind with two mugs of steaming coffee. She motioned Eden to sit on the peacock velvet sofa to the left of the fireplace. Cassy sat opposite. The low coffee table between them was piled with books that Eden could see on closer examination were exclusively devoted to one subject: pyromania.

'So, what do you want to know?' asked Cassy, placing her mug on the table and strapping on her game face.

'I've taken on a cold case, a boy convicted of arson as a teenager. His family died in the fire. He served fifteen years and has recently been released on licence.' Eden took a sip of her coffee. 'He says he's innocent and wants me to help him prove it, and as there are a number of discrepancies in the evidence, I'm persuaded to help.'

'So, what's the problem?'

Eden hesitated. 'I need to know whether he was capable of setting fire to his family and... if he could do it again, to someone else?'

Cassy scrutinised her. Her smile less glossy now.

'Are you asking because you think he might have lit other fires or because you're frightened he might do so in the future, and this time it will be on your watch?'

Eden's response dried on her lips under her friend's quizzical gaze.

'Pyromaniacs are driven by impulse in the same way as kleptomaniacs or gamblers. They are led by an irresistible urge and experience tension or arousal before and sometimes after the act. They've often had an intense fascination with fire for as long as they can remember, which in some cases extends to an obsession with the equipment used to put it out.'

Eden remembered her own fascination as a child watching her father light garden bonfires on chilly Autumn evenings.

'Aren't all children a little obsessed with fire?'

'Yes, but the pyromaniacs' fixation goes well beyond the fascination displayed by other children.'

'How early does this obsession start?'

'Let's just say some little boys who want to be firemen when they grow up need to be pointed in another direction.'

'What do they get out of it?'

'A sense of relief or gratification which can be sexual when lighting or watching the fire or its aftermath. The police know this and often scan bystanders for suspects.'

'Can it be about revenge?'

'A true pyromaniac never sets a fire for revenge or for the insurance money for that matter. The fire is not a means to an end. It's the sole object of their desire.'

'What about if they're drunk?'

'If they're the real deal, they rarely set fires when intoxicated. They'd miss all the fun if they did. They want to relish the full impact of their handiwork. They don't need Dutch courage and there is never any remorse.'

Eden remembered Kit's first response on that fateful night when woken by the police.

'What made the authorities think this boy was a pyromaniac?' Cassy asked.

'He'd been cautioned for setting light to a skip a couple of months before. There had been witnesses. The prosecution seemed to straddle two camps at his trial. Firstly, inferring he was disturbed with a history of fire starting and, secondly, that he was seeking revenge against his stepfather. Add intoxication to the mix, and it amounted to a compelling case.'

'Maybe, for your average jury, but the inference of pyromania could have easily been rebutted by a good defence expert in the field. To hold up one minor incident as evidence of the disorder, especially when others were present, is ridiculous. Fire-starting is a solitary obsession, never communal, and, as I said, never driven by revenge.'

'Perhaps these fires would have been the first of many had he not been locked up?' offered Eden, playing devil's advocate.

'Unlikely. It's true the man hasn't had the opportunity to commit other offences, but if he is a pyromaniac, it would have been picked up by any analyst worth their salt while he was inside. The urge to set fires does not go away without treatment, and for many, not even then. Unless there is something in his records post-incarceration to say he received therapy for the condition, I think you can assume those in the penal system ruled it out soon after his conviction. I don't think we are dealing with a pyromaniac here. What I cannot say with any certainty is whether he is a man capable of using fire as a weapon against those he has a grievance against. I cannot rule him out as the perpetrator of these new atrocities.'

Eden knew her friend was referring to the two recently murdered men. She hadn't needed to mention them. Cassy was no fool. The cases had been widely reported. She had joined the dots without any help from her.

At the door, Cassy gave Eden a hug.

'Keep looking for the discrepancies in the evidence. There is a possibility your client was wrongly convicted. Don't let yourself be distracted by the crime, horrendous as it is. We are all terrified of fire; that's partly the reason we are drawn to it. Don't let yourself be mesmerised by the flames. Fire is a good servant but a bad master.'

TWENTY-SIX

Molly looked up as Eden arrived and nodded in the direction of the waiting area. Kit was sitting there, head down, playing with his fingers. Eden noticed he'd had a haircut and was dressed casually. He looked younger than he had the day he'd visited her office before and less intimidating. The scar across the left side of his face was less obvious now his hair wasn't pulled back into a top knot.

'Morning,' Eden said with mock cheeriness. 'Would you like to follow me?'

Out of the corner of her eye, she saw Molly's shoulders drop. The girl was desperate to join them, but without Agnes, Eden needed her front of house. She felt bad about it, but there it was. She had no intention of ringing her secretary to ask for help. She was still disappointed she'd telephoned the police. A fact she had yet to tell her client, although he had a right to know why all this additional grief was coming his way. She couldn't afford to lose Agnes permanently, but for the moment, she wasn't sure she could trust herself not to lose her temper if she saw her, and that would do no one any good.

When they reached her office, Kit waited for her to settle before taking his own seat. For someone who had spent half his life behind bars, he had surprisingly good manners. The last time they'd been in the room together, she had been intimidated by him. Now the tables were turned. She'd witnessed his distress the day before and glimpsed the boy behind the man on the pages of his statement. She sensed a vulnerability far deeper than his scars.

'Did you sleep okay?'

'Not too bad.'

Not too good either, she guessed.

'I spent an informative evening listening to your police interview,' Eden began. 'I have the transcript here, but I want you to answer my questions relying on your memory alone. I want to hear everything you recall about the day of the fire. I appreciate this will be painful, but I can't stress enough the importance of not censoring your replies.'

Kit shuffled in his seat as if he thought this might be a trap of some sort.

Eden pulled a bottle of water from her desk drawer and handed it to him.

He unscrewed the lid and took a sip.

'This won't be like your police interview. I won't badger you if you can't answer,' she reassured him. 'Don't patch together a memory from the information the police gave you or from the testimony you heard at the trial. If you don't have firsthand evidence, I don't want to hear it, understand?'

Kit nodded.

'Good,' said Eden, leaning back in her chair, 'let's start with that morning.'

Kit looked blankly at her, and for one terrible moment, she thought he was about to get up and run before they'd begun. He took another gulp of water, leaned forward, folded his hands on the desk and closed his eyes the way a child would when trying to remember a story.

'It was just like any other Saturday. I got up and had breakfast.'

'What did you have?'

'Frosties,' a smile played across his lips. 'I always had Frosties.'

'And after breakfast?'

'I helped Ray.'

'Helped him how?'

'Four new bullocks had arrived the day before. They needed tagging. I helped Ray hold them down while he punched their ears. They were always skittish when they first arrived. He'd keep them penned up, knowing we'd have no chance of catching them if he let them out in the field.'

This is good, Eden thought. *He's remembering detail.*

'Was Ray pleased with you for helping him?'

Kit grimaced. 'Nothing much pleased Ray except beer and throwing his weight around, but he gave me money and told me to run down to the village to buy pasties for our lunch. He said I could buy a Coke with the change so yeah, he was in a good mood for him. I remember he said it was good to get me away from the women. He said he could make a half-decent farmer of me if the damn women stopped fussing over me.'

'He meant your mother and sister?'

'Yeah. They'd caught the train to Plymouth first thing. They were looking to buy Tamar's dress for her leavers' ball.'

'So, it was just you and Ray at home during the day.' Eden underlined the note she'd made. 'Carry on, Kit, you're doing really well. You went to the shops, bought the pasties and the Coke and took them back.'

Kit opened his eyes.

'I didn't buy the Coke. I bought a lighter and a pack of Rizlas.'

Eden felt a greasy unease in the pit of her stomach.

'Why did you buy them?'

'I'd nicked some tobacco from Ray's packet that morning and planned to smoke it later.'

'Weren't you afraid he'd miss it?'

'No, he had loads of packs. He had a mate with a van who used to smuggle it over on the ferry from Roscoff.'

'Anything else?'

He hesitated again.

'What?' said Eden, concerned.

'The cider.'

She thought for a minute he was doing exactly what she told him not to and straying into the realms of his police statement.

'I didn't mention the cider,' she said.

'I know, but that's when I got it.'

'You mean you bought it in the shop?'

His head dropped. 'I didn't buy it. I nicked it. I put the bottle inside my jacket.'

'Had you done that before?'

'No.'

'But you'd drunk cider before?'

'Yes, but before, I'd always nicked Ray's Scrumpy or scrounged it from Tamar when she'd bought it for her and her mates.'

'And you drank it in the barn?'

'Mostly, yeah.'

They had strayed off course, but now they were here, she decided to stay with it.

'Where did you put the empty bottles?'

'At the back of the barn behind the farm machinery, or sometimes I smuggled them out and dumped them in the bin. Mostly, I left them in the barn. No one ever bothered to go through the stuff at the back. It was only good for scrap.'

'How much did you drink that particular night?'

'Just the one bottle.'

'But you were drunk when the police found you?'

Eden thought of her own illicit drinking escapades as a teenager. Cider had been the beverage of choice for her and her friends too. She had been a lightweight back then. Her ability to hold her liquor came later with practice, but even she wouldn't have been legless after only one small bottle of cider.

'If all you drank was the one bottle, you wouldn't have been that drunk, surely. What do they hold, a pint?'

'You're thinking of the craft blends you get these days. This was a big plastic litre bottle.'

Eden thought of the Molotov cocktails Kit had been accused of making and of the smashed bottle on the pathway.

'Plastic?'

'Yeah,' Kit frowned.

'And the other times, when you stole from Ray or got it from Tamar, were those bottles plastic too?'

'Yeah, it was always the cheap stuff with the screw tops other than when I drank it straight from Ray's flagon he got filled down the pub.'

'Kit, this is really important. Are you categorically saying there were no glass bottles in the barn?'

'No, not that I knew of, only plastic ones.'

Eden's mind was racing, but she didn't want to push him, not yet.

'What time did your mum and Tamar get home?'

'About half four, five o'clock.'

His eyes lit up when she mentioned the two women.

'Have you remembered something?'

'Only how happy they were when they arrived. They were giggling, and Mum didn't do much of that. I suppose that's why I remember it.'

'And Ray, what was his reaction?'

'He'd gone down the pub as usual. Mum, Tamar and me were going to watch a video.'

'So, all in all, everyone was in a good mood. Nothing happened to upset you. It had been a good day. You hadn't argued with Ray, and Tamar and your mum were happy.'

'Until Ray came back early.'

Eden felt a tingle at the nape of her neck. Up until this point, there was nothing to rile Kit enough to set the fire. She had a feeling that was about to change.

'He'd come home early because there was a hen do down the pub. Ray hated incomers. He came back in a shitty mood and then was angry we were upstairs laughing and that.'

'What happened?'

Kit leaned back in his chair, his hands balled into fists on the desk.

'He kicked off as usual, but this time, Mum stood up to him. She never usually did, but she did that night. I think she was mad because Tamar mentioned his girlfriend.'

'His girlfriend?'

'Tamar accused him of carrying on with his ex, the barmaid down the pub.'

'And was he carrying on with her?'

Kit shrugged. 'Who knows? I wouldn't put it past him. He treated Mum like dirt in every other way. Why wouldn't he fuck her that way as well?'

'Did they fight?'

'No, not really. He stormed off. Mum was working a night shift at the care home, so by the time he got back, she'd gone to work.'

'And Tamar?'

'She was seriously pissed off. He'd told her she looked like a tart in her new dress. She left, saying she was staying at a friend's place. She did that when Mum was on nights.'

'So, you and Ray were in the house on your own once your mum left?'

'Yeah, until I went out to the barn around eleven. Ray had had a skinful by then and was in front of the telly asleep. I climbed out my bedroom window. That's what I always did. I never liked being in the house alone with Ray when he was drunk.'

'Were you frightened of him?'

'Fuck yes. The man had hands like shovels. When he hit you, you knew about it.'

'Did that happen often?'

'At first, before I learnt to read his moods and to avoid him when he'd had a session. Nothing heavy… not by some standards. I met blokes inside who'd been thrashed within an inch of their lives since they were toddlers with no one noticing. Ray would rough me up if I cheeked him, and I'd get the belt if I broke anything or was late with my chores.'

'You didn't tell anyone?'

'What was the point? I'd have been put into care. I didn't want to leave Mum and Tamar there with him on their own. I wasn't the only one on the receiving end of his temper. Mind you, Tamar told me that night someone was looking out for us, and strangely, I remember it made me feel better.'

'Did she say who?'

'No.'

'So, escaping to the barn was a way of avoiding a confrontation?'

'Yeah, he was pissed off, and with Mum and Tamar both gone for the night, I was the only one left for him to pick on.'

Eden's brain was sparking. She flipped over the pages of the notes she'd made the evening before, adrenaline coursing through her.

'Kit, when DI Noble found you, why did you say you had to save your mum and Tamar?'

'I never said that. I told Mr Bassett at the time I didn't, but he didn't believe me. He said I probably couldn't remember saying it because I was drunk. He said it explained my running back to the house to try and save them. He said my injuries were proof of my intention, but I know I didn't say it. I think he thought he was helping me. He thought it would play well with the jury… the fact I was sorry.'

'I believe you. Why would you when you thought your mum and sister weren't there?'

He looked at her open-mouthed, his eyes filled with pain. 'But they were, weren't they? They found their remains.'

'Yes, unfortunately, that's true, but as far as you were *aware* your mother was working all night and Tamar was staying with her friend. Why on earth would you believe they needed saving, and why on earth had they come back that night?'

'I don't know. I've laid awake at night wondering why over the years, wishing they hadn't.'

Tears sparkled in Kit's eyes.

'I'm so sorry,' Eden said, 'but I must ask you one more thing. If not to save your mum and sister, why did you risk your own safety by trying to enter the building.'

'Jasper.'

'Who?'

'Jasper. Ray's dog.'

TWENTY-SEVEN

Eden woke on Tuesday morning with a sinking feeling. The brief spell of euphoria she'd felt after her interview with Kit and on giving Molly the news they'd be taking his case had dissipated like sea mist in the face of the prospect of Gloria le Grice's appearance in front of the magistrates. Her spirits plummeted further as she remembered she needed to be suited and booted, and her only clean blouse was sitting wet in the tumble dryer she'd forgotten to turn on.

She had arranged to meet Gloria outside the magistrates' court at ten sharp. She had precisely one hour to get ready and to get there. Allowing for traffic, she had twenty minutes to dress. She turned the dial of the machine and headed for the shower. By nine thirty, she was on her way, her shirt still clammy. She turned the car heater to high and hoped for the best.

As she pulled into the car park, she spotted Gloria sitting on a bench outside the court building, puffing on a cigarette. She was dressed in a mangey-looking fur coat. Her hair, as usual, was backcombed and sprayed into candyfloss around her wizened face. Eden had no idea what look the woman was aiming for, but given she was wearing Jackie O sunglasses, she guessed fifties film star, although the result was more Lily Savage than Gina Lollobrigida. She wasn't sure the look would impress the magistrates.

'My nerves are in shreds,' Gloria shrieked, stamping out her cigarette with the heel of her red ankle boot. 'The babies know something's up. They sense these things.'

Eden guessed she meant her cats. 'Gloria, you need to calm

down and lose the shades. The magistrates will ask you to remove them to give evidence.'

'I can't, it's the cataracts.'

'What do you mean, the cataracts?' Eden asked, having presumed the woman had donned the sunglasses in an attempt to preserve her anonymity should the local press turn up.

'I had an operation on my left eye last week.'

'You didn't say?'

'I don't like to foist my disability on others.'

'When exactly did you have the op?'

'The day after you called to see me.'

'Friday then, and did it go well?'

'So they say, but I know they're lying. No doubt they want me to come to terms with the horror before they tell me the truth.'

'What horror?'

'Blindness, of course, the loss of my sight,' Gloria said impatiently. 'It'll only be a matter of time before the other one goes. That's what happens when it takes the strain, you know. Well, they can think again if they imagine I'll be getting a guide dog. The babies wouldn't stand for it.'

The woman reached into her bag and took out another cigarette, lifting it to her lips with bony fingers. Eden's mum had undergone a cataract op the year before. She'd understood they were pretty routine. She'd taken her to outpatients and been amazed the whole thing had been completed in less than an hour. She'd needed to wear a patch for a few days but then emerged as good as new.

'I'm sure it's too soon to tell whether it's been successful or not, and shouldn't you be wearing a patch rather than sunglasses?'

Gloria hesitated.

'I'm allergic to sticking plaster. I'm a martyr to eczema.'

'Okay. I'll need to explain this to the magistrates' clerk if you're going to keep the glasses on. Let's get you inside, it's cold out here.'

Gloria reached for her. 'You'll have to lead me. I can't see a thing.'

Eden led Gloria through the double doors into the waiting area.

'Do you need assistance?' an usher asked as Gloria felt for the seat.

'We're fine, thanks,' said Eden, her cheeks reddening as she tried to unpeel her client's painted talons, which were now stopping the circulation in her upper arm.

'Gloria, are you still happy to give evidence? Because if you're not, I will need to let the magistrates know and ask for an adjournment on medical grounds.'

'I'm prepared to fight through the pain if I must, but you will have to help me to the witness box,' Gloria snivelled.

Eden spotted Angie Evans from the CPS approaching.

She and Angie were good friends, and when she indicated with a tilt of her head she'd like a private chat, Eden left Gloria to join her.

'What's with the shades?' asked Angie, making no attempt to conceal her amusement. She had been involved the last time Gloria had been before the bench.

'Cataract op last Friday.'

'And you believe her, do you?' said Angie, in the lilting Welsh accent Eden had heard charm a jury more than once. 'You do know the woman's an inveterate liar, don't you?'

Eden said nothing.

'What are you offering?'

'How do you know I'm offering anything? This is a second offence. And despite what the old girl says, the store detective's evidence is unequivocal. He says he paid particular attention to her because of the peculiar way she was dressed and the equally peculiar way she was behaving. He says he watched her carefully select the items she took. She even put back a couple of packets of tights after checking the sizes before leaving the store without paying for the ones she'd slipped in her bag.'

'So, you're not offering anything then?'

'I didn't say that.'

'Go on.'

'I'd offer community service, but let's face it, I can't see Gloria donning a hi-viz jacket to pick up rubbish in those boots, can you? Plus, there's a danger at her age she might keel over, and that's more paperwork for some poor sod.'

'So?'

'I'll accept a guilty plea, a fine and as the goods stolen were below two hundred quid, six months suspended.'

'Look, make it a fine and a probation order, and subject to Gloria agreeing, we've got a deal.'

Eden could see Angie weighing up the implications.

'Alright, as a favour to you, cariad, but I want a year's probation. I don't want to be back here again in another six months.'

Eden smiled. 'You're not alone there. I'll put it to her, but at the moment, she's adamant she wants her day in court.'

'Then she's a bloody fool. She'll be wasting everyone's time. I've come across this store detective before. He's a compelling witness. No one's going to sway him, not even you.'

'I hear you,' said Eden, turning her back and walking across to Gloria.

'I've spoken to the CPS, and they're willing to make a deal if you're prepared to plead guilty.'

'But I told you I'm innocent.'

'The store detective says he was watching you for some time prior to detaining you. His evidence is not only that he saw you take the items but that you knew exactly what you were looking for. I think, in the face of his evidence, it will be extremely difficult to persuade the magistrates this was an absent-minded mistake on your part. If you plead guilty, the CPS is prepared to accept a fine and a probation order.'

'A fine? I'm a pensioner. I can't afford to pay a fine, and what will this probation order involve?'

'You will be monitored for a year and must not commit any other offence during that period. Or after, come to that.'

'Monitored,' Gloria squawked, removing her glasses and rubbing the bridge of her nose.

Eden could see nothing wrong with the woman's left eye. Certainly nothing to prevent her from applying a slick of blue eyeliner along the lid.

'Will I need to wear one of those ankle tags?'

'No, and you won't have a curfew.'

'They won't come to my house, will they, these probation people?' Gloria asked, foundation settling in her wrinkles as her face crumpled with trepidation.

Eden decided to play her trump card.

'No, and at least this way, you won't have to worry about your cats.'

If the threat of separation from her beloved babies didn't work, nothing would.

Gloria replaced her glasses. 'If you can get them to ditch the fine, it's a deal.'

'I'll do my best,' said Eden.

Twenty minutes later, having agreed the deal and entered a guilty plea, she parted company with Gloria.

'Are you okay to get home under your own steam? I'd offer you a lift, but I have another meeting.'

'I'm fine, a friend is picking me up. I've texted him.'

So much for her temporary blindness, Eden thought as she

watched Gloria walk across the car park with the speed and grace of a gazelle and sidle into the same BMW Eden had seen coming up the drive on the day she'd visited her.

Eden was shaken from her reverie by a voice from behind.

'God almighty, don't tell me you represent Gloria le Grice.'

It was Ross Trenear, grinning like a Cheshire cat.

'You know Gloria?'

'Everyone knows Gloria.'

'How come?' asked Eden, starting to worry she was the only one stumbling in the dark as far as Gloria was concerned.

'Back in the day, she ran a very successful business in Penzance for gentlemen with particular tastes.'

'What sort of tastes?'

'Her escort agency was called "Plumpalicious".'

'You're saying she was a madam for plus-size sex workers?'

'Let's say girls with plenty to go around,' Ross smiled, raising an eyebrow.

'Stop it,' Eden chided, stifling a giggle.

'She never got done for it. She's a shrewd operator, our Gloria.'

'When was this?' asked Eden.

'Oh, fifteen, maybe even twenty years ago. Don't tell me she's still at it. Is that why you're here today? Did one of the chubby chasers get tangled in some giant knickers?'

'You're incorrigible,' said Eden, steering him towards the café entrance. 'I've had enough of Gloria le Grice for one day. Let's get a coffee.'

As they walked through the foyer towards the café, several young women gave Ross the once over. She couldn't blame them; he was a handsome devil. She noticed his sun-bleached hair was longer, more surf dude than detective these days. Tanned and toned in a tight white t-shirt and jeans. Though in his forties, he was still a poster boy for the sport.

They sat with their coffees in the corner of the café.

'You look good,' Eden said, 'retirement obviously suits you.'

'Retirement, you've got to be joking. I've never worked so hard. That wife of mine is a slave driver.'

'How are Karenza and the kids?'

'Good. Piran's moved out. He lives with his girlfriend, Carly. They have a baby boy. I'm a grandfather, would you believe?'

'No, not to look at you,' she smiled.

'Livvy's off to university next year. How about you? Are you with anyone… do you want me to check him out for you? I've got the software to do it.'

'No need. There's no one, not even on the horizon. I'm practically an old maid.'

'You're easy on the eye, brainy and financially independent. What's not to like?'

Eden blushed. Years of feeling like an ungainly red-headed beanpole next to her pert, pretty blonde sister had rendered her uncomfortable with compliments about her looks. She wasn't delusional. She knew she had smashed the ugly duckling mould and turned into a flame-feathered swan in her late teens. Nevertheless, she could never receive a compliment graciously like Thea, as if it was the most natural thing in the world. Compliments were always met with silent embarrassment.

'I'm not very flexible these days,' she said.

Ross began to laugh. 'Too much information…'

'Not that way, you fool. I like my life the way it is. I don't need a man in my life, thank you very much. I've been there once. I'm not going there again. I've got the beach house how I like it, and whilst I can't deny it's a challenge running the business alone, I'm beholden to no one.'

'I get it, but, in my experience, autonomy is overrated. I whine about being tied to the pub and running around after the kids, but I've never been happier. The time when I was on my own, with two failed marriages behind me, was the bleakest of my life. I thank God Karenza took me back.'

'Don't we all? For a while there, you were a pain in the ass.' Ross gave a wry smile. 'What about Luke?'

'What about him?' said Eden.

'Nothing, it's just I always had you down as a couple when you were teenagers and got the feeling there might have been something between you two had your sister not got there first.'

She heard herself stuttering; 'I couldn't... not with Luke. Not after Thea, and it's not that kind of relationship. We're friends, that's all. I see a lot of him because of Flora.'

She was gabbling, and she could tell by the smirk on his face she was less convincing with every line. She was relieved when he changed the subject.

'So, down to business. This cold case you want me to have a look at?'

Eden reached into her briefcase and pulled out her file.

She spent the best part of an hour running through the transcripts with Ross, filling him in on Kit's history, her impressions of him and the discrepancies in the police evidence. The more they talked, the more engrossed Ross became. Little by little, the surfing dude paddled off into the sunset, and the detective engaged.

'Here,' Eden said, slipping the file across the desk, 'I've put together a brief just like I would to counsel, along with my own notes and copies of the original statements and transcripts. 'Read it and let me know what you think?'

She knew by the way he took the file without the slightest hesitation that Ross was hooked. He kissed her on her cheek as they parted.

As she watched him walk away, she wondered why she'd never been able to nab a man as easy to fathom as Ross. She knew he drove other people mad, Luke included, but she didn't see it herself. He was laid back and fun. Yes, he could be reckless, and seemed to attract trouble, but she got him.

Her mobile rang. It was Kit.

'They're watching me.'

'Who?'

'The police. They've got a car parked in the old quarry just outside the village. I think they've also had a word with the staff at the pub. I was putting out the bin and one of them snapped a photo of me on his phone. He didn't even try to hide what he was doing. When I asked what he was up to, he didn't answer. He had a smirk on his face like he knew he was in the right.'

Eden felt her hackles rise. *How dare they? This was harassment.* Well, she'd see about that.

'Look, my parents have a caravan they rent out sometimes. It's empty at the moment and at the end of a long private road. I want you to stay there for a few days. It's not right you feel you have to stay cooped up in that cottage because other people don't know how to behave. The police are clearly encouraging the villagers to ostracise you. You've served your time and earned the right to live peacefully.'

'I couldn't impose. It wouldn't feel right.'

'I insist. I need to be able to speak to you regularly. I won't put up with them scrutinising your every move or mine, come to that.'

'But won't you need to ask your parents first?'

'You leave that to me.'

Eden thought of the Amnesty International poster on the wall of her mother's potting shed and knew her parents would be only too willing to assist. They were, after all, a couple of old hippies, always ready to stick it to the man. Hopefully, he wouldn't have to be there for long, and he'd be self-sufficient in the caravan. They never let it out in the winter. As long as he didn't mind the isolation or the cold, he'd be fine.

'How long will it take you to pack a bag?'
'Ten minutes tops.'
'Okay, I'll be there in twenty minutes to pick you up.'

TWENTY-EIGHT

Luke was at the coffee machine when Nathan and Rosie walked in. On seeing him, Nathan took a left turn and headed for the gents. Luke wouldn't have thought anything of it but for the sheepish look on the young detective's face and the knowledge Nathan had a serious caffeine habit. He hardly ever saw him without a mug in his hand. Maybe he needed to watch his intake these days, with a new baby at home waking him in the middle of the night. He might need all the sleep he could get. He himself never drank coffee after four pm. Rosie had headed straight to her desk without saying a word to anyone. Perhaps Nathan and Rosie had had words. It happened when partners were cooped up in a car together on surveillance jobs. It was hardly scintillating stuff, boring as hell, not to mention in most cases fruitless, but it was the job, and let's face it they weren't only there to chart Retallick's every move, they were there to prevent him from killing anyone else until they had gathered enough evidence to nail him.

Luke decided to take a detour on the way back to his room to see what was up.

'How did you get on?' he asked Rosie, who, on spotting his approach, had turned her attention to her computer screen.

'Rosie?'

'Yes, sir?' she said, as if hearing him for the first time.

'How did you get on?'

'Fine, he didn't move last night.'

'Did he go anywhere this morning?'

'Well, the thing is.'

Luke caught a glimpse of Nathan out of the corner of his eye doing a three-sixty on spotting him at Rosie's desk.

'Rosie, what the hell's going on? Have you two fallen out or something?'

'No, sir, nothing like that.'

Luke couldn't be bothered with this.

'Did the other team turn up on time? Are they in place outside the village?'

'They're not at Malpas, sir. We didn't see much point in them being there.'

'Of course, there's a point,' Luke said, exacerbation creeping into his tone as he wondered what planet his subordinates were on, thinking they had the right to countermand his decisions. 'We need to keep the pressure on Retallick. If we do that, he'll take risks and slip up.'

'He isn't there anymore.'

'What do you mean, he isn't there anymore? If he's not there, where the hell is he?'

Luke was aware he was shouting and that the rest of the room had fallen silent.

'He left with Eden Gray. She turned up at his place late morning. He came out carrying a suitcase and they left together.'

Luke was beginning to worry now.

'Please tell me she didn't take him to the train station?'

'No... no. Don't worry, sir, he's still in the county.'

'Where then, for god's sake? Spit it out.'

'She drove him to her parents' place.'

Luke couldn't quite believe what he was hearing.

'We followed the car to their smallholding. She stayed for about twenty minutes, then left without him.'

Luke slammed his fist down on Rosie's desk, making her keyboard jump. The eyes of every member of the team followed him back to his office. He was furious. How could Eden be so reckless, and how could her mother and father be complicit? He expected this kind of bat-shit madness from Thea, but Eden had a sensible head on her shoulders. She was harbouring a convicted felon and the principal suspect in a murder investigation. It was one thing to represent Retallick; it was her job, but this was beyond the pale. That he could do nothing about it made it worse, as did the certainty she'd say she'd been forced into it because his team were harassing her client. He had eyes on Retallick because it was his job to protect the public.

He took his job seriously, although not as seriously as he took the obligation to protect his child. Eden's madcap family could take what risk they liked with their own safety, but they weren't going to take risks with Flora. She was precious, and however much Thea objected, he had custody. He didn't care if he had to employ a nanny to pick her up from school and look after her when he was working, she would not be going to her grandparents or to Eden's place for as long as that man was free. It wouldn't be easy. Flora would want to know why all contact had been curtailed with her closest family, and he could hardly tell her it was because they had a psychotic serial killer living in the garden. He couldn't stop her seeing Thea, but he could make sure she saw her on his terms, at his place and when he was around. She could take it or leave it. Beggars couldn't be choosers. The rap on his office door made him jump. It was Denise.

'We've had a lead on the clothes. A charity shop in town has a bag full of clothes they found on the doorstep that look like they might be the ones Graham White was wearing. They saw the appeal for information on the local news.'

Luke could barely hide his excitement as he grabbed his coat from the back of the chair. 'Come on.' They were in the car before he asked where they were heading.

'Age Concern. One of the volunteers opened the bag this morning. Apparently, people drop them off all the time.'

'Any idea who dropped this one off?'

'No, it was left outside the door overnight.'

'CCTV?'

'Nothing at that end of town.'

'Tell me it hasn't been touched?' Luke was already worrying about cross-contamination.

'Do you want the good news or the bad?'

'The bad, always the bad first.'

'It's been handled, but the good news is they always wear gloves to unload the bags. According to the woman I spoke to, they've had a few nasty shocks in the past. Apparently, not everyone donates clean clothes.'

Luke grimaced at the thought.

'This could be it, Denise, the break we've been waiting for. This could be the thing that gets Retallick banged up for good.'

***

The woman had the clothes waiting on the table in the back room of the shop when they arrived. She looked pleased with herself.

'I said it, as soon as I pulled out the sports jacket that looks like the one they're talking about on the telly. Didn't I say that, Jeanie?'

'You did, that's what she said.'

'And when I saw the symbol on the tie, you know, the bowling club, I was certain.'

'She was certain,' chipped in the sidekick.

Luke was sure he heard a snigger escape from Denise.

'I left the rest in the bag, and I called you straight away. Do you think they're the ones you're after?' she said, her eyes alight with excitement.

'We won't know until we've tested them, but I'm hopeful,'

said Luke, holding up the sports jacket before carefully slipping it into a clear plastic evidence bag.

'There's a hat in the right pocket, and I assume you're taking the whole bag… to be examined, I mean?' said the woman.

'Yes,' said Luke.

'You'll be putting something in the tin then?'

'I'm sorry?' said Luke bemused.

'We can't let any items off the premises without a contribution. We haven't had the chance to price the clothes like we do normally, but I tell you straight, that jacket's as good as new.'

'Wool too, not polyester,' said her friend.

Luke reached into his back pocket and pulled a twenty-pound note from his wallet.

The woman's eyes stayed fixed on the brown leather.

He pulled out another note. 'Is that enough?' he asked.

'That'll be fine.'

He caught Denise's eye before she turned away, a grin plastered across her face as the woman slipped the folded notes into the donation tin on top of the counter. Thanking the volunteers again, they headed back to the car. Luke turned to Denise.

'We need to get Graham White's daughter in to identify the clothes before we send them off to forensics. They look right, but we haven't got money to burn on wild goose chases. She'll know for certain what's his.'

'It's odd, don't you think?' said Denise, lifting the boot to deposit the evidence bag.

'What's odd?'

'That the perpetrator didn't burn the clothes. He must have known there was a chance someone would bring them in once we released the info to the media. It's almost as if he's taunting us.'

'You mean he's smart enough not to have left DNA, and he wants to see us get egg on our faces?'

'There's that, I suppose, but I was thinking more that it's as if he's scattering breadcrumbs for us to follow. It's as if he wants us to catch him.'

Luke said nothing. He was thinking of Kit Retallick making himself cosy at Eden's parents' house. Of Thea revelling in getting one over on him, and wiping the smile off their faces as he placed the handcuffs on Retallick's wrists. The man had better enjoy his rural idyll while he could because soon he'd be back where he should be, and they could all heave a sigh of relief.

***

White's daughter stared at the clothing laid out on the table. Every now and again, she patted her eyes with a tissue. She had down tools and come as soon as they'd called her.

'Yes,' she whispered, 'they're Dad's. That's his jacket and his bowling tie,' she said, her voice choked. 'I recognise it all except the hat,' she said, pointing to the khaki green beanie sitting above a pair of brown loafers.

'Are you sure?' said Luke. 'It was found in the pocket of the jacket.'

'Dad would never wear something like that, not even in cold weather. He never wore hats. He was proud he still had a full head of hair. He was fastidious about it.'

Luke shot Denise a knowing glance.

'Thank you so much, you've been really helpful. I know it couldn't have been an easy thing to do.'

'You're going to catch whoever did this, aren't you?'

'We'll do our best, and finding the clothes is a big step in the right direction.'

'You'll let me know if you get someone before you release the news to the press. I'll need to prepare my children. They've taken the loss of their grandfather badly.'

'Of course we will,' reassured Denise.

'And when will the body be released so we can bury Dad? Relatives keep calling, and I don't know what to say. It's all so awful,' she sobbed.

'The coroner's office will call you shortly,' reassured Luke.

The woman's husband was waiting outside, and Denise marshalled her out to join him. When she returned, Luke was looking at the label inside the beanie.

'Superdry. Not likely to be a brand chosen by a bloke in his late sixties. I think she's right. This could belong to our killer.'

'Or someone could have stuffed it into the bag while it was sat outside the charity shop?' said Denise.

'Oh, come on, show a bit of faith. Retallick's slipped up. Get this lot off to forensics ASAP. Tell them to look for a DNA match with Retallick and to pay particular attention to the hat.'

'Okay, boss,' said Denise.

Luke didn't like the *boss,* not from her, or the fact she didn't look convinced.

TWENTY-NINE

Ross arrived back in St. Ives, a man on a mission. He needed to approach this challenge with the mindset of a time and motion expert if he was going to juggle a full-on investigation with his shifts at the pub. Karenza always said women were better at multitasking, and she was right. He knew once he read Eden's files, the case would be all he thought of. He'd smile his way through the customers' small talk and make sure there wasn't too much head on their pints, but he knew from experience where his own head would be. No more lying awake wondering if they should take on more staff for the Christmas rush or whether the takings could run to a new glass washer. True, he'd be batting for the opposite team, looking for clues to innocence rather than guilt, but the obsession would be the same: the suspect and the crime.

A wave of excitement coursed through him for the first time since he'd resigned. He felt wired and ready to go, like a car recharged after grinding to an undignified yet inevitable halt. He had known he'd have to leave the force after what he'd done. It hadn't mattered to the powers that be he'd delivered the goods. Pretending to be on leave and heading off to Portugal to hunt down a murder suspect was bound to do more than raise eyebrows, not to mention the fact he'd almost single-handedly scuppered a combined task force operation in the process. Well, you couldn't write it, could you?

He had jumped before he was pushed. Luke Parish had been sympathetic, and he had nothing against him. He'd always been a good governor and a friend of sorts, although they never socialised out of work hours. Nevertheless, it would be satisfying to show him what he was missing. He had to admit the case had only become interesting to him when he knew Luke had Retallick in his sights for the murder of the two men. Before that, it had been a cold case investigation without any real incentive other than the money, of course, which would definitely come in handy. The man was already out of prison, and these things were generally nit-picking academic exercises best suited to lawyers like Eden rather than policemen. A double murder, though, was different. It was very much up his alley.

He wouldn't tell Karenza about the link between Retallick and the two men if she asked what he was working on. He'd stick to the cold case. She'd only worry he was stepping over the mark with his amateur sleuthing.

She was in the bar clearing up after the lunchtime session when he arrived.

'So, how did it go with Eden?' she asked, deftly manoeuvring two empty glasses with one hand while wiping down the table with the other.

'Good… it was good.'

'So, you've got your first case then?'

'Yeah, I suppose so. I'm just looking through the paperwork at the moment.'

'I see.'

What her *I see* meant wasn't clear. Her attention was fixed on the tabletop as she spoke. Much as he loved his wife, she had the power to make him nervous, like a playground friend who invites you over and then gives you a Chinese burn.

When she finally looked up, he was relieved her blue eyes twinkled with optimism rather than scepticism and he relaxed.

'Go on then, I can see you're itching to make a start on that file under your arm.'

'You sure you don't need me down here?'

Karenza cast her eye around the empty bar. 'I think I'll

manage,' she said. 'Help yourself to something from the fridge before you go. There's not much at home. I don't suppose you've had lunch.'

'I had a bacon sandwich in the court canteen.'

'I hope you kept the receipt to add to your expenses,' Karenza smiled. 'Isn't that what you PIs do?'

'I'm not sure what they do. I keep thinking of Poirot or Magnum.'

'Well think again because moustaches and Hawaiian shirts have never floated my boat. Although when I think of it, those tight shorts he used to wear...'

'Who, Poirot?' Ross laughed, grabbing Karenza around the waist and pulling her to him, 'tight shorts, eh... I'll have to see what I can do.'

Karenza flicked him across the buttocks with her cloth as he released her to lean across and grab a beer from behind the bar. Kissing her on the way out, he headed for the cottage next door. He'd have the place to himself for a couple of hours until Livvy got home from college. Feet up on the sofa, he began reading Eden's file.

***

Ross rang Eden that evening to confirm he'd decided to take the case. She hadn't seemed at all surprised. He told her he would start the next day, searching out anyone who knew the family well enough to know who might have a grievance against them sufficient to kill them.

He told her he'd decided to begin with Laura Tremlett, the only person still alive who had given evidence for the defence at Retallick's trial. As it happened, she'd been surprisingly easy to find. One call to the newsagents in Morvah had led to the present owners providing him with the name of the residential home in Mounts Bay where she now lived. He'd rung ahead and been told by an officious-sounding woman not to come until the residents had finished their breakfast at ten thirty. He'd also been advised as he was not a visitor on their list, it would be up to Mrs Tremlett whether or not she agreed to see him.

THIRTY

It was the first clear morning they'd had for a week, and as he rounded the corner into Penzance, his heart was warmed by the watery sunlight licking the bay. There was no surf to speak of, but you couldn't have everything. Perhaps it was just as well. He had no time for distractions today.

Mounts Bay Care Home was on the main road. It had once no doubt been a grand private house with an equally grand entrance and grounds. Sold off in lots long ago to developers, it now sat amid a hotchpotch of bungalows and holiday flats, the only land around it being the ugly tarmacked car park to the front.

He sat in the car waiting for the clock to tick past ten, thinking about who he would have interviewed as SIO had the boy not been so obviously in the frame.

Firstly, there was Shona, the barmaid having an affair with Ray.

The relationship had been long-term. Kit had said as much in his interview with Eden. Ray had dated her before he'd met Kit's mother. She was married. That's a lot of baggage to put up with unless he had feelings for the woman.

Then there was her husband. According to Kit, everyone in the village knew about the relationship. It couldn't have been easy for him, knowing people were laughing behind his back. The jealous husband number one in the true crime suspect manual. Why had no one interviewed him?

And what about Kit's mother? There was nothing to say she didn't start the fire. Plenty of people got caught in the crossfire of their own violent crimes. She'd been told that night Ray was dipping his wick somewhere else. She'd been angry and had threatened him. She was meant to be working the nightshift at the care home but left before her shift was over. Why? Did she want to have it out with Ray? Maybe she was suspicious Shona might be in the house with him. When the cat's away and all that. What had made her down tools and leave that night?

The same could be asked about Kit's sister, Tamar, a pretty name after the river separating Cornwall from Devon or England if you think like a true Cornishman. He slipped the photograph of Tamar Retallick from his file. Pretty name for a pretty girl. Slender, with elfin features, big brown eyes and long dark hair almost reaching her waist, she was a teenage boy's dream or nightmare, depending on whether or not his tender heart remained intact. Had she had a row with a boyfriend that night? Had some horny dirtbag full of hormones decided to teach her a lesson? The girl had been off to university that autumn. He thought of Livvy, about to embark on the same journey. He hoped she'd come back and work in the county once her studies were over, but it was unlikely. Good jobs were few and far between, mostly zero-hours contracts and seasonal work. Unlike his son Piran, who had settled down with a local girl and was earning his living fishing with his grandfather, Livvy would probably have to raise her family outside the county. Ross couldn't bring himself to think about it.

He looked down at the photo of the girl. Where had she been going to stay that evening? Why had she changed her mind, and why hadn't the police taken a statement from her friends?

He hoped Laura Tremlett might be able to give some answers, although he had no idea whether she'd be up to it. For all he knew, she might have dementia or some other mind-affecting affliction and not be able to tell him anything. He wasn't sure what he was going to do if she couldn't help him.

At twenty past, he headed up the granite steps to the front

porch and pressed the buzzer.

'Hello, it's DI…' He stopped himself just in time. 'Ross Trenear, I called earlier about a visit with Laura Tremlett.'

No one answered, but Ross heard the click of the front door unlocking and entered.

A buxom woman in her late thirties wearing a pink uniform met him in the foyer.

'Laura's heading back to her room. She should be ready for you in five minutes. Can you sign the visitors' book and jot down your car reg so we know you're not some emmet taking the piss.'

The smile on the woman's face belied the aggressive tone. He wouldn't like to be the sorry-assed tourist who took her on.

Ross picked up the pen attached with string to the visitor's book and signed in.

'Make sure you use the sanitiser too. COVID's never over as far as we're concerned.'

'No, I suppose we can't be complacent,' Ross agreed, giving his hands a squirt.

The woman looked vaguely familiar, but then again, it had to be expected when you ran a busy pub. Karenza was great at remembering the customers' faces, even those of the visitors who only darkened their door once a year. She remembered where they were from and how many kids they had. She always said he was never interested because they hadn't committed a crime.

'You don't recognise me, do you?' said the woman.

Ross wondered if he'd ever arrested her… no, if he had, he would have remembered, once again proving Karenza right.

'I can't quite place the face.'

'Debbie Carveth, Morris now. We were at school together. I was in the year below you. Mr Peters's class. I had mousy hair and sang in the school choir.'

Ross didn't have a clue.

'Ah, yes, Debbie. How are you? Are you still singing?'

'You needn't lie. There's no reason why you should remember me. I was shy back then. I remember you, though. All us girls fancied you. You've kept yourself fit,' she said, poking at his abs.

Well, she's certainly tackled her shyness, thought Ross, his face reddening.

'Thanks.'

'I was there when Matron took your call earlier. I'm just about to go off duty, but I had a chat with Laura in the breakfast room to make sure you wouldn't have a wasted journey. I told her you were a policeman, and it was just a routine call.'

'I'm not actually a p…'

She talked over him.

'I told her I was at school with you and you were lovely.'

'Thanks,' repeated Ross, wishing the floor would swallow him up.

'Anyways, it didn't matter in the end because when I told her your name, she said she knew your mother. She went to school with her. Imagine… what a coincidence, me going to school with you and her going to school with your mum.'

'Yeah, freaky,' said Ross, wondering how to politely escape.

Debbie looked down at her watch. 'I must go. I've got to get the shopping in before I go home for a kip. I'm back on again tonight. Laura's in room seventeen, down the corridor and turn left. Her name and photo are on the door.'

As she headed out the door, she paused to kiss him on the cheek. 'I've been wanting to do that for years,' she whispered, 'wait till I tell the girls I've kissed Ross Trenear, they'll never believe it.'

Ross couldn't get away fast enough.

The voice answering his knock was thin and tinny. Ross

paused, worried how frail this woman was and whether it was appropriate to rake up old memories she might think best forgotten.

Laura Tremlett was sitting in the bay window in a yellow armchair so plump she looked as if she was being devoured by it. She had a spectacular view right across the bay to St. Michael's Mount, which Ross guessed wasn't being paid for by the council. No doubt her life savings were slipping away with the tide.

She looked up as he entered, rheumy blue eyes creasing at the corners as she smiled her welcome. 'Come in and have a seat by me.'

He joined her, reaching out his hand to introduce himself.

'No need for formality. Now, can I call one of the girls to get you some tea… or coffee if you prefer? They have the real stuff here, you know, not instant.'

'Thanks, but no, I'm fine,' said Ross.

The old lady looked as neat as a pin, her silvery hair cut into a stylish bob. He'd worked out she must be in her eighties. Although her twisted fingers and swollen knuckles were testament to arthritis, her eyes still had a twinkle of youthful mischief.

'That mouthy Debbie said you're a policeman like your father was.'

'I *was* a policeman, but not anymore. I'm a private investigator.'

The words sounded odd in his mouth like he had somebody else's teeth in.

The woman looked at him quizzically.

'I don't blame you. Being a policeman these days must be a thankless task. You lot can't seem to do right by anyone. The public complain about you not catching criminals then moan about how you do it when you do. I'd like to see how they'd cope if you all down tools and let them get on with it. They'd soon realise what it's like to deal with some of the scum you've got to handle with kid gloves. Not like when your dad was on the beat. He was a lovely man, your dad. He didn't take any prisoners, mind,' she laughed at the pun. 'I mean, he was old school, but he knew everyone and everyone knew him. He could put you in your place with one of his looks. You know the look I mean.'

'I do,' said Ross, knowing exactly the look she meant.

'How's your mum? Jenna and I were in primary school together. We ended up at different secondary schools, but we always kept in touch.'

'Good,' said Ross, 'still living on her own in the bungalow in St. Ives. I live in the town with my wife and kids, so I keep an eye on her.'

'You see, that's the difference… family. Me and my Denzel couldn't have kids. If we had, I probably wouldn't be in this bloody place. You resist as long as you can, but then you have a fall like I did, only a small one mind, in the garden, and it saps your confidence, and you start to worry. So, I bit the bullet and I booked myself in here. It's not bad as far as these places go, but it's not like your own home. Jenna's lucky to have you,' Laura said wistfully, reaching across to touch Ross's hand.

No matter how nice the home might be, he could never envisage his mother living in a place like this.

'Don't ever get old. People only see what's missing,' Laura said, twisting a thin gold wedding band hung on a chain around her neck. 'They don't see what's still there if they only took the trouble to look,' she sighed.

Ross felt a lump in his throat.

Laura moved her hand away, leaning back into the cushions of the enormous chair.

'Listen to me harping on. Debbie didn't say what you were investigating. Whatever it is, I'm not sure I can be of much help stuck in here. I've got the view, but I can't see much of the street. Or is it about Matron and the gardener? Has her husband finally cottoned on? Like we need a gardener here,' she scoffed.

Ross smiled, 'No, nothing like that, it's about a cold case I'm investigating. Do you remember the name Kit Retallick?'

The woman's smile slipped as her attention was drawn out of the window towards the bay.

'Oh, I'll never forget that name or that poor girl.'

'You mean Tamar?'

'Yes, Tamar.' There was a tremble in the woman's voice not there before and she suddenly looked frail.

'That stepfather was a brute. Their mother, Lilah Polglaze, was a lovely woman, hardworking and friendly but timid, you know the way some are when they've got a bully for a husband? She was always apologising for herself like he was a real prize, whereas everyone knew he was a drunk and a philanderer.'

Ross seized his chance. 'I understand he was having an affair at the time of the fire?'

'Shona Bryant, the barmaid at the pub. She was no better than she ought to have been either. Her husband at home in a wheelchair and her off gallivanting doing god knows what. I felt sorry for him. Best thing that ever happened to him, her leaving. He met a woman, a widow. They still live in the village.'

Ross's heart sank. There was no way anyone in a wheelchair could have covered the terrain leading to the farmhouse, especially at night. He could cross Shona's husband off his list of alternative suspects.

'Do you know where Shona is now?'

'Don't know and don't suppose anyone cares. I never understood why the landlord employed her, given her reputation. Well, it gives the wrong impression, doesn't it, having someone like her behind the bar?'

Ross thought this was a tad judgemental. Surely, having an

affair these days didn't brand you a scarlet woman. If it did, there would be plenty wearing red.

'You mean because of her adultery?'

'There's that, I suppose, but I meant the other stuff, taking money for sex. She was little more than a common prostitute.'

'Do you think Ray might have been paying her?'

'No, not Ray. He was more likely to take a cut of her earnings.'

Ross made a note.

'What about Tamar and Kit? What were they like? I know you gave evidence for the defence at the trial.'

'That backfired, didn't it? Everything I said in support of the boy was twisted to make him appear more disturbed than he was.'

'You don't think Kit did it?'

'Didn't then and don't now. He didn't have that kind of malice in him. He was a strange boy, a bit of a loner, but gentle like his mum, not vindictive. His sister was a darling. I can tell you if I had been lucky to have a daughter, I would have chosen one like her. I still miss her, you know.'

'She got on well with her brother?'

'Oh my, yes. She adored him. It was Kit this and Kit that. She hated the idea of leaving him behind when she went to university.'

'You know she wasn't meant to be there that evening. She was supposed to be staying with friends.'

'So I heard. Fate can be cruel. She often stayed with friends at weekends when her mother worked nights. She even stayed with me above the shop a couple of times. She told me she didn't like being in the house alone with Ray.'

Ross didn't know how to put this delicately.

'Do you think he was abusing her?'

The woman looked at him sternly. 'No, not that. He had

Shona for that, and she was enough for any man, I can tell you. I think Tamar was afraid of her temper. Whenever there was no one to stop her, she'd get in a row with Ray, and he'd take it out on her mother or the boy. Tamar wasn't like Lilah. She was feisty. Not afraid to speak her mind.'

'Did she ever talk to you about boyfriends?'

'Why do you ask?'

'Nothing specific. She was a pretty girl, and Kit seemed to think she might have been seeing someone. Someone she said could protect them.'

'The police asked me the same thing back then, and I said no, but afterwards, I wondered if I'd got that wrong. She'd started dressing for work. Before, it had been jeans and a hoodie. Then suddenly, it was a nice top or a smart dress. I half expected some boy to turn up in the shop, but he never did, leastwise no one she would look at twice. It was odd really because she never talked about boys, but I got the feeling there was something going on.'

Ross scribbled down a note. He noticed Laura was shuffling in her seat, and he wondered if he should ask if she needed some help to get out of the chair.

'Look, I mustn't keep you any longer. You've been a great help. One last thing. What did you think about the detective who headed up the investigation?'

'Detective Inspector Noble. It might have been his name, but it wasn't his nature, that's for sure. I didn't like him one bit. The way he twisted everything I said. I don't think he bothered to look anywhere else other than the boy. All he was interested in was getting his conviction and his face in the papers. I tried at the time to tell him about Shona and her relationship with Ray, and he wasn't interested.'

Ross thanked her again, promising he would bring his mum down to visit sometime. He meant it. He liked this woman. A visit would be good for both of them.

As he headed for the door, Laura called after him.

'He's out, isn't he?'

Ross hesitated, wondering if she was worried about the prospect of Kit Retallick being on the loose.

'Yes, yes, he is.'

'Not before time. You give him my best if you see him, and make sure you put things right for that young man. If there was ever a miscarriage of justice, this was it, and someone deserves to pay.'

THIRTY-ONE

'A weasel. Untrustworthy.'

'Are you saying he was bent?'

'Your father had his suspicions, although he couldn't prove it. Noble was too clever for that, but your father didn't like working with him, that's for certain. He had to watch his back when he was around. He was careful to note everything down because Noble had a happy knack of changing his story. He didn't trust him not to drop him in the shit.'

Ross's mother never swore, and he laughed. He'd called in on the way home to see how she was and to ask about DI Noble on the off chance she might remember the man. She spotted the schoolboy smirk as she looked up from her ironing.

'I'm not kidding. Dad got on with everyone, even the lowlifes he put away. They all knew when your dad was the arresting officer, they'd get a fair crack. He'd worked hard to get the community's trust. They came to him with information, knowing he'd be discreet. Brett Noble was a different animal altogether. Oh, he was charming alright, a real lounge lizard type, and handsome too, and he knew it. He made my flesh crawl. I wouldn't trust that man as far as I could throw him. Your dad was relieved when he moved up country.'

'When?'

'Oh, I don't know, just before Dad retired. He was pleased he wouldn't be taking over from him. He would not have been happy handing his legacy over to that man. It was a shock to his superior's mind. They'd reckoned on him stepping up and had to recruit elsewhere.'

'Did Dad know why he chose to leave just when his career

seemed to be on the rise?'

'No, it was as much a shock to him as everyone else. He speculated of course. Noble hadn't made many mates down here. He wasn't married, so he had no ties to speak of. Not everyone takes to living here. People see it in the summer when it's bustling, but you and I know out of season it's another story. He was ambitious. Perhaps he could see there were better opportunities back where he'd come from. He asked for a transfer, so he obviously had a plan.'

'And Dad didn't hear of him after?'

'Well if he did, he never said anything to me.'

Ross decided to introduce the subject of the fire.

'I met an old friend of yours today.'

'Who?'

'Laura Tremlett, she said to remember her to you.'

'Laura, where on earth did you see her? I heard she sold the newsagents and moved into a care home in Marazion.'

'That's right, I went there to interview her.'

'About what?'

'Ah, just some case I'm looking at.'

'Looking at for who?'

'For Eden, it's an old case.'

He wasn't sure how well his mum would take to the idea of him working for a defence lawyer. She knew Eden. She was a close family friend, but nonetheless, they were a family of coppers. His grandad and his dad. She hadn't been thrilled when he left the force.

'So, is this the start of this PI business Karenza's told me about?'

'I suppose so,' he said, feeling like he was the one about to be interrogated.

'Hmm,' she said, lifting another tea towel from the laundry basket.

'It's a case you might remember. It happened in Morvah years ago. A fire… the family died. The son was convicted of manslaughter?'

'Christopher Retallick.'

'You remember it then?'

'Hard to forget something like that. Is that why you were asking about Noble?'

'Was Dad involved in the investigation?'

'No, more's the pity. Brett Noble was the SIO. It was just after Dad had his operation for a slipped disc. He was off for four months. Worst four months of my life. He was a terrible patient. He wasn't used to doing nothing. It drove him mad.'

'Dad wasn't involved at all?'

'No.'

Ross couldn't deny he was relieved. If something went wrong with this, or worse still, he dug up evidence suggesting the investigation had been compromised, his father's involvement could have complicated matters. It didn't mean his dad hadn't had an opinion on it. It would have been the biggest case his colleagues had on their books. He would have been itching to look at the evidence.

'Do you remember if Dad had any thoughts on the case at the time?'

'He did. He called in, asking if he could help from his bed. You know, look at the statements and the forensics when they came in, but Noble was having none of it. He was quite short with Dad. Told him they had it all tied up and that he should concentrate on getting himself better and leave this to a younger man. He inferred your father was past it. You can imagine how that went down.'

'Not well.'

'No.'

'What was it Dad didn't like about the case?'

'The speed at which they laid the blame on the boy. He thought it was too tidy. The investigation was all done and dusted in a month. Of course, he didn't like Noble, and it didn't sit well with him that he solved the case so quickly. I remember we had a row when I suggested he might be prejudiced.'

'Do you think that's what it was, sour grapes?'

'Back then, maybe, but then when I read about the trial and how awful that stepfather was and the evidence of the boy's gran, how much he loved his sister and his mum, I wasn't so sure. Your dad always said plenty of people had it in for Ray Polglaze but that no one ever considered it could have been one of them. That boy was an easy target, and Noble was lazy enough to make the evidence fit if it suited him.'

Ross had enough to be going on with, but it might be useful to arrange a catch-up between his mum and Laura Tremlett. Now he'd stirred the pot, who knew what might bubble to the surface?

***

Ross rang Eden that evening with an update.

'The old lady hasn't changed her opinion. She still thinks the boy was innocent.'

'Did she have anything new to say?'

'Not new exactly, but she confirmed a lot of what Retallick told you about Ray Polglaze being involved with Shona Bryant. I was hoping her husband might be in the frame, but the bloke is in a wheelchair… he was at the time too. There's no way he could have done it. Him and Shona split up afterwards. Mrs Tremlett hasn't a clue where Shona is now. I'm hoping the ex will be able to help me out there. Shona's certainly someone we need to talk to, along with Brett Noble, of course. I'll fill you in when we meet. I was wondering whether you'd like to come along tomorrow to interview Bryant. He still lives in the same house and was in the phone book so I took a chance and gave him a call. He's happy to talk, but you never know if that will last. I thought it best to strike while the iron's hot.'

Eden was pleased she'd got Ross on board. He had that pushiness that came with years of being a policeman knocking on doors. She would have pussyfooted around Bryant, not wanting to offend.

'I can't. I've got too much on, but if you need anything from me, give me a call. What time are you meeting him?'

'I'm dropping my mum off to see Laura Tremlett at eleven. They're old friends, as it happens. I'm off to meet him straight after.'

'Let me know how you get on.'

'Will do.'

THIRTY-TWO

Kit sat on the steps of the caravan with the doors open. They'd been shut when he first arrived, but it felt claustrophobic. Eden hadn't said it was a gypsy caravan he'd be staying in. Like his nan's cottage, the interior had been designed to appeal to holidaymakers, although compared to this, the cottage seemed bland. He imagined this would be described in the brochure as quirky or eclectic with its yellow walls and cerise and gold paisley curtains. There was a raised bed at one end above which the barrelled ceiling was painted to imitate a starry sky.

He had to admire the use of space. Beneath the bed was a neat row of painted drawers, and along another wall, scaled to fit perfectly, a run of cobalt blue units housing a sink and microwave. Built-in seating, piled high with flamboyantly patterned cushions, added to the laidback bohemian feel. As the last of the day's sunlight bounced off the mirror-framed bedstead, the place lit up like a box of jewels.

Eden had told him her parents had been inspired by a trip to India as she'd walked him to a separate wooden building containing something called a composting toilet. She'd explained it didn't use running water but worked perfectly well with the use of sawdust and hay, producing clean, non-smelly human manure for the garden.

Kit said nothing. He had, in his time, shared a toilet with another prisoner in a three-by-three metre cell. The smell back then had been the least of his worries. There was a small potbellied stove at one end of the caravan. Eden had pulled a coffee pot from one of the cupboards. It was the metal Italian kind with a hexagonal lid he'd seen in films. She'd brought the ground coffee with her, and he was glad she showed him how to fill it because he'd never have fathomed it out himself.

He looked across the open fields towards the house. Someone had done a good job with the smallholding. He could see the ground had been tilled, ready for next spring's vegetable crops. Ray had told him how the frost helped break up the soil into a fine crumb. He'd said it was best to let nature do its work before layering it with manure as a mulch to keep the weeds down and build in warmth to give the seeds a good start. He didn't know whether it was true or not, but Ray's crops always seemed to do well enough. He noticed at the end of the field was a patch of orchard. The trees were bare this time of year, but he imagined in spring, they'd be frothy with blossom.

The coffee was coming to a boil, and he got up to lift the pot from the stove. Unhooking one of the brightly painted tin mugs from above the kitchen cabinets, he poured the dark, steaming brew and headed back to the steps.

The last of the day was dipping behind the trees. It would be a cold night, and when he'd finished his coffee, he'd go and collect kindling to keep the fire going. He'd be cosy under the goose feather duvet. He might even leave the door open. He'd kept the door locked in the village. He hadn't felt safe enough to do anything else, but here he'd be fine. He hadn't been sleeping well. The last good night's sleep he'd enjoyed had been at the pub, where he'd drifted off easily amidst the noise of people moving about. The cottage had been too quiet, and he'd been unable to settle. He had forgotten what it was like to be alone in a space.

After he skirted the boundaries of the field for twigs to stock the fire, he lay on the bed and stared up at the starry-painted sky. He wondered what the police would do when they realised he'd left the village. He couldn't understand why they were watching him. He'd come back to prove his innocence. He wasn't going anywhere now someone was finally taking him seriously. There was no denying his connection with Vincent and White, and he had to admit if he were a policeman, he'd be suspicious too, but he hadn't had anything to do with their deaths. Thank god Eden believed him. If she hadn't, he'd be going mad right now.

She'd told him on the way here she'd employed a private investigator, an ex-detective who had already begun interviewing people. She hadn't said who. He would have been worried about the expense had he not decided to sell his nan's cottage. He realised now he'd been naive, thinking he could live in the village. He'd felt more trapped there than he had in prison. He'd put it on the market straight away in the hope it would sell quickly. With the money, he'd buy something more modest, perhaps something a bit like this, but with a smaller house and more land, and an outbuilding he could convert into a workshop.

He couldn't bear the thought of getting a job. He'd have to explain why, at his age, he'd never been employed. If he was honest and said it was because he'd been in prison, people were bound to be nosey and ask what he'd done, and he couldn't face that. No, he'd set up his own business, making garden furniture or even fitting out places like this. Whoever had done the carpentry in the caravan had done a good job, but he could do it just as well, and there must be work around if you had skills.

He'd made furniture in prison. Benches and picnic tables for public parks. He'd been good at it, and unlike most, he'd taken pride in his work. The bloke who taught them said he had a feel for the wood and had shown him how to use the router to create decorative work on the back of the seats.

He'd need to learn to drive, of course. That would be the first thing on his list, and once he'd passed his test, he'd buy a van or a pick-up to carry the furniture. He could make it work if he put his mind to it, and when things were slack, he could subsidise his income with a bit of agricultural labouring. He'd heard on the local news that since Brexit, farmers in Cornwall were having a hard job getting people to pick the cabbages and daffodils in spring. He could do that if push came to shove.

He found comfort in his imaginings, the idea he could build himself a future. He had his nan to thank for it. She'd stuck with him and had left him everything she had. Nan had always been someone to rely on. If she had only been there when he was arrested things might have been so different. His mind involuntarily drifted back to White.

His nan had never liked the headmaster. She complained to Mr Bassett how he'd ingratiated himself with the police and how he should have called her to sit with him in the hospital instead of White taking it upon himself to act in *loco parentis*. She wouldn't have let the police interview him when he was still so poorly. She said that's what did it for him and perhaps with hindsight, she'd been right. Although he hadn't seen it that way at the time. He'd been glad to have the teacher there. He'd been scared, and to have him beside his bed made him feel safe.

White had been kind to him, well, kinder than he'd ever been at school. There, he'd seemed embarrassed by him. He was always pulling up the other boys for having the wrong shoes or not tying their ties properly, but he never commented about his unwashed uniform or his lack of PE kit. He'd pass him in the corridors as if he were invisible. He'd only acknowledged his existence after the fire at school. He recalled how surprised he'd looked when Tamar turned up. As if it had clicked for the first time, he was the younger brother of the model pupil he'd sent off the year before to sixth form college. White talked about Tamar in the hospital, about what a waste it was she'd died. He'd gone on about how he'd expected great things of her and would still like to know her A-level results when they came through. As if they mattered.

As for Vincent, he'd only met the man twice. That first time at school, after he was called in by child services to assess him for ADHD. Kit remembered the man's long hair below his collar, unlike his own, which Ray had shorn off with an electric razor when they'd had a letter sent home from school about nits. He remembered Vincent had tears in his eyes when he saw the bruises on his arms and legs and asked him how he got them. The second time, he'd come to the farm. Ray had set Jasper on him and said he was nothing but a streak of piss, and he'd better not show his face around there again or he'd shoot him. He never saw him again, but Vincent seemed to know an awful lot about him, nevertheless. He'd spent half a day in the witness box talking about him, reading from the reports he'd made, detailing the visits to the farm and the meetings he'd had with Ray and his mum. He guessed Ray must have had a change of heart and decided to talk to the bloke. Perhaps he'd sniffed money in the offing, extra benefits or freebies if they co-operated. It was strange his mum never mentioned it, though and how the man hadn't talked to him.

In the distance, he could hear the jackdaws coming home to roost in the rookery beyond the farmhouse. He felt comfort in their chattering and slept soundly until woken by a hairy bear of a dog licking his face the following morning.

THIRTY-THREE

Ross took the coast road, shadowing the old tinner's trail. This was not the Roseland with its manicured palms or St. Ives with its artistic bent and relentless bustle. You could smell the deprivation in the ozone. Here, it was not hard to believe Cornwall was one of the poorest counties in the country.

The far west of the peninsula bore the brunt of the Atlantic breakers and the scars of an industrial past. The place screamed of toil and hardship. It had once been one of the most industrialised places on earth. Imagine what that meant when it had been taken away, when the mine engines ground to a halt, and the last shift whistle blew. The glorious landscape was salve to the wound, but the pain of the past was not forgotten.

Bryant lived in a nineteen seventies bungalow on the road between Morvah and Pendeen. It was tidy, with a wide gateway and concrete path, which Ross guessed gave him easy access for his wheelchair. A dark-haired woman with a broad, welcoming smile let him in.

'Steve's in the front room, go through,' she said.

The man sat in his wheelchair in the dated conservatory. The view across open fields towards the sea was unexpected. If this was somewhere more accessible, Ross imagined a second homeowner would have knocked down this modest property to build a glass monolith in its place. It would have sat incongruously in the shadow of the derelict mine amid the workingmen's club and the fishermen's mission.

'I'll fetch you some tea,' said the woman, beckoning Ross to take the wicker seat in the window next to Bryant.

'Rain expected later.'

'So I hear,' said Ross, who would like a pound for every conversation that started with a weather reference. It was a British trait that came naturally to an island nation and, to the storm-watching Cornish, an obligatory prelude.

After the tea and niceties were over, Bryant began in earnest.

'It was like any other night. Shona left for her shift at six. I didn't think anything of it when she didn't come home straight after. She often stayed for a lock-in or went on somewhere… to Newquay or Penzance to meet up with friends. She sometimes stayed over, but she usually called if she was going to do that. I thought maybe her phone had run out of battery or she'd had a few too many. It was only when she didn't come back the next morning I started to worry and began calling her friends, but none of them had seen her. I called the pub. They said she left straight after her shift, well, a little earlier actually after getting a phone call. They didn't say who from, only that it was a man. They knew that much because someone else got to the phone first and passed it on to Shona. They didn't say much else; they were too eager to tell me about the fire up at the farm and that Ray Polglaze was dead.'

Ross longed to ask what the man's reaction had been to the news but sensed he had more to say.

'I rang the police and told them Shona was missing. The fella in charge of the inquiry into the fire came around.'

'DI Noble?' said Ross, wondering why Noble had come around in the middle of a murder enquiry unless he had suspicions. The usual procedure would have been to refer it to the missing persons team.

'Yeah, that's him.'

'And?'

'He said Shona couldn't be registered as a missing person for at least twenty-four hours. To be honest, he treated me as if I was wasting his time. Don't get me wrong, I understood he had a lot on his plate, and to be honest, I expected someone junior in uniform to come around.'

So would I, thought Ross.

'His attitude when he got here stank. It got personal very quickly, and he was vicious about Shona. He said it was common knowledge she had affairs and was promiscuous. He could see I was worried sick, but all he was interested in doing was bad-mouthing her. It was like he wanted to shock me into thinking I was well rid. Only it didn't work. The thing was, I knew all about the other men. It was part of the deal.'

'The deal?'

The man sighed. 'When I met Shona, I was a fit young buck working on building sites. She was always wild… you know, exciting. I like to think I was the same. We were a good match. We'd been going out for a couple of years, saving up to travel and get engaged somewhere exotic, Thailand or Bali. The plan was to work our way around the globe before we settled down. Then this happened.'

He looked down at his legs.

'Do you mind me asking how?'

'An accident on the site. I fell from the scaffolding. My own fault. I was being reckless, cutting corners to get the job done quickly. I got an insurance payout, but because of my contributory negligence, it wasn't as much as it should have been. I knew early on I'd be paralysed for the rest of my life, and trust me, no amount of money can compensate you for that. I didn't take it well. Twenty-five years old, knowing your life's going to be full of *nevers*. Never walk again, never have kids, never have a proper sex life. I did everything I could to push her away, but Shona stuck with me. Plenty of others wouldn't have. I didn't expect her to be faithful. How could I expect that of her?'

'Did you know Shona was in a relationship with Ray?'

'Yeah, he was one of the very few she cared about. I'll never know why. He was a mean bastard, especially in drink, but she must have seen something in him the rest of us didn't. Then again, she's a sucker for a sob story. I think that's how it started. Back then, Ray was coping with the farm while caring for his elderly parents. It was soon after we moved here from London. We used the money from my insurance to buy this place, but we had nothing spare. I'd started a course in computer programming. Something I could do from home. Shona started doing shifts in the pub and the odd cleaning job. She cleaned for old Mr and Mrs Polglaze. She got to know Ray, and one thing led to another.'

'How did she take it when she heard he was getting married?'

'How could she take it? She'd told him she'd never leave me. After his parents died, I dare say he wanted more, and when she wasn't up for that, he looked elsewhere. They split up for a while, but it was one of those relationships that's never properly laid to rest. I think she always thought he'd be there for her, and when she heard from someone else, he'd got married behind her back, and the wife was bringing her kids to the farm, she lost it for a while. We couldn't have kids see, so I think that hit her the hardest. She needn't have worried. Ray was hardly what you'd call a family man.'

'Did you tell DI Noble Shona was having an affair with Ray?'

'I didn't need to, he already knew. He said it was probably the last straw when she heard Ray had been killed in the fire. He said she probably packed her bags and fucked off.'

'And that was it? He didn't say anything else… that he would open a missing person case once she'd been missing the requisite time?'

'No. In fact, he threatened me.'

'Threatened you?'

'I took it as a threat. He said if I was going to pursue this, it might open up a can of worms for me.'

'How come?'

'I thought at first he meant about Shona, you know, about her sleeping around and that.'

'But he didn't?'

'No, he said if I were to pursue this, I could find myself a suspect in an investigation, and they'd have to bring me in for questioning about the fire at the farm. He even went on about how it was no fun being disabled behind bars. Like it's a never-ending party out here; insensitive sod.'

'He said that?'

'Yeah. What's more, I could tell he meant it. I was so relieved when a couple of days later, Shona texted me. She said she was sorry, but she couldn't imagine living in the village without Ray. She'd decided to go back to London and was staying with friends until she found a job and somewhere to live permanently. She said I could keep the house as I'd paid for it with my insurance money and that she hoped I had a happy life. She said she'd tried her best, but living the way we were did neither of us any good and Ray's death had brought it home to her.'

'Did you try and contact her or these friends she was staying with?'

'I texted back asking her to come home and talk things over and later asking her if she wanted her clothes and stuff, but she never answered. I guessed she wanted a clean break, and I respected her wishes. I didn't want her to change her mind out of pity for me. She'd sacrificed enough over the years.'

'Did you tell all this to Noble?'

'I did. I rang him as soon as I got the text, and he was nice as pie. He as good as said I should forget about Shona… do what she'd said and get on with the rest of my life.'

'And you've not heard from Shona since?'

'No. The least I could do was let her go, let her have her freedom.'

'She never filed for divorce?'

'No, and neither did I. I would give it to her if she asked, but she never has and I feel it's her choice. Linda here is a widow, aren't you, love?' He glanced up at the woman standing next to him, his eyes tender as he reached up to cover the hand she had laid on his shoulder. 'She never wants to marry again. Neither of us is looking to replace what we had. We get on well and are very fond of each other, and that's good enough for us.'

'I don't suppose you have the telephone numbers for Shona's friends, the ones she was likely to be staying with in London when she left?'

'I've got her old address book. I think that has her numbers in it, but I'm not sure how useful it will be all these years later. I'll circle the ones that were closest to her, but it's a long time ago.'

'If you don't mind, that would be great. I'll bring it back when I've finished with it.'

'Not much point. I don't have any need of it.'

Ross left the house with the address book clutched in his hand and a bad taste in his mouth. There was something very wrong here. He couldn't quite put his finger on what. Everything pointed to Shona lighting that fire and running off, but Noble had not even considered the possibility. He'd dismissed her husband's concerns and made no attempt to trace her once she'd made contact. Why the hell not? She had to be a person of interest, given her relationship with Ray.

Everything came back to Noble and how he had carried out his investigation. Ross was no defence lawyer, but he bloody well knew if he had been, he would have made use of the fact a victim's girlfriend had disappeared the night he'd been killed and hadn't been seen since. That little snippet of information had never been available to the defence. He needed to find out where Noble was now. He needed to talk to the man.

THIRTY-FOUR

'Did you have a good visit?'

'We did, but don't you go getting any ideas. If you think you're putting me in a place like that, you can think again.'

'As if.'

'Just so we're clear.'

'What did you talk about?'

'You mean, did we talk about Kit Retallick?' I'm your mother. I know what you mean. Well, for your information, we did. Laura seemed worried about something when I first arrived, and I asked her if it was to do with your visit. Truth be told, I didn't want her thinking I was there just to smooth the way for you to ask more questions. She's an old friend, and at our age, we can do without more sleepless nights. She said it wasn't you. You were the perfect gentleman apparently, but she was worried she'd not been truthful with you and it had played on her mind since.'

'Not truthful about what?'

'About the girl, about Tamar and her boyfriend.'

Ross sat up straighter in his seat.

'She said she hadn't wanted to talk ill of the dead. The Retallick girl obviously meant a lot to her, and she didn't feel she could betray her confidence. She said she'd done that once before, and it had done no good.'

Ross turned off the ignition and faced his mother. 'What about the boyfriend?'

'She was seeing an older man. Laura asked the girl if he was married, and she said definitely not, but when I say older…'

'How much older?'

'About twenty years.'

Ross couldn't hide his shock.

'Twenty?'

His mother nodded.

'How long had it been going on for when Laura found out?'

His mother took a deep breath. 'That's where Laura's worries stemmed from, about a year and a half. They met when she'd just turned sixteen.'

'Sixteen!' Ross was incredulous. The girl was over the age of consent, but she was still a child in his book.

'Did this man have sex with her? Was she groomed?'

His thoughts ran to Livvy and what he'd do to any middle-aged man who laid his hands on her.

'Not according to the girl. She was adamant about that. She said he was waiting until she was eighteen, that they were in love.'

Love, my ass, thought Ross, seething at the thought of it.

'Laura had been scared it was the stepfather and had been about to report it to the police, but when she'd broached the subject, the girl had been disgusted she could even think such a thing. Laura racked her brains trying to work out who it might be, knowing the girl didn't go far, but no one seemed to fit the bill. In the end, she told her if she didn't end it, she'd tell her mother and that if Lilah Polglaze told Ray, he'd kill the bloke. Mind you, it might have been the one useful thing he ever did.'

'Did Tamar end it?'

'Laura thought she had. When she raised the issue, the girl said it was over, and she didn't want to dwell on it. Laura tried to explain why she'd felt she had to threaten to tell her mother, and Tamar said she understood, but their relationship was never the same. Laura told me it damn near broke her heart, but it was a price she'd been prepared to pay to get her away from this man.'

'Well, if she didn't have any idea, then we haven't got much hope of finding out who he was all these years after it ended.'

'Well, that's the thing.'

'What?'

'It didn't end when Laura thought. The day before the girl died, Laura saw her getting into a red Audi.'

'That could have been anyone, a parent of a school friend or some youngster using his dad's car. We can't say for certain it was this man.'

'No, not for certain, but Laura said whoever it was had parked around the back out of sight. She only spotted him because she was putting empty boxes in the outhouse. There's plenty of parking to the front of the shop, and the girl left via the front door when she finished her shift but had walked around the corner to meet him. It was clear whoever was driving that car didn't want to be seen.'

'Did Laura confront Tamar about it?'

'No, she did what she'd said she'd do. She rang the girl's mother.'

'And what did she do about it?'

'She didn't have time to do anything. Laura rang her on the evening of the fire. She rang the house first and got no answer, so assumed Ray was in the pub, and Lilah was working. She rang the care home and spoke to her.'

'What did she say?'

'She thanked Laura for letting her know and asked if she could rely on her discretion not to tell anyone else.'

'And Mrs Tremlett still has no idea who it was? She didn't recognise him or the car?'

'I'm afraid not.'

Ross couldn't hide his disappointment and was about to leave when his mother stopped him.

'Hang on, there's something else she said you need to know.'

'Go on then.'

'She said it was her who rang the fire brigade to report the fire. She'd tried to call Lilah back at work but was told she'd gone home. She'd been too worried to sleep and had gone to check out the farm to make sure Tamar and her mum were all right. She got as far as the end of the village and saw the smoke. She called from the phone box. She didn't leave her name; she was so worried it was all her fault.'

THIRTY-FIVE

Ross called Eden to tell her the news. Not only had Shona Bryant absconded on the night of the fire, but having carried out a search when he'd got home, he could find neither hide nor hair of her since. She had no employment record. Her bank account hadn't been touched. There was no trace of her on social media. She was, for all intents and purposes, a ghost.

He'd rung the six closest friends circled by Bryant in her address book. All had confirmed they hadn't had contact with her since she left Ray. Only one had thought it odd and had rung the Devon and Cornwall Police after hearing through the grapevine about Shona's text to Steve. She thought Steve's story didn't ring true, but when they rang her back confirming the text had come from Shona's phone, and they had no suspicions, she left it. She'd assumed Shona was grieving over Ray and would get in touch in her own good time. When she never did, she and Shona's other friends guessed she'd made a fresh start somewhere new. They'd speculated she might be travelling or even living off some sugar daddy she'd picked up on a cruise. Ross didn't have the heart to tell the woman her friend's passport had run out long ago and had never been renewed.

'And Shona's disappearance is only part of the story,' Ross said, breaking the news of Tamar's affair.

Eden was understandably shocked, and when he divulged the age gap, he thought she'd burst a blood vessel.

'No one in their right mind could think a relationship like that was healthy,' she said.

'But the million-dollar question is whether Laura Tremlett's phone call triggered something? It could have been the reason why Lilah left work early and was at the farm that night.'

'And was she brave enough to keep the news from Ray, knowing he might hear about it from someone else, and she'd pay the price if he did?' added Ross. 'Ray was no saint, but even he would have thought it was sick. If she told him that night, he wouldn't have rested until he found out who the man was.'

'The problem is this is all conjecture. We can't know any of it for certain.'

'Not all of it. Shona's disappearance is fact, and then there's the phone call to her before she left the pub.'

'What phone call?'

'Sorry, I forgot to say. According to her husband, Shona got a phone call at the pub that evening. It was from a man. We don't know who, but she left early. What if it was Ray? He may have called her to tell her Lilah had found out about them and to call off the relationship for a second time. What if she snapped and decided to tackle her problems head-on?'

'It certainly raises questions. Thanks, Ross, you've done a brilliant job. I'm going to go and talk to Kit about this older man. He might be able to cast some light on who he was.'

'Okay, I'll concentrate on Noble. We need to know why he didn't pursue Shona's disappearance… oh, and one more thing. The anonymous call from the phone box on the night of the fire, that was Laura.'

'Well, at least that's one mystery solved,' said Eden.

***

Kit was in the caravan when Eden arrived. Castro was on the bed having made himself at home. She wasn't sure whether his residency was an indication of Kit's good character or the Labrador's love of a good fire. Castro wasn't stupid. The caravan was toasty, unlike the icy corridors of her parents' house.

Kit made a pot of coffee.

'You said on the phone you had some news?'

'It's not a magic bullet, but Ross has turned up some interesting information.'

'Information?'

'About Shona Bryant. She hasn't been seen since the night of the fire.'

Kit looked aghast.

'She left before her shift ended that night and never went home. What's more, she doesn't figure anywhere.'

Kit looked blankly at her.

'A lot has changed since you went away. None of our lives are private anymore. If you have someone's last address and their national insurance number, you can find just about anything, add social media into the equation, and you can build a pretty good picture. Shona's profile shows no activity since that night except for a text message to her husband received two days after she disappeared. Other than that, she's broken off ties with everyone.'

'I didn't know,' Kit said. Eden guessed he was realising the world had moved on and how ill-equipped he was to deal with it.

'We know Shona and Ray had begun seeing each other again. We know your mum found out that night. Ray might have told her their relationship was on hold, and she could have reacted badly. We cannot rule out that she set the fire then disappeared.'

Kit's face lit up. 'You think we might be able to prove that?'

'We don't need to prove it. We need to show it's a possibility that wasn't explored at the time of your trial. Shona's husband confirmed the police showed no interest in investigating her disappearance despite knowing about her and Ray.'

'And they should have,' said Kit.

He was on his feet now, hopping from foot to foot like an

excitable child.

'Yes, I think they should.' Eden paused. 'There's something else I need to tell you. Perhaps you ought to sit down for this.'

Kit's enthusiasm wilted as he sat on the edge of the bed. Eden could tell this was a man used to having his bubble burst.

'It's about Tamar and the man she was seeing.'

'What man?'

'According to Laura Tremlett, your sister was seeing a man much older than her.'

'What do you mean, seeing…'

'I mean romantically.'

'How much older?'

'Substantially older, by about twenty years.'

Kit grimaced in disbelief.

'She also believes her relationship with this man began when she was sixteen or even earlier.'

Kit leapt up and began to pace the tiny floor space. 'I don't believe it. Why would she want to be with an old man? My sister was beautiful. All the boys at college fancied her. She could have had her pick.'

'Who knows, some girls find boys their own age immature. Maybe she was seeking protection from someone older, someone she felt safe with. You said yourself your sister told you someone was looking out for you. It's unlikely she'd say that about a boy her own age.'

'I thought she meant one of her friends' parents or maybe even a teacher at college. I never imagined… it's disgusting… who was this man?'

'I don't know, but Laura Tremlett was concerned enough to tell your mum about it.'

Deflated, he sat back on the edge of the bed.

'Mum knew?'

'She did, but not until the evening of the fire.'

He didn't seem to hear her.

'I can't even imagine where she'd meet someone like that. She was always busy with her studies. She was going to university.'

The conversation was interrupted by a loud buzzing above the caravan. Castro stirred and began to growl.

'What the hell's that noise?' said Kit, straining to look through the skylight, then opening the caravan door and stepping out into the cold.

Eden followed.

They looked up at the drone hovering above their heads.

You've got to be joking, thought Eden, imagining the press had got wind of Kit's release and wondering if Luke had leaked the news in a fit of peeve. She barely had time to process this and lift her mobile from her pocket before she heard police sirens.

Luke and Denise Charlton were leading the charge.

She listened, her gaze oscillating between Kit and Denise as the DS arrested her client for the murder of Graham White.

Luke whispered one sentence in her ear as they watched a uniformed officer fix the handcuffs. 'DNA never lies.'

'What DNA, where are you taking him?'

'Hopefully back where he belongs,' replied Luke, his hand hovering above Kit's head to protect it as he deposited him in the back seat of the police car. It seemed like a futile gesture, given he was intent on throwing the man to the wolves.

'But he was on the train from London.'

Luke ignored her.

Eden raced past her parents back to her car.

They stood by the front door, their expressions impassive. Only Castro protested Kit's innocence, running around in circles barking as police officers searched the caravan.

Eden's hands were sweating as she grabbed the gearstick to reverse the car. As soon as she had the police vehicles in her sight, she rang Molly.

'Hi, Molly, I'm going to need you to cancel my appointments. I'm so sorry I keep dropping you in at the deep end.'

'I hope it's nothing serious?'

'Kit's been arrested for the murder of Graham White.'

There was a long pause at the other end of the phone. When Molly eventually spoke, her voice had a wounded quality.

'Do you think it's true? Do you think Agnes was right all along?'

Eden couldn't bring herself to answer. Kit had told her he had an alibi but if there was DNA evidence to link him to White's murder, they'd both been duped. It didn't matter whether he was innocent of his original crime or not. All their efforts would count for nothing; their belief in him misplaced. They'd wasted time, money and, worse still, she'd invited Kit like a vampire into her parent's home. You got what you deserved when you were foolish enough to do that. Part of her wanted to wash her hands of him there and then, let him try his luck with the duty solicitor. She guillotined the thought as soon as it arrived. She had to know what Luke meant by DNA evidence. She also needed to look Kit in the eye. Knowing for certain he was guilty of White's murder would release her. Once she'd done that, she could turn her back on him. Lawyers defended the guilty all the time, but only idiots defended clients who lied to them.

THIRTY-SIX

The mood at the station was a mix of jubilation and relief. She couldn't blame them. If they were right, they'd solved at least one of the murders within two weeks. What's more, they'd done it without outside help. There would be many looking on from other forces who would have thought it beyond them. This was a coup, but for Eden, it was a disaster. Eventually, Denise came to collect her.

'He's ready for you if you'd like a private word.'

'No, it's fine. I'm happy we go straight to interview. Luke said there's new DNA evidence, no doubt he'll produce it.'

Denise looked surprised. She couldn't know Eden was as eager as Luke to see Kit's reaction to this bombshell.

'Okay, if you're sure.' Denise showed her into the interview room.

Kit looked bewildered; his face ashen, his scar angry and raised. She sat next to him without saying a word, ignoring his attempts to catch her eye.

Luke appeared in the doorway holding a plastic evidence bag in his right hand. He nodded to Denise to start recording the interview. After the usual introductions, he reminded Kit he was under caution and had been arrested for the murder of Graham White.

'I know you've been interviewed in respect of this crime before and have denied it, but new evidence has come to light that indicates conclusively you were lying at your previous interview. I'm going to show you that evidence now.'

'For the benefit of the recording, DCI Parish is showing Mr Retallick an evidence bag containing a khaki-coloured knitted hat,' said Denise.

'Do you recognise this hat, Christopher? It's okay, you can take the bag. Have a good look at it. I can also tell you it has a Superdry label.'

Luke slid the bag towards him. Kit took it with the timidity of a mouse sniffing at a piece of cheese in a trap.

'Is that your hat, Mr Retallick?'

'I'm not sure. It looks like my hat, but I'm not sure it's mine.'

'But you do have a hat like this one?'

'I do,' Kit said, his trembling fingers leaving sweat marks on the bag.

Professional integrity pinched at Eden's conscience.

'There must be dozens of hats like that in circulation. This could be anyone's hat.'

It was a stupid thing to say, and she knew what was coming next. She'd known it the minute Luke produced the plastic bag. She'd foolishly provided a drum roll to his tah-dah reveal.

'True… true,' he said indulgently, 'but this one was found among Graham White's clothes, and this one is covered in your client's DNA.'

Eden longed to wipe the smug look from his face.

She watched the sucker punch travel through Kit's body, turning his backbone to jelly.

'But how… I didn't. I swear, I didn't… I haven't been anywhere near Mr White since my trial.'

'That isn't true, is it Christopher? Otherwise, why would your DNA be all over a hat found in his jacket pocket? You killed him. You tracked him down, chained his feet and hands and set him alight.' Luke spat the words at Kit. 'If you wish to continue to deny it, go ahead, but we're going to charge you with this and on this evidence, and with your record, trust me, you will be convicted. The question is whether you are prepared to confess here and now and make it easier on yourself. I'm not offering you anything… let's be clear on that. I saw what you did to that man. You are going to jail, probably for the rest of your miserable life. Confessing now may just mean you can serve out your sentence at your old prison and won't have to start working your way up the food chain all over again. It could mean the difference between you surviving or not.'

'I think my client needs a break.'

Luke looked reluctant, but Denise intervened, pausing the tape to suspend the interview.

Once the detectives had left the room, Eden turned her attention to Kit.

'If you want me to continue to advise you, you need to tell me the truth. Did you kill Graham White?'

'No, I swear.'

'Kit, that's your hat with your DNA all over it.'

'Could they be tricking me like the last time? Maybe it's just a hat and they're lying about the DNA?'

'No, not this time, and to be honest, I'm having difficulty believing you at the moment. I'll stay to the end of this interview, but you'll have to get yourself a new solicitor. I won't act for someone who deliberately lies to me.'

The man looked even more dejected when faced with her brittle lack of sympathy. He began to sob, tears tracking his cheeks as his words caught like barbed wire in his throat.

'Please… please don't give up on me. I can't go back… I can't. I had the hat when I went back to the farm. I had it after Mr White was killed.'

He hadn't told her he'd been to Morvah.

'When did you visit the farm?'

'The day after I saw you. I had it then. I know I did. I wore a scarf and the hat. I didn't want anyone to recognise me.'

'Did you have it when you got back?'

She could see his mind working.

'Yes… yes, I did. I wore it when I went to get a haircut.'

Eden remembered noticing he'd been to the barbers when she'd seen him for the second time in her office.

'And since?'

'I don't know, I can't remember wearing it since then.'

'Think carefully, where would it be now if you still have it?'

'I don't know. I couldn't find it when I packed to go to the caravan. I thought I might need it.'

He leaned forward, his head in his hands. 'I can't think… why can't I think?'

Eden touched his sleeve, her original disappointment and anger dissipating as the building blocks of a theory she couldn't fully construct began to stack up.

'Kit, can you remember if it was there when the police searched the cottage on the Saturday morning?'

'I don't know. I suppose so, but I can't say for certain. They arrived before I had time to unpack. I can't remember if I wore it in the taxi.'

'I'm going to have a word with them. I need to check something.'

Denise was in the corridor outside.

Eden banged on the door.

'Can I have a word?'

'Is everything okay?' asked Denise.

'The hat… was it logged when you searched the Malpas property?'

Denise frowned. 'I don't know. I can check, but I hope you're not suggesting we planted it?'

'Not at the moment.'

'Good, because you'd be accusing Luke and I. We were the ones who collected it from the charity shop and inspected the clothes when we got them back to the station. We found the hat folded in the pocket of the sports jacket.'

'Hang on a second. Where exactly did you find the clothes?'

No one had told her about the charity shop. It was her own fault. She'd not asked any questions before the interview. She'd been too riled up to follow her usual procedure.

'They were left in a bag outside Age Concern in the High Street.'

'And you believe Kit left them there?'

'We don't know who left them. There are no cameras nearby.'

Luke walked around the corner carrying a coffee.

'What's going on?'

'I'm explaining to Eden how we recovered the victim's clothes.'

'And the hat with Retallick's DNA all over it,' he added.

'I've asked to see the log of the search you carried out at the property in Malpas. I want to know if the hat was there two days after the murder.'

'You're not seriously going to argue we planted it?'

'I'm not arguing anything other than this feels wrong.'

Denise glanced at Luke, and Eden spotted a shard of concern in her eyes.

'I'm surprised you don't think the same. You have to admit it's odd. White's clothes turning up outside a charity shop days after the murder?'

'We ran an appeal, remember. Whoever left them could have found them earlier but only realised their importance after seeing the appeal,' said Luke.

'Setting aside for the moment the anomaly that the murderer didn't destroy the evidence in the first place, why did the person who discovered them not bring them to the station?'

'Who knows? Maybe they didn't want to get involved, or maybe there was a bit of cash in the pocket, and they'd spent it. There could be any number of reasons why they wanted anonymity.'

'I can think of one,' said Eden. 'I assume you couldn't identify the hat as belonging to the victim?'

'Correct.'

'So, you're saying the killer was careless?'

'It would have been easy enough to slip the hat into the bag by mistake when stripping and re-dressing the victim.'

'But it wasn't slipped into the bag, was it? It was folded in the victim's jacket pocket. What's more, if it's in the police log, the killer did it after the event. That means it had to be placed there on purpose. He goes to all that trouble to commit the crime and then leaves evidence leading directly back to him. Why?'

She could see from Luke's expression the penny had finally dropped.

'Denise, check the log to see if the hat was there when we searched the cottage,' he said reluctantly.

Denise disappeared down the corridor, leaving Luke and Eden alone.

'The man sitting in that interview room has spent all his adult life behind bars. He claims he's innocent of the crime that put him there. Yet you're saying the first thing he does when he gets out is to commit another crime, equally heinous, leaving evidence in his wake bound to result in his conviction and his being frog-marched back to prison. Surely you can see the lack of logic?'

'So, you do think we planted the evidence.'

'No, I'm not saying you did. I'm saying someone did. I presume that someone is the killer.'

Denise was back.

'I've checked the photos. We didn't log it, but it's there sitting on top of the chest of drawers in the bedroom.'

'Fuck,' said Luke, coffee spilling from his cup.

'Look, if you think Retallick is the kind of man who would plan his crime then give you the keys to his jail cell to make a point or to gain notoriety, then go ahead and charge him, but I don't think he's that man. I don't think he's insane or narcissistic, and what's more, I don't think he committed the original crime. In fact, Ross has uncovered evidence to suggest there were several other suspects with far greater motives than him who should have been investigated.'

Luke's eyes widened as he wiped the coffee from his lapel.

'Ross?'

'He's taken on the case for me. It's his first fully-fledged PI job.'

Luke looked as if he was about to say something but thought better of it.

'I'm sorry, sir, but I think Eden's right. I said at the time… when we picked up the clothes, it's all too neat,' said Denise, 'and we still have to overcome his alibi. This has to be watertight if the CPS are going to run with this.'

'Okay… okay, let's take a breath here. Let's say we were to go along with this bullshit, accepting as a prerequisite that no one in this station is complicit in this. How and when did the killer get hold of Retallick's hat in the first place?'

'That's what we need to find out. You were watching the cottage, so I assume we can rule out anybody breaking in and stealing it, which means the killer and Kit had to cross paths. My client's in a mess at the moment. He can't think straight. He doesn't even know for certain when he last had the hat, let alone who else could have it. I need the chance to talk to him away from here, to try and get him to remember when he last had it. Today, that's all I need. You can charge him tomorrow.'

'And tonight? I hope you don't intend taking him back to your parents' place?'

'No, I appreciate now that was a stupid idea. You can put the surveillance back on him, it doesn't matter now. Twenty-four hours, that's all I'm asking.'

'Fine, but that's it. If you come up with nothing, I charge him tomorrow, and you can make your arguments in court.'

'Agreed, and thanks, Luke. I know what you're risking.'

'Me? I'm not risking anything, but trust me, if he absconds, I'll see you're struck off for aiding and abetting. Friend or no friend.'

THIRTY-SEVEN

'Kit, I need you to think. Were you wearing the hat when you left the barbers?'

'I can't remember.'

As soon as Luke had bailed Kit to return the next day, pending further investigation, they headed back to Malpas. Eden didn't know what to expect and was surprised how modern and cosy the cottage was with its porridge-coloured walls and seagrass carpeting. Very hygge, but they weren't there to talk about the décor. Kit made tea, and they retreated into the sitting room.

'Why don't we try the method we used the other day at my office to recall the night of the fire? I noticed you closed your eyes. It seemed to help you visualise it.'

'Do you think it might work?'

'We've got nothing to lose.'

Kit sat back in his chair and let his lids droop.

'Let's start with the basics. Where did you go for your haircut?'

'The barbers in River Street.'

'What were you wearing?'

'Jeans, jumper, blue donkey jacket and the hat, of course.'

'Are you sure about the hat?'

'My hair was a mess. I was sick of that awful topknot. I'd let it grow too long in prison. We used to have a volunteer who came in, and he did a good job, but he stopped about six months before I got out. His replacement was a short back and sides merchant, and I knew he wouldn't think about the scar. I need something on my collar and a fringe that can hide it a bit. It won't make it disappear, but a good haircut helps.'

Eden remembered how much better he'd looked the second time they'd met in her office.

'Was there anyone else in the barbers when you got there?'

'It was quiet. I picked a weekday because I knew it would be packed on Saturday morning. There were a couple of men there when I arrived. One was having a haircut, the other was having a professional shave, the full works… hot towels and all that.' Kit opened his eyes. 'When did that start to be a thing? Men going out for a shave. Like in old American films.'

'It's been popular for a while now. It followed on from the trend for beards a few years back. Men are into personal grooming as much as women these days. You'll have to bear that in mind when you start dating. A quick spray of Lynx under the armpits doesn't hack it anymore.'

'I won't need to bother if I'm back inside,' Kit said glumly. 'Anyway, I don't think about things like that.'

'You look just fine,' said Eden, her heart swelling for the young man.

Kit, blushing, closed his eyes again, more to hide his embarrassment than to assist with his recollection, Eden guessed.

'Okay, so you sat in the barber's chair and took off the hat. Where did you put it?'

'I didn't sit down right away. I took off the hat, slipped it into my coat pocket, then hung my jacket on the coat stand by the door.'

'Then you took your seat?'

'Not straight away. I waited by the reception desk for the girl to show me to the chair. I had to wait a couple of minutes because the bloke who came in after me was asking her about the products.'

'Products?'

'He wanted to know which shampoo was best for his hair

type and whether he should use gel or balm. Half of it was stuff I'd never heard of. When she sold him a tiny pot of gunk for thirty quid, I started to wonder whether I'd picked the right place or ought to try somewhere else. I was worried what a haircut might cost in a place like that, but I didn't get the chance to bolt. As soon as she'd finished serving him, she led me to the chair and put one of those rubber collars around my shoulders. Then she had to rush off again because the bloke knocked over the coat stand on his way out.'

'Knocked it over?'

'Yeah, the coats went flying. He was so embarrassed he left the hair balm on the windowsill by the door. The receptionist ran after him, but he'd already gone. He didn't come back for it either. Thirty quid down the pan.'

'Do you think the man could have taken your hat? Are you sure you didn't recognise him?'

'I didn't really look at him, not face on. I was standing by the desk, and he was slightly behind me to the left, by the shelf where the products were.'

'Can you describe him?'

'Oldish, tallish… like I said, I didn't really get a good look. I tend not to stare at people. I suppose I'm used to them staring at me rather than the other way around. I try not to invite attention if I can help it.'

'Did anyone else come in when you were there?'

'No, the other customers finished off, and then I was the only one left.'

'Did they have coats on the coat stand?'

'No idea. I think there were others hanging there when I arrived, but they could have belonged to the staff.'

'Kit, this is important. Did you put the hat back on before you left?'

'I didn't. I'd paid a fortune for that haircut. I wasn't going to cover it with a skanky old hat. I remember I wanted to leave the barber a tip. He was nice. He didn't mention the scar once, but I could tell he was aware of it and doing his best, you know, to conceal it. I paid with my card, and I was worried he might not get a cut, so I reached in my pocket for some cash and realised I didn't have any.'

His eyes, wide as saucers, stared at Eden.

'I didn't have any notes or coins… or the hat.'

Eden imagined the unknown man knocking over the coat stand and taking the opportunity to pilfer the hat from Kit's pocket while the coats were on the floor. The fact he left his purchase and didn't come back for it was certainly odd, but none of this helped if Kit had no idea who the culprit was.

.

THIRTY-EIGHT

Ross called Jake Fairchild at the station. He and Jake went back a long way. Jake had been a young PC when his dad had been DCI and he'd watched Ross's back over the years as a favour to his old boss.

'Ex-detective Trenear, what can I do for you? I hear you've started up as a private investigator. I suppose it's better than pounding warehouse floors as a security guard. So, is this a social call, or are you looking for information and hoping I'll sing like a canary?'

'How are you, Jake? How's Julie and the grandkids?'

'Bloody brilliant. I can't wait to retire from this lot and spend more time with them. I missed out on my own kids growing up. But I don't need to tell you that. You've got the t-shirt.'

'How much longer have you got to go now?'

'Twelve months, three weeks and two days, and I've done my thirty years. Then me and Julie will be off on a cruise around the Med. Of course, you're already living the dream.'

'Not quite. Remember,, my kids are a long way off being independent, but at least I can hand my grandson back to his parents when I've had enough. I expect you've heard I'm a grandad too now.'

'Never.'

'Straight up, Piran's got a little boy.'

'Good god, where does the time go?'

'Tell me about it. Funnily enough, I'm calling about a blast from the past. Do you remember a detective who worked with Dad just before he retired? DS Noble?'

Jake huffed on the other end of the phone. 'How could I

forget that gobshite.'

'You weren't a fan then?'

'You could say that. Neither was your dad, if I remember rightly.'

'Do you know where he went after he left the Devon and Cornwall Force? I heard he got transferred?'

'Hereford. He made DCI, though Christ knows how. I can only guess he used the same tactics he did when he was down here.'

'Which were?'

'Suck up to the brass and throw your colleagues under the bus. He was a master of self-promotion. Everything your dad hated. Why the hell are you asking about him?'

'It's for Mum, really. She's asked me to sort out Dad's old papers, you know, reading his diaries and that. He mentions him, that's all.'

'Which cases, I might remember them?'

Ross had no intention of mentioning Retallick by name.

'Oh, you know, just the ones around that time. How could I find out where he is now?'

'He would have retired, but I do know he was heavily involved with the Police Federation. He might even have been on the committee at one stage. I'm sure if you look on their website, you'll find something.'

'Thanks, Jake. We'll have to get together for a drink sometime. Bring Julie down to the pub. Karenza would love to see you both.'

'I might take you up on that,' said Jake.

***

After a bit of digging, Ross found Noble. In fact, it was hard not to find an article in the back copies of the *West Mercia Police*

Federation magazine where he didn't figure. The last one was in 2021, a feature about his retirement. There was a photograph of Noble with his wife and two teenage sons.

They were standing in the garden of a smart double-bayed red-brick detached. All four of them smiling broadly. The boys standing either side of him were tall and stocky like their father. The mother looked younger than her husband, and at first, Ross thought she was Noble's daughter until he read the caption underneath.

"I look forward to spending more time with my lovely wife, Elaine," said former DCI Brett Noble. "Although, with my two boys intent on joining the ranks, I don't expect I'll ever really say goodbye to the force."

Ross contemplated how he was going to sell a trip to Hereford to Karenza. It would mean an overnight stay. He wondered if he could combine it with a weekend away for the two of them. He'd have to square it with Eden, of course. She might insist he telephone Noble instead. He hoped not. A conversation over the telephone wouldn't be as revealing as a face-to-face interview. If he phoned, Noble was likely to give him the bum's rush. That was harder to do if he visited in person. He didn't intend to tell him why he wanted to see him. The plan was to say he was compiling a family history about his dad for his mum. Much the same story he'd spun for Jake. He'd say his name had come up and as he was in the area, he'd decided to look up this old colleague of his father's who worked for the Police Federation. Once he caught him unawares and he'd relaxed, he'd casually drop the Retallick case into the mix. He'd say his dad had always thought of it as the one that got away… the one he would have loved to have worked on, and how he'd been so impressed Noble had solved it so quickly and how disappointed he'd been that he hadn't become his successor when he retired. He'd appeal to the man's vanity.

The door behind him opened and Karenza came in carrying

a mug of coffee.

'This place is a tip,' she said, grabbing a coaster before putting the mug down. 'You're going to have to get yourself a filing cabinet to store all this paperwork and a better printer. That one is on its last legs. By the way, if you're looking for the file you were working on the other day, it's in the bottom drawer of the desk. It was strewn all over the floor and I needed to hoover.'

'Sorry,' said Ross. 'How do you fancy a trip to Hereford?'

'Hereford?'

'It's a case I'm working on. I thought we might sneak a weekend off. I'm sure the staff would cover for us. They'd be glad of the extra cash in the lead-up to Christmas. You'd like that, wouldn't you?'

Karenza put her arms around his neck and leaned over his shoulder to look at the screen.

'Who are they?'

'An ex-policeman I need to interview and his family.'

Karenza peered closer. 'It's not the woman you're investigating then. It looks just like her… older, but it's her, isn't it?'

'What woman?'

'The one in the photo. The pretty girl with the long dark hair. I picked up her photo from the floor.'

Ross stared blankly at her.

'Oh, for god's sake, shift,' she said, pushing him to the side and pulling open the bottom drawer of the desk. She shuffled through the file and lifted out the photograph of Tamar Retallick from amongst the papers.

'There,' she said, slamming it down on the table triumphantly, 'that's her in the photo on the screen.'

Ross looked at the face of the young woman and back to the shot of Noble's wife.

'Zoom in. Surely you can see it. They are one and the same.'

Ross did as she suggested and zoomed in on the face of Elaine Noble.

'Look at her eyes. Those eyes are unmistakable,' said Karenza.

Ross's heart was racing. 'What the… fuck?'

THIRTY-NINE

Eden's mobile rang. It was Ross. She was dreading the call. Telling him they were dropping the case because Kit was going to be charged with the murder of Graham White would be difficult. It was his first case as a PI. He was bound to be disappointed, but he'd been clear from the outset he would not help her save someone he felt was guilty and knowing how your average policeman thought about DNA evidence, he would agree with Luke. Her client was banged to rights. He, like Luke, would think he should be back behind bars. She let the call go to voicemail.

She was certain Kit would be charged the next day. Even if they traced the culprit from the barbers, how on earth could they prove he stole the hat, let alone planted it with White's clothes? Unless he had some obvious connection with the case, or his DNA was on the hat, it was a non-starter. From the look on Kit's face, he knew so too.

'Look, we'll pick this up tomorrow. I'm going to head off now. It'll give you time to think. If anything else comes to mind, you've got my number. You never know, you might remember the man's face if you're not trying so hard.'

'Will you be with me when they charge me?'

'Of course I will.'

'Can you meet me at the station? I'll call you. I assume I'll get my phone call.'

'I don't mind coming here first thing.'

'I'd prefer it if you didn't.'

'Okay, whatever you want,' said Eden, getting up from the sofa and heading for the door.

Kit called after her as she reached the bottom of the steps.

'Thanks for all you've done for me. I know you tried, and I want you to know I really appreciate it.'

Eden turned one more time to look at the pale young man standing in the doorway before she got into her car and drove away.

She hoped he'd get a good night's sleep but knew in her heart he wouldn't. She passed the car park at Boscawen Park, where she'd seen the angry lines running along Kit's wrist. Her head was pounding. She suddenly felt uneasy about leaving him in the cottage on his own. Why didn't he want her to call there in the morning? What if he had decided to do something drastic and didn't want her to be the one to find him? She knew how hard it was for him to face going back to prison. He was on licence, and for an offence like this, he wouldn't have a chance of getting bail. He'd be back inside by this time tomorrow. She spun the car around and headed back to the cottage.

All the lights were out. She ran up the steps to the front door and rang the bell. No one answered. She banged on the door. Still nothing. She climbed over the narrow border across the path and banged on the window of the sitting room.

Please, God, please. I was only gone a few minutes. Surely, he couldn't have done anything yet.

Her throat felt tight as she shouted through the letterbox. 'Kit... Kit, it's me, Eden. Come to the door, let me in please... please.'

The relief was almost unbearable as she saw the young man walk down the stairs, pulling his jumper back over his head as he opened the door.

'Eden, did you leave something behind?'

'You, I left you behind. You shouldn't be on your own tonight.'

He looked relieved. 'Are you taking me back to the caravan?'

She remembered her promise to Luke.

'No… no you're going to stay with me.'

***

Ross was waiting outside in his car when Eden and Kit arrived at the beach house. As soon as they pulled up, he jumped out to meet them.

'Don't you ever answer your phone?'

'I'm sorry, I was at the station for most of the morning and then at Kit's place. There's not a very good signal in Malpas,' Eden lied.

Kit stood by the bonnet, waiting to be introduced.

'Kit, this is Ross. He's the private detective I told you about.'

'Hi,' Ross smiled, offering his hand. 'Good, now the introductions are over, are you going to invite me inside? It's bloody freezing on this clifftop.'

Once inside, Eden poked at the ashes in the wood burner until they glowed before throwing on a couple of logs.

'The spare room is at the top of the stairs, to the left,' she said to Kit.

'Are you sure?' Kit frowned.

'We've already been over this. Go and get yourself settled. Help yourself to a shower and I'll make a pot of tea for us all.' As soon as she was certain Kit was out of earshot, she turned to Ross.

'They're going to charge him tomorrow with the murder of Graham White.'

'On what evidence?'

'They found the victim's clothes.'

'I saw the appeal on the local news. I didn't think they had a cat in hell's chance of finding them.'

'Well, they have. They were dropped outside a charity shop,

and Kit's hat, with his DNA on, was found in White's jacket pocket.'

'How convenient.'

'I'm glad you think that too, because I believe it was planted.'

'Look, Eden, I told you when we started all this, I won't go up against my old team.'

'You can relax. I'm not saying it was anyone from your *old team*. I think someone else did it. I think someone who was following Kit stole the hat and planted it among White's clothes.'

She went on to explain about the barber's shop and the man who knocked over the coat stand but noticed, to her discomfort, the more she talked, the more fidgety Ross became. It was as if he couldn't wait for her to finish. Consequently, her story sounded less and less solid to her and by the time she got to the part where Kit looked in his pocket and the hat was missing, the law of diminishing returns had reduced her theory to a big fat zero.

'You don't believe me, do you?'

Ross remained distracted. 'Yeah, yeah, I do, it's just I've got something way more important to tell you.'

'More important. How can anything be more important than saving him from going back to prison?'

'Nothing, of course not, but look, it's easier if I show you,' Ross said, pulling his laptop from its case. 'What's your Wi-Fi password?'

Eden retrieved a small card from a shelf next to the television, and Ross connected his device. Within seconds, he had retrieved the photo of Noble and his family.

'See?' he said.

'What are we looking at?' asked Eden as she shuffled next to him on the sofa.

'DCI Noble, his two sons and his wife, Elaine, taken in 2021 just before he retired.'

'You found him then?'

'Yes, with a bit of help from Jake Fairchild. He lives in Hereford.'

'You didn't tell Jake why you were looking for him, did you?'

'Give me some credit, of course not.'

'Have you arranged to talk to him? Because if you have, I think you should hold back. There's really no point carrying on with this now Kit's facing this new charge. I need to concentrate on his defence. I'll pay what I owe you, of course.'

'Look again.'

Eden was becoming frustrated with all this cloak-and-dagger stuff.

'Can't we do this later? I wanted to talk to you about the chances of finding this man before Kit comes back down. I've got a feeling you're going to tell me it's hopeless and he's going to be so disappointed. I think I might have got his hopes up for nothing. He's vulnerable. It's why I insisted he come back here tonight. I was worried he might do something stupid.'

Ross didn't answer. Instead, he retrieved the photo of seventeen-year-old Tamar Retallick from his laptop case.

'That's Kit's sister, Tamar,' said Eden, confused.

'I know. Now look at the woman in the photograph.'

Just as he had done at home with Karenza, Ross zoomed in on the beautiful face of Noble's wife. 'Do you see it?'

'I'm not sure…'

'It took me a while too. Karenza saw it right away, but she's good with faces. Me, I'm not so hot, but I got there in the end.'

Eden squinted at the photo, then slowly, very slowly, puzzlement turned to disbelief.

'Elaine Noble is Tamar Retallick,' said Ross triumphantly. 'Noble is the older man Tamar told Laura Tremlett about.'

'Jesus Christ… what does this mean?'

'It means Noble had a very real reason for setting that fire and for wanting to frame Kit. He was in a secret relationship with his sister. A relationship that, in all likelihood, began when she was underage. What's more, thanks to Laura Tremlett, everyone was about to find out.'

Eden heard footsteps on the landing. She looked at Ross and knew both of them were thinking the same thing. How were they going to break the news to Kit that the sister he believed dead was alive? Eden half expected Ross to slam down the lid of his laptop like a teenager caught watching porn, but he didn't.

Kit came and stood awkwardly beside the fire.

'Did you find everything you needed? There's an extra blanket on top of the wardrobe,' Eden said.

'You have a lovely place here. I can't thank you enough for this. It's nice to have company.' He hesitated as if he sensed they'd been deep in conversation before he arrived. 'If you two need to talk, I'm happy to make myself scarce?'

'No,' said Ross, 'actually it's you we need to talk to. We've got something to show you… something that might come as a bit of a shock.'

Kit's face dropped.

'Can you come over here for a second? I need you to look at what's on my laptop,' said Ross, making room for Kit to sit between him and Eden.

'Take a look at this. Is there anyone in the picture you recognise?'

Kit looked at the photo for several seconds, during which Eden was bursting to say something.

'I can't believe you found him so quickly,' Kit said.

'Him?' said Eden.

'The man from the barber shop, the one we think stole my hat.'

'Are you sure?' asked Eden.

'Positive.'

Eden could feel the adrenaline pumping.

'Look closely, Kit. Do you recognise him from before?' asked Ross. 'I'm not talking about the barbershop now. I mean, from before you went to prison?'

Kit studied the photograph. When he looked up, his eyes were on fire.

'It's him, isn't it… the detective… DS Noble?' Kit's voice trembled with anger at the realisation this face, once a symbol of authority, was, in truth, a mask of deceit.

'Yes, it's him with his wife and sons,' said Eden.

Kit peered at the photograph again. 'She looks a bit like my mum… I mean how my mum used to look when I was little, before Ray,' he said.

Ross shot Eden a desperate look, the tension clearly too much for him.

Eden shook her head, a warning to say nothing. They needed Kit to see this for himself.

'Is that… oh my god! Is that my sister… is that Tamar?'

Eden could feel Kit's body trembling next to hers. She was pretty certain had he not been wedged between her and Ross, he would have collapsed.

Ross closed the laptop and rested Kit's back against the sofa. 'Have you got something you can give him? He's in shock?'

Eden ran to the kitchen and brought back a shot of whiskey. Kit took the glass and downed it in one.

'I need some air,' he said.

He swayed as he got to his feet and Ross steadied him. 'I'll take him,' he said to Eden, 'you call Luke.'

As soon as they were safely outside, Eden did just that.

She wasn't sure if he was tired or exasperated. Whichever, he didn't exactly sound pleased to hear her voice.

'There's something you need to see.'

'Can't it wait until tomorrow when I arrest him? Like I said, you'll have all the time in the world to put your case once he's charged.'

'No, it won't wait. You need to see this now,' she said sharply. 'If you don't, you might make the biggest mistake of your career.'

She heard him sigh.

'Are you at the cottage?'

'No, we're at my place.'

'What… you're there on your own with him?' he yelled.

Eden held the phone away from her ear.

'Calm down, Ross is here too. Look, come, please. We'll tell you everything when you get here.'

She sensed his reluctance waver.

'I'll leave now.'

***

By the time Luke arrived forty minutes later, Kit had revived, although he still couldn't seem to believe his eyes despite staring at the photograph several more times.

'Do you think he's kept her prisoner all these years? Do you think he forced her to have the children? I need to see her. I need to talk to her… to find out what he's done.'

'The police will find out. There will be plenty of time for you to talk to her then. First they need to find Noble.'

Eden, like everyone else, had read the tabloid stories about young women being abducted and kept in underground bunkers, raped and forced to have babies only to be discovered by chance years later, broken and traumatised. The woman in the photo standing proudly beside her husband and children was something else. She'd told Laura Tremlett all those years before she loved this man. There was nothing in her expression to indicate anything had changed. Whether Kit could ever accept that was another matter.

Over the next hour and a half, Ross appraised Luke with all the evidence he had gathered about Shona Bryant's disappearance and Noble's affair with Tamar. When they finished, Kit confirmed his identification of Noble as the man in the barbershop.

'Can you stay here with these two?' Luke asked Ross. 'It's a lot for him to take in and I'm not sure Eden can cope on her own.'

Ross was pretty sure Eden could cope with anything anyone could throw at her right now. She, like him, was so pumped that relaxing was not an option. Nevertheless, he was happy to agree to wait until they heard from Luke.

When he called Karenza to say he wouldn't be home until late, she wasn't in the least bit surprised.

They eventually persuaded Kit to go to bed.

Luke called around midnight to tell them the West Mercia Police had apprehended Elaine Noble but that her husband had not been there when they had taken her into custody. He, according to her, was on a two-week walking holiday in west Wales with a couple of retired cronies from the force. She rang him every night to catch up with his progress and to chat about their sons. When she'd rung him from the station in Hereford to tell him a police car would be arriving to take her to Cornwall the next morning, he'd decided to cut his holiday short.

'You mean he's heading back to Hereford?' said Ross.

'I mean, he's coming here. He's volunteered to come in for questioning. He's arriving at eleven o'clock tomorrow morning.'

FORTY

The tension at the station as they waited for Noble to arrive was palpable. At ten to eleven, there was little sound to be heard other than the occasional ringing of a telephone no one intended to answer.

Jake Fairchild stood at the front desk like a barman in a western, waiting for the gunslinger to kick the saloon door in and start shooting.

'Are you sure he said eleven and not high noon?' he said as Luke joined him.

At eleven on the dot, a blue Range Rover drew into the car park and Brett Noble got out.

'We'll caution him here at the desk, Jake, then take him through to the interview room.'

'As you like, so long as I'm not expected to spend more than two minutes with that arrogant asshole.'

Noble sauntered in as if he owned the place. Cool as the proverbial cucumber. He was an imposing man. Tall, thickset and powerful. Though grey-haired and in his mid-fifties, he had presence, and Luke could see only too well how he would have easily intimidated the fourteen-year-old Kit Retallick.

'Hello, Jake, he said, approaching the desk and emptying out his pockets. 'Still here then, I see.'

The words, designed to cut through flesh like a scalpel, were delivered with a wry smile. To his credit, Jake ignored the slight as he loaded Noble's keys and wallet into a plastic bag.

As Luke delivered the caution, you could have heard a pin drop. It stayed that way until Noble was ensconced downstairs. Only then did the building exhale.

Noble swaggered into the interview room, raking over the interior as if re-living past triumphs. 'Same old shithole,' he sneered.

Luke bit his lip.

'You've declined legal representation?'

'I have. Why waste money on lawyers? Bloodsucking parasites. We all know why I'm here. I don't need a phone call or anyone to hold my hand. All I need to know from you is when my wife is arriving. I won't be talking to anyone until I know she's here and she's okay.'

Luke looked at Denise for guidance.

'ETA between one and two pm.'

'Then it's a coffee for me and a copy of the local paper. It would be good to catch up on what's going on these days in the back of beyond. Oh, and a couple of biscuits on the side wouldn't go amiss.'

Luke wanted to thump him.

***

Noble was not the only person eager for Elaine to arrive. Kit had woken at six thirty determined to be at the station to meet her, despite being told by Luke and Ross that was neither possible nor advisable.

Eden had spent a restless night. Nothing could have prepared her for the revelation about Tamar. She'd watched Ross and Luke bat information back and forth, piecing together various scenarios the evening before. There was a competitive element between them she found amusing. Yet, despite all their efforts, by the time the pair left, they were certain of only two things. Brett Noble had framed Kit for the manslaughter of his family and had likely planted evidence with the aim of framing him again, this time for the murder of Graham White. The only explanation they had for the second was to cover the first, and the impetus for the original crime was his illicit relationship with an underage girl. Other than that, the thing had more holes than a string vest.

They still had no solid evidence he'd lit the fire at the farm or any idea why White and Vincent had to die or whether it was Noble who killed them or hired someone to do it for him. All that planning and the viciousness of the crimes had to be more than an extreme measure to land his wife's brother back in jail.

Eventful though the day had been, they all knew if real progress was to be made, it would happen today. Whether they would get answers from Noble remained to be seen. Much as she would have liked to be optimistic, Eden was not convinced her client could be saved.

FORTY-ONE

Denise was taken aback by the resemblance between the woman and her brother. It was not only the physical similarities that struck her, the same dark hair and fine-boned features, but also their mannerisms.

It was clear from the outset Elaine Noble thought she was there to talk about her husband.

'Where's Brett?' she asked as Denise and Rosie walked her to the interview room.

'Your husband's in the cells awaiting interview.'

'In the cells?'

She sounded surprised as if she expected him to be waiting for her in the canteen or in the incident room, telling the rest of them how to do their job.

'Can I see him?'

'Perhaps later, after we've talked. We'll see how things go, shall we?'

Denise did not want to caution Elaine at this stage. Luke had disagreed at first but eventually had seen the logic in letting her continue to believe she was here as a witness to what had happened all those years ago rather than a suspect. They had to accept, given her age and vulnerability at the time, she might herself be a victim. She might not have been given any choice but to go along with her lover. Until they got her side of the story, they could not assume she was a party to any of this.

As soon as they were seated, Denise advised Elaine she was there to help with their enquiries concerning the fire at her family farm; that the interview would be recorded and she had the right to legal representation. Once Denise was certain she understood, she decided to move the conversation away from Brett Noble for the time being and concentrate instead on Kit.

'I've met your brother. You look remarkably alike… apart from the scar, of course.'

The woman raised her hand to her own left cheek.

'It's a shame, really,' said Denise. 'If not for that, he'd be a very handsome young man.'

'How is he?' asked Elaine, her voice thin and wistful.

'How do you think? It's quite a shock learning the sister you're supposed to have murdered is alive and well and married to the detective who put you away for killing her. By the way, what do you prefer to be called, Elaine or Tamar? I like Tamar myself. Elaine sounds old-fashioned for someone your age. Did Brett choose it for you, or did you pick it yourself?'

Elaine looked up, chin quivering.

Denise leaned forward, elbows resting on the desk.

'How did this happen, Elaine? How on earth did you end up here? You weren't the first, and you won't be the last teenager to fall for an older man. God knows I had a terrible crush on Brad Pitt when I was fifteen, and what is he now, almost sixty? You would have grown out of Brett and moved on to someone your own age. You would have gone to uni and had loads of boyfriends before you settled down. Your brother wouldn't have spent most of his adult life in prison, and your mum would still be alive. So, we have to ask, how did it come to this?'

Denise looked up to the ceiling, her hands raised as if expecting divine intervention to provide the answer. When she looked back at Elaine, she could see her eyes brimming with tears.

'It was my fault, not his.'

'You mean Kit?'

'No, Brett. I caused it all. He was just protecting me.'

'Protecting you how? What happened that night?'

Rosie looked at Denise for the cue to caution the woman. Denise shook her head.

'Go on, Elaine.'

'Mum called me from work that night.'

Denise pushed the box of tissues towards her. She took one, blew her nose, straightened in her seat and continued. 'She told me to get myself home and she'd meet me there in half an hour.'

'Did she say why she needed you to do that?'

'No, but I thought it was something to do with the row we'd had earlier with Ray. I'd let slip he was still carrying on with his ex. I thought Mum had finally seen sense and decided to leave him. I thought she had chosen to do it that night when he was flat-out drunk, and she needed my help to get our stuff together and leave before he woke up.'

'How did you feel about that?'

'Over the moon. It was what Kit and I had wanted from the day we arrived in that dump. We'd be safe… Mum would be safe.'

'What happened when you got home?'

'Mum was already there. I expected to see our bags packed, but she was sitting at the kitchen table and she was angry.'

'With Ray?'

'No, with me.'

'Laura, my boss at the newsagents, had told her I was seeing an older man and that it had been going on since I was fifteen. She started shouting as soon as I walked in, wanting to know who this man was and whether we'd had sex and if I'd taken precautions. She went on and on about how she wasn't going to let me ruin my life and how she'd see to it he went to prison once she found out who he was. She woke Ray with all her shouting.'

'Where was Ray?'

'In the sitting room in front of the telly, sleeping it off as usual. He burst in and demanded to know what we were doing there. He told Mum to get back to work and leave him in peace. It was the first time I'd ever been glad to see him. I thought Mum would never say anything with him there; she'd know he'd kick off big time. She'd drop it for now and I'd have time to warn Brett, but I was wrong. She blurted it out, and you could see from Ray's face he was loving every minute of it. As if he'd been proved right about me. That I was the little slut he'd always said I was.'

'What did he do?'

'He went for me. He pushed me down on the chair and stood there looming over me, a big hulk of ugliness demanding to know who the man was and what we'd done together. Disgusting, lewd words spilling from his filthy mouth. I thought he was going to hit me, but looking back, he was enjoying it too much to finish it so soon. I tried to get up, but he pushed me back down. Then Mum stepped in as if she'd suddenly realised what she'd done. She grabbed him and he turned on her. He was shouting in her face, saying it was all down to her… like mother like daughter. He grabbed her by the throat and wrestled her to the ground. I remember his hands, those huge white knuckles around Mum's neck and her legs kicking. I got up from the chair and threw it at him. He didn't even look up. I picked up a frying pan from the draining board, and I hit him hard on the back of the head, twice, three times, I don't know how many. I carried on hitting and hitting him until he let go of her neck and fell on top of her. I rolled him off her and hit him again and again and again, until I couldn't see his ugly face anymore.'

Elaine squirmed in disgust at the memory.

Denise, whose chest felt tight with the effort of keeping silent, finally spoke.

'He was dead?'

Elaine nodded.

'And your mother?'

'I thought at first she had passed out, and I tried to revive her. I lifted her head… felt for a pulse. I tried to pump her chest. I pumped and pumped; you know the way it's done on the telly?' Tears were coursing down Elaine's cheeks now, dripping off her chin as her voice cracked. 'I couldn't face the fact she'd gone.'

'How long were you there alone?'

'I don't know.'

She had a faraway look about her as she wiped away her tears with the back of her hand. 'It seemed like forever. Then I rang Brett. I told him what had happened and he came straight away.'

'What did he do when he saw the bodies?'

'He told me to go back to his place and stay there. He took my phone and told me not to talk to anyone. He said he'd deal with it.'

'What did you think he meant by that?'

Elaine shrugged.

'When did you first hear about the fire?'

'He told me when he got home in the early hours of the morning.'

Denise glanced at Rosie.

'Let's end this here for the time being,' she said. 'Elaine, are you willing to give a written statement detailing exactly what you've told us?'

Elaine looked drained.

'Can I have a minute?'

'Of course. Rosie is going to caution you now and will help you write your statement up for signature. Before you do that, I'm obliged to advise you again of your right to legal advice. Do you want a solicitor present?'

'No, it's time the truth came out. You need to know this wasn't Brett's fault. This was all me. All he ever did was love me.'

Rosie followed Denise to the door. 'What if she changes her mind? None of this is admissible? She's committed murder and she could get away with it because we failed to follow procedure.'

'She won't change her mind. She's doing this to protect her husband the way he protected her back then. She's sacrificing herself for him, not knowing what he really is. It just goes to show love really is blind.'

FORTY-TWO

When Denise broke the news to Luke about Elaine Noble's confession, he could have kissed her. He made do with a friendly pat on the back.

'She told you everything?'

'Up to the point when Brett took over, but yeah, she confirmed she killed Ray Polglaze in an attempt to save her mother. I don't think it will take much to get her to confirm Brett lit the fire to cover it up.'

'That might not be necessary. Armed with what she's told you, I might get it from the horse's mouth.'

'You think he'll fess up to it that easily?'

'I think he'll be completely thrown when I tell him his wife has confessed to murder. Well done, Denise, this is really great work.'

'To be honest, she was ready to tell her story. I didn't have to work that hard.'

'Nevertheless, it's our inroad to getting something more from him, and it was a brilliant idea to lie about what time she'd get here. You fooled me, that's for certain. We'll stick to the timeline we've given him. He's expecting Elaine to arrive between one and two. We'll let him stew until half past. He won't have a clue we've had the time to interview her already until I drop the bombshell.'

'Do you want me to call Eden with an update? You know she'll have a hard job stopping Retallick from coming in. If I can tell her we're making progress, she might be able to persuade him to hold fast for another hour or two.'

'Okay, but don't give away too much. We don't want to get

her hopes up yet. Until Noble confesses to lighting the fire and framing the boy, her client is still a guilty man.'

***

Noble folded the newspaper neatly and placed it on the table in front of him as Luke entered the room.

'Good to see you've made the front page, Inspector, even if it is for all the wrong reasons. They don't think much of your detecting skills, do they?'

'I'm hoping to rectify that sooner than they think,' said Luke.

'Optimism, in the face of adversity, that's what I like to see, that good old British fighting spirit. Keep calm and carry on.'

Luke checked himself. He refused to let this prick get to him.

'Has my wife arrived yet?'

'She has.'

'Where is she?'

'Having coffee, I believe.'

'Is she okay? This would have been very stressful for her. That lot in Hereford had better not have upset her. I might be retired, but I still have influence where it counts there.'

Not here, though, thought Luke. *Here you answer to me.*

'Did she look pale? She has a tendency towards anaemia. She gets very tired if she doesn't eat regular meals or take her iron tablets.'

Luke hesitated as if re-examining her appearance from memory.

'I have to say, she looked much better after she unburdened herself.'

'What do you mean unburdened herself?' Noble asked.

'What I said. You're right; when she turned up, she looked tired and drawn, but after she confessed, she seemed much better. I suppose that's what happens when you clear your conscience.'

The smugness slipped from Noble's face. 'Confessed to what?'

'The murder of Ray Polglaze.'

'You're bluffing. You haven't had time to interview her, let alone get a confession.'

'You mean like this one?' Luke said, pulling a copy of Elaine Noble's signed statement from his file. 'Take a look if you don't believe me.'

He slipped the piece of paper across the desk to Noble.

'But you said she'd be arriving between one and two. She's only just got here.'

'That's my DS for you. She's a brilliant detective, but as for timekeeping…'

'You lied,' spat Noble, his face twisting with rage and frustration.

'I know, it's terrible, isn't it?' said Luke, grinning. 'Now, how about we cut the crap. We have half the story. How about you tell us the rest?' We know you lit the fire to cover up what your girlfriend did to her stepfather. Kit Retallick didn't light that fire. You lied about the Molotov cocktails. I'm amazed how anyone believed that shit. This is Cornwall, not bloody Beirut. You framed that poor boy so you and his sister could start a new life and live happily ever after.'

'And why shouldn't we? We'd done nothing wrong. It was all in the filthy minds of other people like that interfering bitch Tamar worked for. If she had kept her mouth shut, none of this would have happened. She, like the rest of them, thought the worst, whereas the truth was, I never had sex with her, not fully, until much later.'

'That may be so, but who will believe you? You've read the local paper. Not much happens down here to get them excited, but they'll have a field day with this. The nationals will pick it up, and things will only get worse when the trial starts. You and I know it will go on for months, and your boys will suffer the gory details every day on the news. They're at the right age to be targeted on social media, and I doubt they'll make it into the force with their background. A murderess for a mother, a bent, paedophile copper for a dad. It doesn't bode well. Of course, if you plead guilty, there'll be less fuss. The press will lose interest sooner, and of course, you wouldn't be wasting any more valuable police time.'

Noble banged his fists down on the table. 'Shut your fucking mouth. I want to see my wife… I want to see her now. You won't get another word out of me until I see Elaine.'

FORTY-THREE

After some discussion and the laying down of a few ground rules, namely that Denise and Rosie would remain in the room throughout, Noble got his wish.

The minute Elaine walked through the door, his demeanour changed. His thunderous rage was replaced with sky-blue tenderness. The couple clung to each other for a long time without saying a single word before Noble, holding his wife at arm's length, asked, 'Are the boys alright?'

'They're fine. They have no idea about this. They're with your sister. She drove down overnight. She's taken them back to Essex with her.'

Denise couldn't imagine Noble with a sister. She didn't know why. Maybe it was because he exuded the archetypal traits of an only child: self-confidence, ambition and independence. She knew these because she was an only child herself and had looked them up more than once. She wondered whether he was as close to his sister as Kit and Tamar Retallick had once been.

Eventually, the couple pulled apart. Noble dragged two chairs together, and they sat, eyes fixed on each other as if they were the only ones in the room.

'I know you've confessed. I've read your statement. Did they advise you could have a solicitor present? Did they caution you before the interview? If they didn't, they're in breach of PACE, and everything you've said is inadmissible. You can retract it, my love… you made it under duress.'

Rosie glared at Denise. Denise knew she hadn't followed procedure. It had got results, but just as Rosie had warned, the whole thing could fall apart if the woman followed her husband's advice. Denise could feel sweat gathering on her back and under her collar.

'Brett, I know my rights. How could I have lived with you for all these years and not know them?' Elaine smiled, reaching out to touch her husband's hand. I needed to tell the truth. I've needed to do it for a very long time. Now you need to do the same for my brother's sake. I can't live with what we did to him anymore. I won't live with guilt and regret for the rest of my life. If you don't tell them everything, I will.'

'You know what it will mean, don't you?'

'I do, but I'm prepared to face it. We've had a wonderful life together. We have two incredible boys, but it's been at a terrible cost. I thought I could deal with it, knowing Kit was out of prison, but somehow, it's made it worse. I long to see him, but how can I look him in the eye, knowing what we've done to him? This has hung over us for too long. It's time to free ourselves of it.'

Noble looked deflated as his head bent towards hers. 'You don't know everything I've done… terrible… terrible things, to keep you safe… to stop the truth coming out. I can't bear the thought you'll hate me when you know what I've done.'

'I could never hate you. You saved me, Brett. No matter what you've done, I will always be there for you, just as I know you will always be there for me.' She looked around the room. 'None of this matters, not this place or these people. None of this is real. The only thing that matters… the only thing that's real is you and me.'

Denise would have found it touching had it not been so sickening.

FORTY-FOUR

Luke let Noble regain his composure before he began the formal interview, and by the time Denise turned on the recorder, he was ready to talk.

'You have to understand I didn't set out to frame the boy. I didn't set out to do any of it. I just needed to cover up what Tamar had done. People were dead. Nothing I could do could change that, but I could save her. I was in a panic. I knew if the police interviewed her, she'd go to pieces and tell them about us. She'd have no choice if she intended to argue self-defence. They'd want to know what started the row, and as soon as my name came up, and it would, I'd be suspended. Any chance I had of controlling the investigation would go out the window. It would all come out: the nosey newsagent's call and her mother summoning her to the farm to have it out with her. The Tremlett woman would tell them how long our affair had been going on. I'd lose my job and go to prison. I'd be labelled a sex offender, a nonce. We all know what happens to them inside. It was unthinkable.'

Noble took a sip of water.

'I was sweating like a pig. There was an old oil fire in the room. I tried to turn it off. It was too hot to think. Then it came to me, the way things do sometimes when the adrenaline's pumping and your brain is firing on all cylinders. If I kicked the fire over and set the place alight, there would be no evidence, and the boy would get the blame. It seemed the obvious solution.'

'Where did you think he was?'

'In his room asleep. The way I saw it. He'd die of smoke

inhalation without waking up, and what would he have left to live for?'

'So, you set the fire, planning to kill him and, in the process, destroy the crime scene.'

It was the first time Noble looked ashamed as if Luke had insulted his professional integrity.

'It was all for Tamar. She had to be seen to have had nothing to do with it. She had to be able to keep to her story.'

'Which was?'

'She went to a party in St. Ives, stayed overnight with friends and the first she heard of the fire was the next morning. I knew if I could make sure I was the one who interviewed her, I could pretend I'd corroborated her story. She was off to uni soon. Once she was out of the county, people would forget about her. There was no reason for her to ever come back. I would get a transfer, and we could be together.'

'So what changed?'

'She turned up.'

'Who?'

'Shona Bryant, Ray's girlfriend. He must have called her earlier. I suppose the pair thought Lilah was working. I'd slipped out back to get more fuel. I needed the place to go up quickly, like a tinder box, before the boy woke. I remembered Tamar had told me Ray broke all the rules, keeping flammable chemicals in an unlocked shed close to the house. She'd said the fumes drifted into her bedroom sometimes and gave her a headache. Shona must have let herself in. She was there in the kitchen, crouched over Ray's body when I got back. I thought, at first, she was Tamar. She had the same long dark hair. I was about to tell her to do what I'd told her and go back to the flat when she turned, and I saw it was Shona. As soon as she saw me, she started to scream. She was hysterical. I thought she'd wake the boy. I grabbed her. I had to shut her up, but she was strong. She was scratching at my face and neck. I couldn't risk marks all over my face. I thumped her, and once she was out cold, I held a cushion over her face. She came around once, for just a second, then went limp. Don't you see I had no choice?'

'We all have a choice,' said Luke from behind gritted teeth. 'What then?'

'I set the fire and left.'

'When did you realise Kit wasn't in the house?'

'Once I was outside. I needed to wait long enough to be sure the flames had caught. I needn't have worried. The place went up in seconds. I was looking around, trying to see if I could take a different route out of the place that wouldn't involve me walking back down the lane to the road where I might be spotted when I noticed a light on in the barn. I ran up there and found the boy asleep. I knew I didn't have time to drag him back to the farmhouse. The place was already ablaze and someone would report it soon. Smoke was already billowing towards the village, and the damn dog was barking. I'd forgotten about the dog. I think that's what woke the boy, the bloody dog howling. I couldn't stop Kit once he woke and smelt the fire. He was drunk and ranting. He got up and raced down to the farm. He kept shouting about the dog. I couldn't understand. What kind of kid worries about a dog when his family are burning to death?'

The kind who believes his family aren't anywhere near the place, thought Luke.

'I caught up with him and managed to stop him running into the house, but not before the debris from the porch fell on him and burnt his face. Then I heard the sirens and saw the fire engines coming up the lane.'

'How did you explain your presence to the fire crew?'

'I didn't need to. They didn't ask. I showed them my warrant card, and they assumed I'd been called to the scene. I had the boy in custody by then. I told them he was known to me and that I had arrested him on suspicion of lighting the fire. He was carted off to the ambulance to be treated for his burns. The fire was raging. They could tell by the colour of the smoke there were chemicals inside. The scene was volatile, given all the stuff around the back. Some of the canisters in the shed had already exploded. It was too risky for them to enter the building, and in any event, they were certain anyone inside was already dead. There was nothing they could do but secure the perimeter and wait for it to burn itself out. I remember it was so damn hot you couldn't get anywhere near it. You could feel your skin bubbling, like crackling on the Sunday joint.'

Luke did his best to dispel the image.

'How did you manipulate the evidence?'

'That was the easy part. The boy had already done half the job for me. He was drunk and susceptible to suggestion. I found his shirt and the kerosene in the barn. The very fact he was there and not in bed was suspicious. If I didn't know better, I would have thought he did it. It was no surprise, given his history, everyone else did.'

'What did you tell Tamar when you got back to the flat?'

'The truth.'

'Come on... you can't expect us to believe she agreed to frame her little brother for this?'

'What choice did she have? She thought she'd killed a man. Her mother was dead. I admitted I'd had to kill Shona. After some persuasion, she could see that Shona turning up could be a blessing in disguise. I was confident there was no way any DNA evidence would survive that fire and that if they did find three bodies, they would assume one was hers. We had a chance to move on. Of course, I was right. That's exactly the conclusion they reached when she didn't turn up the next day.'

Luke had read the report. The forensics team had ascertained there was not enough autosomal DNA left to identify the victims, and the assumption had been made the burnt remains belonged to Ray, Tamar and her mother. These days, of course, they could find enough material in the ash to carry out an analysis, but back then, it was a different matter.

'I hid her in my flat for two weeks before moving her to a place I rented in Plymouth. She was in a state. I needed to keep her close. At first, she wavered all the time and was all for telling the truth until I told her what would happen to us. We would go to jail and Kit would be put in care. She already knew my views on Kit, that he had problems and without any support, they'd only get worse. I did my best to persuade her he'd be okay. Unlike her, he wouldn't be tried as an adult. That wherever he was sent, it wouldn't be like prison. He'd get therapy and an education, whereas in care, a fourteen-year-old boy with behavioural problems was unlikely to be fostered and would slip through the net. With her in prison and his mother dead, what chance would he have?'

'So, you eventually convinced her to go along with the story?'

'Yes, but I still sensed resistance and was worried she'd change her mind once the trial started. There was always the sneaking suspicion she didn't trust my opinion of her brother. That's why I needed Vincent and White. I had to be sure she believed me, and for her to be certain, she had to hear it from someone other than me.

'I needed their testimony to back me up. White was easy; he didn't like the boy. I sensed that the day I was called to the school after Kit lit the fire. A kid like him brought down the tone. It was all about how things looked to White, and there was the other thing, of course.'

'What other thing?'

'Let's say Mr White wasn't the pillar of respectability he claimed to be.'

'In what way?'

'I found out by chance. I needed to know more about Shona Bryant. I had to know if she'd be missed… whether anyone was likely to kick up a stink about her having disappeared. As it happened, she had a record for soliciting and guess who came up as one of her punters? Graham White. He'd been let off with a warning, but nevertheless, if it came out, I'm not sure the local authority or the PTA would be pleased to have a man like him in charge of their children's education. He was married with a daughter. He had a lot to lose, and he'd been caught with his pants down, or rather his flies open and Shona Bryant's head in his lap.'

'And Vincent?'

Noble stretched his arms above his head and yawned.

'I'm tired. I'm not saying anything else until I get some sleep.'

Denise turned off the tape. When Noble was certain he wasn't being recorded, he spoke again.

'If you want me to talk more about White and Vincent, I'll need some guarantees.'

'Guarantees about what?'

'That you leave my wife out of this.'

'You know I can't promise to do that. She killed a man and perverted the course of justice.'

'She was seventeen, for Christ's sake.'

Luke wanted to point out he hadn't afforded Kit any mercy despite his age.

'My evidence will be Ray was still alive when I got there. Unconscious but alive. I'll say it was me who finished him off and forced her to go along with the story, and you can whistle for a conviction on Vincent and White. You've got nothing on me as far as they're concerned. On the other hand, if you do this deal, I'll tell you everything.'

'We've got the hat you planted.'

'Noble laughed. 'Good luck with that. Pure conjecture. It

leads to Kit, not to me. You won't find any of my DNA on either of them. You won't find my DNA anywhere. If you really want to hear what happened to that pair and get yourself a conviction, you give me that guarantee. I won't settle for a maybe or a promise. I want it on the record and sanctioned from the top. Without that, you'll get nothing more from me.'

FORTY-FIVE

It took Luke the rest of the day and a fair part of the next to secure a piece of paper signed by the DPP confirming the Crown Prosecution Service could grant immunity to Elaine Noble. Brett Noble had woken in the middle of the night demanding they ensure that the notice contained both her real name and her alias; such was his mistrust of the system he had championed all his working life. Once he had eaten breakfast and been allowed to call his solicitor to confirm the document was valid, he was ready to talk.

'It's tempting to think in black and white, don't you think? To believe there are two types of men, good or bad, but there's a third type, the weak. Don't get me wrong, weak men have their uses. They're easy to bend, easy to threaten, but you can never trust them. They are instinctively disloyal creatures. White and Vincent were weak men. Different kinds of weakness, of course, but the same in many ways. White was willing to be led by the nose as long as he could see an advantage for himself. Vincent, the liberal do-gooder, afraid of being seen for the cowardly fraud he really was. Had they been good men, they would never have allowed themselves to be compromised in the first place. Had they been bad men, I could have relied on their silence. Now, all these years later, their weakness has come home to haunt them.'

'How did you get them to meet you?'

'We'd kept in touch. It wasn't difficult to convince them. Vincent, full of remorse, wanted reassurance he had done his best. White, as usual, worried for his own neck. Both were looking to me to protect them from whatever punishment the boy intended to dole out now he was free and looking for justice. It was easy reeling them in. Although it wasn't until I found out Kit's release date and he was travelling down on the evening of the Festival of Lights that the pieces slotted together. Serendipity, that's what they call it, isn't it, when things come together so perfectly by chance?'

It was clear to Luke this man's ego would keep him talking. He decided not to interrupt more than absolutely necessary with questions. He had a feeling if he gave him enough rope, he'd hang himself without any prompting.

'I met Vincent in the County Arms that afternoon. He hadn't changed much. The shitty corduroy jacket with leather patches on the elbows had gone, and the hair was shorter, but he still had the look of a social worker. If you've had any involvement with the system, you know that look. The pained expression saying *I really care,* when in fact, they're wondering *which one of the sorry sad bastards on my list is this? Is this the kid with the alcoholic mother or the one whose uncle felt him up?* I slipped the drugs into his drink?'

'You used ketamine?'

'Yeah, it's quick, especially if you're not a user.'

'What did you talk about?' asked Luke.

'Vincent was a whiner,' Noble continued. 'You know the type. In this game, you come across them all the time. He started by saying he'd tried several times to write to the boy when he was inside but had never been able to get it right and ended up burning all the letters. He said he'd carried the guilt with him but felt he would be able to move on if he could only meet and apologise in person, and could I arrange it?'

'What was your response?' asked Luke.

"Apologise for what?" I said, "You were just doing your job. It wasn't your fault the stepfather would never let you in when you called."

"I know," he said, "but I should have told someone about

the problems I was having. I should have admitted I was too scared to go around there. I should have asked for help from someone more senior."

'I told him not to beat himself up. Anyone would have been scared of that gorilla. What with him and that bloody dog he kept. That dog would have had your leg off if Polglaze ordered it to go for you.'

"As soon as you opened the farm gate, it was there," he said.

'Do you know his eyes were fixed and glassy when he said that as if the scruffy mutt was still on his trail? I patted him on the back. A bit of reassurance goes a long way with his type, as you know.'

Luke resented Noble trying to cast him in the same mould as himself. He was nothing like this man. They had the badge in common, but that was it.

'I told him he was new to the job, and with all those other cases to deal with and not enough time to go around, anyone would have struggled. I reassured him at least he'd tried. He'd turned up... what two or three times at the farm, and given the last time, the week before the fire, Ray had pointed a shotgun at him, he'd done his best.'

"He threatened to blow my brains out if I showed my face around there again," he whinged.

"What were you supposed to do when faced with that sort of behaviour?" I said. "It wasn't as if the boy was prepared to help. You tried talking to him at school after he set that first fire, but he'd never say a thing. He wouldn't help himself despite all the opportunities you gave him. You did your best. You pieced the case together from what little you had. I get it, but I'm not sure the authorities would see it that way. You know what the current climate is like. Investigations into this and that, scrutinising what people in positions of power did and didn't do years ago with no regard to what it was like back when the thing happened, no idea of context. No one is safe these days. The fact you falsified the records… they would take a dim view of that. Unfair, I know, but there it is."

'He buckled when I said that, his Adam's apple bobbing as he grabbed the bar like he might topple. I told him he couldn't meet his wife in the state he was in. I said I'd give him a lift home. I told him to get in the back seat because I had my costume for the parade on the passenger seat. The back windows of the Range Rover are blacked out, you see. By the time I'd hit the roundabout into town he was sparked out.'

'What time was this?'

'Around four thirty. I parked up under the viaduct around the back of an old, abandoned garage off St. George's Road and left him there while I went to meet White. I'd told him I'd meet him at the bandstand in the gardens behind the court building. I used to walk through there sometimes when I was on the job. I arrested a couple of blokes for gross indecency once. It's peaceful, and I've always loved brass bands. Orchestras are for toffs in my book, but your brass band, that's music for the common man. The man who gets his hands dirty. It was getting dark by the time White got there. I watched him arriving from a distance. His hair grey, portlier than I remembered. He had to hold the railings to haul himself up the steps. I guessed that might be something to do with his heart condition. I knew he'd had a pacemaker fitted just before he retired. He was dressed smartly, though, just like always, navy sports jacket, white shirt, old school tie. A picture of respectability on the outside. I'd barely sat down when he started questioning me like I was one of his bloody school kids.'

Noble mimicked White, putting on a plummy, supercilious accent.

"What are we going to do about this?"

'*We*, I thought, *we* aren't going to do anything. You'll leave the dirty work to me as per bloody usual.'

"I really don't need all this dragged up again at my age," he said. "I can't believe they've let him out before he's served his sentence. They must realise he'll do it again. They must know he's dangerous."

"Apparently, he's reformed," I said, enjoying every minute of the old sod's discomfort.

"But you said on the phone you'd heard from your sources inside that he's looking to come after the people who had put him away, and I'm on that list. Can't you threaten him, tell him to leave me alone? Perhaps advise him to leave the county and start up somewhere new?"

'He was absolutely serious when he asked me that. I told him I could, but it was risky. He might run to the police, and I was sure he wouldn't want that.'

"So, what are we going to do? I have a reputation to protect. I have a daughter and grandchildren to think of," he said, his face all red and sweaty. That's when I offered him a swig of whiskey to calm his nerves. He knocked back the lot. I had to prize the flask out of his sticky, fat fingers.'

"Don't worry about a thing," I said. "Retallick arrives this evening, and I'll meet him at the station. I'll let him know he's not wanted here. I'll give him cash to turn around and go back the way he came."

'He thanked me, but his words were slurred. I could tell the drug was working when he lifted his hand to loosen his collar. I suggested he take off his jacket and tie. He tried to get up but immediately fell back into his seat. I offered to help him. By now, his hands were like two wet fish in his lap, his shirt gaping, showing off his flabby white gut. It was easy from there on in swapping the clothes with the ones in my bag, then fixing cuffs round his wrists and ankles.'

'And the fire?' asked Luke.

'I took the thermos from my bag and poured the petrol over his feet and hands. The flames caught quickly. He moaned and twitched a bit as the fire licked at his ankles and fingers, but not much considering. Then again, the fire was never meant to kill him. The drugs would do that job well enough with his heart condition. The old git must have been tougher than I thought. I tell you straight, when I looked back at him silhouetted in that bandstand, hands and feet aglow like beacons, I never thought he'd make it to hospital.'

Luke's stomach heaved.

'Was it really necessary to kill him… and in the way you did?'

'You had to think it was Retallick… it had to be obvious. What was I meant to do, run him over with my car? Scare him into having a heart attack? What good would that have done? The finger wouldn't have pointed at Kit. I'd kept tabs on the boy over the years to make sure he was okay. I do have some conscience, you know, despite what you think. I wanted him to be safe, and I was pleased he'd got an education like I said he would. I was able to tell Elaine, and it made her feel better about the whole thing, almost like we'd been justified, but then, when I heard he was going to be out on licence and the word was he was looking to re-open his case, I got worried. I didn't want him sniffing around. When I heard he'd tracked down a lawyer, I knew I had to stop this before it began. Elaine had started saying she'd like to see him, not meet him, of course, but see him at a distance. I couldn't have that either. It was all too risky, and the only solution was to rid myself of the two men who could cast doubt on the conviction and pin it on Kit. He'd be back inside for the rest of his life. Job done.'

'And the change of clothes, what was all that about?'

'The same thing. It was the sort of stunt a nutter would pull, and it gave me a means to plant evidence. The mask was an impulse buy… an afterthought but a nice touch, don't you think? A traitor's mask for a traitor? It tickled me when I thought of the tat I'd picked to dress him in. I wanted him to look like the shabby, rancid old fucker he really was.'

Luke remembered DC Rosie Bray's comments at the beginning of the investigation. She'd been right. Noble was making a point when he dressed White in those clothes. Luke needed a break. He was having difficulty being in the same room as this man.

'I think we should take a comfort break here.'

Denise paused the tape.

***

'Jesus Christ,' said Luke, once he and Denise left the room. 'Can you believe the arrogance? He's actually bragging about what he's done.'

'He was so different with his wife before, so gentle and considerate. You wouldn't think it was the same man.'

'I don't mind telling you, I'm having difficulty keeping it together in there. I want to jump over that bloody desk and punch the sick bastard.'

'He wouldn't take any notice if you did. In fact, he'd revel in it. He's a raving narcissist and craves control. Unpalatable as it is, we have to give it to him. We'll get our confession but on his terms. We can live with that, surely?'

Luke took a deep breath. 'It's because he's police, and you and I know what he's done will reflect on the whole force. We've seen it too many times lately. The public are losing confidence. He's not a minor player, either. The trust that officers like him destroy takes years to rebuild.'

'Have a coffee, take a walk, and when we go in again, remember not only are you on the brink of righting a terrible injustice, you're about to nail a serial killer.'

Luke smiled but knew it was a hollow sort of justice.

FORTY-SIX

'Okay, let's get this over with,' said Luke

Noble glanced up as they walked in. Despite the numbers stacking up, he didn't look like a serial killer. He looked like someone's grandad or the bloke from the Rotary Club, but Luke and Denise both knew what he was. He could dress it up any way he liked. He could pretend he'd done it all for love, but they knew from the way he'd told the story that he'd taken a perverse pleasure in everything he'd done. He was a man who enjoyed power, and what greater power trip was there than taking another's life?

Denise re-convened the interview.

'Tell us about Vincent,' said Luke.

'He was where I'd left him when I got back, laid out fast asleep in the back of the Range Rover. I chucked White's clothes in the boot and retrieved the masks.'

'You wore a mask too?'

'Of course, why wouldn't I? If I hadn't, someone might have identified me on CCTV.'

He looked at Luke as if he was stupid to think otherwise.

'Vincent was groggy when I woke him, and for a second, I was worried I'd been a tad heavy-handed with the ketamine. The man needed to be able to stand up at the very least. To my relief, he came around when I waved the smelling salts under his nose. I needed him to be with it enough to sit up for me to put the wire frame squarely on his shoulders.'

'Didn't anyone see you?' said Luke.

'No one gave us a second glance. What with the noise of the crowd and the parade, we looked like participants. I half carried him back along St. George's Road, masks lit up. They cost a bit, but I suppose there's a lot of hard work goes into making them. Ingenious, really, how they're able to get the features out of nothing more than paper and glue. The most difficult part was the waiting. I needed to time it just right. The more commotion I created, the easier it would be for me to slip away. I waited until I reckoned the first of the procession had reached the pyre at the park, then I set the sparks flying. A squirt of lighter fuel and the mask went up. He just stood there. I thought for a moment he might collapse where he stood, but then the adrenaline cut in. The paper burned away in no time, leaving the wire frame on his shoulders glowing red- then white-hot and his clothes caught. He ran. I could guess the rest. No point hanging around. I legged it back to the car. I got out through Hendra before the police arrived and put up the roadblocks.'

Luke thought of Flora and the way she'd spoken about the man on fire at the dinner table, so matter of fact. The difference was she was a child. This man was an abomination.

***

As they walked Noble back to the front desk to be charged, every single officer lining the corridor turned their back on him and faced the wall in a physical display of disrespect. Only Jake Fairchild met his eye as he read the charges. He did not smile or engage in conversation with his old colleague, and when he'd finished, he, too, turned his back on him as if he were not worth his contempt.

FORTY-SEVEN

It fell to Eden to break the news to Kit that his sister had been in cahoots with Noble all along.

At first, he refused to believe it. 'She wouldn't do that. He made her. I know he did.'

'She was only a kid herself. She thought she was doing the right thing by you. Noble had convinced her you needed help.'

Eden defended the girl not because she believed Elaine Noble to be innocent in all this but because Kit needed to believe it. He was desperate to see his sister. Up until the point Noble was charged with the three counts of murder, it had been impossible. Only after his confession did they get the go-ahead.

He'd asked Eden if she could be with him when he met her for the first time. They knew by then Elaine would not face charges. Luke had told her about the deal they'd struck with Noble to secure her freedom. She was heading back to Hereford that afternoon. The station had thrown in a free ride in a squad car. Denise arranged to drive her to Eden's place on the way.

Kit had not been able to settle all morning. Eventually, she'd persuaded him to go for a walk on the beach. He'd arrived back sand-blasted and cold but no calmer. As soon as brother and sister fell into each other's arms, however, the years seemed to melt away.

Eden swallowed the lump growing in her throat. 'Denise and I will give you some privacy. We'll be in the kitchen if you need us.'

Kit stared at this woman, who looked so much like his mother. The same mouth, the same caramel-coloured eyes and when she spoke, the same Cornish lilt to her voice.

'I'm so sorry, Kit. I knew nothing about the two men. I had no idea Brett could do such a thing.'

'I know none of this is your fault. It was him, that man.'

'Kit…'

'He groomed you… raped you. He was a grown man. You were a child, but don't worry, it's over now, Tamar. We can be together again. You can forget he ever existed.'

She edged away from him. 'Please don't call me that. My name's Elaine, and I don't want to forget him. I love him.'

'What?'

'I love him, Kit. I always have. We have two sons together. We can't pretend none of this ever happened. I can't forget the last seventeen years.'

'But what about me?'

Tamar reached out and touched Kit's face. 'I never stopped thinking about you, not for a single day, but I can't be responsible for you. You're a grown man. Neither of us are the people we were then. We're strangers. I have my own family to think about.'

Kit's stomach roiled. He had imagined they would be together; that was how they'd get through this. He'd imagined meeting his nephews. They weren't to blame; they were innocent bystanders. They would need a father figure now Noble was in jail.

Tamar sobbed, 'I need him, Kit. I don't know how I'll cope without him,' she said, turning her face away from him.

He grabbed her arm. 'You'll have me.'

She looked him straight in the eye. 'I don't want you… I want him.' It was as if she had plunged a knife into his wretched heart.

EPILOGUE

Kit was in the office building shelves in the basement. He'd already fitted the new window. It was the perfect space for Molly's new office after she qualified.

She finished her training contract at the end of the month, and unsurprisingly Eden had decided to take her on full-time as an assistant solicitor. It was she who had prepared the paperwork for Kit's application to the Court of Appeal to quash his conviction and who was in the midst of finalising his compensation claim for submission to the Justice Secretary.

Agnes had just delivered a cup of tea to Eden and advised her that when he'd finished downstairs, Kit had promised to build her a gazebo in her back garden. Needless to say her opinion of Kit Retallick had drastically changed. Eden thought it must be a huge relief for her secretary. She had always trusted Douglas Bassett's judgment until Kit's case. It would be a comfort for her to know he had been right about the boy all along and that in doing what he'd asked of her and saving the files from destruction, she had, in a roundabout way, proved it. He could now be re-instated to his rightful position of legal superstar in her memory.

Luke arrived with Flora later that morning, having just returned from seeing Thea and Rafi off. Eden's mother and father had been relieved when Thea broke the news they had decided to go on a couples retreat in an attempt to re-kindle their flagging relationship and then move back to Scotland. Thea's newfound obsession with cooking had left the kitchen dishevelled, her mother mystified and her father bereft. Eden remained out of pocket with no mention of when her loan might be paid back, but all in all, it seemed a fair price to pay.

Luke had started to find a life-work balance. How long he could maintain the equilibrium was another matter, but he was doing his best to spend time with his daughter, and their relationship could only improve now that Thea was out of the picture. He even met up with Ross occasionally for the odd pint.

The solving of the murders had been a significant feather in Luke's cap, a feather he acknowledged he would never have plucked without Ross's help. With the approval of his superiors, he had gone back to Ross with an offer to come back to the force shortly after.

Whilst the offer was graciously received, it had been declined. Ross had plans of his own. In fact, he'd rung Eden that very morning to say he was off to Bristol to collect an old friend of theirs, Claire McBride. Claire had been a lawyer until she had been charged with falsifying a will. There had been extenuating circumstances, and, in the round, no one had been harmed, leastwise not by her. Nevertheless, she had been struck off and, with no chance of practising law again, was looking for a new job, and Ross had one lined up.

He saw Claire as a valuable addition to his new PI business, and Eden had to admit they would make an excellent team. She was sure she'd call upon their services regularly.

'Are you here for a reason?' she asked Luke. 'Or have you just brought this one for a tickle?' She grabbed Flora, tickling the little girl until she wriggled and squealed.

'I hear you used to represent someone called Gloria la Grice.'

Eden wondered where this was going.

'Yes,' she said tentatively, 'why?'

'She's just been arrested.'

'Not again, what's she stolen this time?'

'She's not stolen anything, although I'm told there's a regular Aladdin's cave in her living room. You remember that trafficking case we were sent from Bristol that I couldn't handle because I was busy with the murder inquiries? Well, the NCA became involved.'

'What's that got to do with Gloria?'

'They found the girls in her house holed up on the first floor.'

Eden released Flora.

'What?'

'They're perfectly fine. They've been well looked after. They were kept warm and were especially well-fed. Apparently, Gloria's what they call a feeder.'

Eden thought back to her conversation with Ross.

'There was quite a tussle when they tried to arrest her. The women all piled in to protect her, said Luke. 'They needn't have worried. The old dear fought like a tiger.'

'I bet she did,' said Eden, thinking about Gloria's shopping sprees. The tampons, the lipsticks, the carefully chosen tights, and not to mention the dapper chauffeur in the blue BMW.

'Don't tell me she's asked for me?'

'No, she's got a solicitor lined up. A bigger fish than you, apparently, paid for by a wealthy *friend*. They've taken her back to Bristol to be interviewed. You've been sacked.'

'Thank god for small mercies,' said Eden.

'Hang on… you don't get off so lightly.'

Eden couldn't read the huge grin pasted across his face.

'She gave your name as someone who might be willing to look after her cats.'

'She what… well, I'm afraid that's impossible, I'm allergic.'

'Since when?' Luke laughed.

'Since right now.'

'Eden, do you think you could come and check the shelving is as you want it?'

It was Kit calling from the basement stairs.

'I have to go,' Eden said, pleased to end this particular

conversation. 'He wants to finish today. He's got loads of work lined up. He was so lucky to sell the cottage quickly. His new place is perfect for his business.'

'Okay, we'll catch up with you later,' he said with a wide smile. She was glad they were friends again.

Kit had bought a smallholding just outside St. Agnes near to Eden's parents. It had a workshop and woodshed, and he seemed happy there. It had taken him a while to deal with Tamar's rejection. She had wounded him, and for a couple of months, Eden had worried he might not recover. Molly had helped. She needed his input to build his case. She was scrupulous in monitoring his moods and letting Eden know when he was particularly down. Little by little, he had rallied. He'd put on weight and looked better for it, and most impressive of all, he'd learned to drive. He had gained his independence and his self-esteem.

The shelving looked great, as did the rest of the room, and Molly was thrilled with the results.

'It looks wonderful, Kit,' said Eden.

She ran her hand along the length of the smooth-edged oak shelving. When she came to the far end, she paused as she felt an indentation, barely noticeable but definitely there.

'I've signed it,' he said.

'For posterity,' Agnes chipped in.

Eden remembered Kit's initials carved into Douglas Bassett's desk.

All Kit had ever wanted was to be heard. He had carved his name back then to prove he existed in a world that didn't care about a skinny kid with attitude. She hoped he knew he had value and that the carving of his name this time symbolised something else: pride. Pride in his work and in the man, despite all the odds, he had become.

***

Kit loaded his tools into his van. He had plans that evening and was eager to get home.

Home. Such a small word with so many meanings. For most, he imagined it meant a haven... a safe place. Home had never been a safe place for him. The farm certainly wasn't safe, nor prison or the spell he'd spent at his nan's cottage when he'd got out. He had a hint of it when he stayed in the gypsy caravan at Eden's parents' place until the police arrived, but that hardly counted. Now, for the first time ever, home felt like a safe place.

Eden had worried he might choose a place somewhere isolated. He imagined she'd thought he'd put up barricades and become like Ray, reclusive and suspicious of strangers. He was pretty sure it was why she'd got her estate agent friend to point him in the direction of the smallholding near her parents' house so she could keep an eye on him. Perhaps she'd been worried he might do something silly. What a strange phrase that was. It conjured images of party pranks and circus clowns, whereas he knew from bitter experience there was nothing remotely amusing about trying to end your life. She needn't have worried, though. All that was in the past.

She had dealt with her concerns by forcing him to be sociable. Though perfectly capable themselves, Eden's parents had asked him if he would mind walking Castro every day. They said the dog had taken a shine to him and needed exercise. He found it hard to say no, even though he knew they saw it as a means for him to meet people and that the lazy dog would far rather spend time sniffing around their garden than running on the beach. The ruse had proved successful.

Complete strangers engaged you in conversation when you had a dog, especially one as friendly as Castro. Eventually, the conversations turned from the dog to him and what he did.

When he told them, they often knew someone who needed work done. They'd take his name and number, and before he knew it, he'd have another job on the go, and so, little by little, his business grew. Once they'd invited him into their home, as long as he was reliable, did a good job and wasn't overly expensive, they trusted him and invited him onto the darts team down the pub and to the annual shoot on the land outside the village. Somewhere along the way, he'd become part of the community. Tonight, he'd been invited to a thirtieth birthday party.

He had not seen Tamar since their meeting at Eden's. His sister had been right; they were different people. Noble was in prison and deserved to be there, but he was sorry she was alone. He realised now, dead or not, she'd been lost to him the night of the fire. They communicated through solicitors. Ray had apparently left everything to his mother, but as she technically died before him, his assets, such as they were, passed under his will to him and Tamar. As Tamar had not been convicted of his murder, she was entitled like him to benefit. It had been a shock Ray had even considered them, but Kit guessed the man had no one else in his life and would not have wanted it to go to the Duchy of Cornwall, which Eden explained was what happened if you died intestate with no relatives. Neither he nor Tamar wanted any of it.

They did, however, insist the farmhouse should be raised to the ground, its scar expunged from the landscape forever.

As for his own scars, he seemed to notice them less and less these days when he looked in the mirror. To those who asked, he said he'd been injured in a fire and received nothing but sympathy. If they knew anything of his story, they never let on.

He had lost so much that night, his family, his freedom, but most of all, he had lost hope. Once hope was dead, there was nothing left to live for. Now he had gained it back, there were endless possibilities to explore. There was a smell of spring in the air, and for starters, he'd bought a new shirt to wear.

Who knew? Maybe he might even find love.

THE END

A LETTER TO MY READERS

Thank you for taking the time to read *A BAPTISM OF FIRE*. I hope you enjoyed it. If you did I would be lovely if you could leave a review on Amazon. As an author it is a great thrill to know someone has enjoyed your work and it will help other readers discover my books.

I have always been fascinated by the schizophrenic character of the windswept Cornish peninsula my family has been lucky enough to call home for generations. Occupied by a cast of reluctant bedfellows; city-slick escapees and us locals who carry the remnants of our myth-ridden history etched on our backs like tattoos, it teeters between the bucket and spade domesticity of modern-day tourism and a superstitious past, riddled with Pagan traditions. The resultant clash of cultures and sensibilities causes friction, resentment and drama. My aim, through my writing is to explore what happens when these divergent worlds collide to expose a darker reality at odds with the picture-perfect landscape. Whilst I was lucky to enjoy a fantastically satisfying career as a lawyer I cannot now imagine anything more joyous than being able to sit at my desk and write knowing others might read and connect with my words. Cornwall has captured the hearts and imagination of countless wonderful writers through the decades; their vivid images now woven into its rich tapestry. If I can add one colourful stitch I will be happy.

My novels can be read as standalones or as a series. Characters pop up from time to time and others will feature in a particular story. Let me know which characters you would like to see more of in the future, I'd love to find out. Hopefully over time you will feel as much a part of their community as I do.

ABOUT JULIE EVANS

After training as a lawyer, Julie returned to her native Cornwall to establish her own law firm and to raise her three children. After years building a successful legal practice it was time for a new adventure and she decided to write the stories she had formulated in her head over the years about her community and the lives of those who find themselves on the wrong side of the law.

If you would like to read more about her, visit her at www.cornishcrimeauthor.com where you will be given the opportunity to join her readers' club and receive free downloads and inside information only available to members, including a FREE novella in the CORNISH CRIME series, *THE DEADLY CHOICE*.

BOOKS IN THE CORNISH CRIME SERIES

RAGE

A SISTERHOOD OF SILENCE

THE BITTER FRUIT BENEATH

THE POISON PROMISE

A BAPTISM OF FIRE

Printed in Great Britain
by Amazon